MYSTERIOUS WAYS

THE WITCHES OF CANYON ROAD:
BOOK THREE

CHRISTINE POPE

DARK VALENTINE PRESS

MYSTERIOUS WAYS

Copyright © 2018 by Christine Pope

ISBN: 978-1-946435-15-6

Published by Dark Valentine Press

Cover design by Lou Harper

Print formatting by Indie Author Services

1

PARTINGS

Miranda McAllister

Rafe wouldn't let me drive him over to his parents' house. Just as well, probably, since I didn't have my I.D., no way of proving that I even had a license. But with both of us reeling from the shocking news of his mother's death, a death most certainly caused by some very nasty dark magic, I'd wanted to do at least one small thing for Rafe, wanted to help however I could. He still wore the same cold, stony expression that had settled on his features as soon as we heard the news, an expression that betrayed nothing of what he might be feeling.

His mother is dead, I thought. *How the hell do you think he's feeling?*

That question was a lot more complicated

than it might have been for most people, however. My fiancé and Genoveva Castillo hadn't exactly shared what you would call a warm and loving relationship. All his life, she'd tried to control him, and he'd fought back every way he knew how. And a large part of their fractious interactions had to do with me.

Well, not because of anything I'd personally done. No, it was more that Rafe had hated being saddled with an arranged marriage, no matter who he was being forced to marry. I couldn't really blame him for feeling that way; I'd had my own rebellious thoughts on the subject as well, although most of the time, I'd done what I could to look at the whole thing as an adventure. We had gotten off to a rocky start, but we'd both come to realize that we were just as intended for one another as a *prima*—a clan's head witch—and her consort, even though I certainly wasn't the *prima* of the Castillo clan.

No, that would be Rafe's older sister, Louisa, now that Genoveva was gone.

The reality of her death hadn't truly sunk in yet. Maybe it would all start to feel real once I was surrounded by Rafe's family, could share in their loss. The horrible thing was that—well, all of it was horrible, but the circumstances just provided an additional dollop of irony—from what Cat, Rafe's younger sister, had told us, it sounded as though Genoveva had basically dropped dead in the middle of the wake for their cousin Marco, right in front of more than a hundred Castillo relatives.

I knew Simon Gutierrez was behind all this.

No, Simon Escobar, I reminded myself. Gutierrez was his mother's last name, and for all I knew, it was the name Simon used most of the time—I didn't know for sure, since he'd told me so many lies—but his true lineage came from the dark warlock who'd been his father, Joaquin Escobar. Even twenty-plus years after Joaquin's death, that name was powerful enough to evoke a shudder in most of Arizona's witches and warlocks.

The Castillos hadn't suffered much at his hands, although Rafe's grandmother had given her life to ensure that my parents would triumph over Escobar in the end. Now, though, Joaquin Escobar's son had brought the fight to their territory.

How he'd managed this particular bit of mayhem, I didn't know. Genoveva Castillo was the *prima* of her clan, a woman who commanded formidable powers. But Simon's magic was at an entirely different level than hers, since he was the son of a *prima* and a *primus*, the male equivalent of a *prima*. Yes, I was also the offspring of two clan leaders, but neither one of them was as strong as Joaquin Escobar had been, and I knew my powers weren't equal to Simon's.

Up until a week ago, I hadn't known that I possessed any real powers at all.

I glanced over at Rafe. His jaw was set, his gaze fully fixed on the road—probably because that way, he wouldn't have to look at me. Honestly, I didn't even know what to say to him. I had a feeling that any condolences I offered would have fallen dreadfully flat.

And past all of that, I couldn't help but think this was all my fault. If Simon hadn't developed an unhealthy obsession with me, then he wouldn't have seen Rafe as a rival, wouldn't have used his powers to strike out at the Castillo clan to get revenge on Rafe for helping me to escape the estate where I'd been staying with Simon.

If Simon could kill Genoveva—a terrible stratagem I knew had been deployed to throw the Castillos into chaos—then no one was truly safe. I'd cast a spell of protection over Rafe's house, and I intended to do the same when we got to the enormous hacienda-style mansion that had been Genoveva's home, but I didn't think I could protect everyone. The Castillos would have to pitch in and deploy their own measures to defend themselves against Simon Escobar's dark magic, or else…well, I didn't want to think what might happen if their defenses weren't up to the task.

Rafe pulled up to the house, but cars blocked the driveway and circled the block. The vehicles were here because of all the Castillo relatives who had come to attend their cousin Marco's wake, Marco, who had also died by Simon's hand, if indirectly. I supposed I should have thought of how everyone would still be lingering at the house, but clearly I wasn't the only one who'd been blindsided, because Rafe cursed under his breath and went around the block again so he could cut over to the next street and park there.

We both got out of the car. Instinctively, I went to him and took his hand in mine. His fingers felt cold, and for a second he didn't respond. Then his grip tightened, hanging on to me like a drowning man reaching for salvation.

I didn't tell him it was going to be okay, because that was probably a lie. But I did look up at him and say, "I'm here, Rafe."

He didn't quite smile, but one corner of his mouth lifted slightly. "I know, Miranda. And thank God for you. I don't—" The words broke off there, and I could see his jaw clench. "I'm not sure how I'm supposed to do this."

What could I say? So far, I'd never experienced any real loss, no real grief. Oh, of course there had been older members of the McAllister and Wilcox clans who'd passed on during my lifetime, but I hadn't been close to any of them. I still had both my parents, had my Great-Aunt Rachel and her husband Tobias, had Cousin Lucas and Margot and so many others. Of course, most of Rafe's family was also still alive, but the loss of a mother had to hit far too close to home, even a mother who'd done her best to be as prickly and difficult as possible.

We went up the walk to the wide front door, which was ancient oak barred with dark iron. A funeral wreath hung on it; Genoveva Castillo had always been someone to follow the conventions. Looking at it, I had to remind myself that the wreath had been placed there for Rafe's cousin Marco, and not for Genoveva herself. That time of mourning would come next—if Simon Escobar allowed us that time. I worried that Genoveva's murder was only the opening salvo, and what was to come next might even be worse. How much worse, I didn't know, but if Simon was good at anything, it was at leaving death and destruction in his wake.

Rafe didn't bother to knock, only opened the door so we could both enter. Of course there was no point in standing on ceremony, since this was the house he'd grown up in, the place that had been his home until a few years ago. The large entry with its formal round table in the center—now topped by an arrangement of white lilies and palm fronds—was empty, but I could hear a murmur of voices coming from the living room.

We'd barely stepped inside before Cat and Rafe's middle sister, Malena, came up to him, sobbing, her dark eyes wet and bloodshot, sleek black hair starting to come loose from the low knot she wore at the back of her neck. He didn't say anything, only awkwardly folded them both in his arms while I stood quietly to one side and took a quick glance around the room. All of the Castillos present were understandably subdued, most of them damp-eyed and solemn. Past Rafe and Cat and Malena, I saw Louisa coming toward us, her head held high and still perfectly coiffed, even as her eyes gleamed bright with unshed tears.

"Rafe," she said quietly, and Cat and Malena stepped away so the new *prima* could approach her brother.

He reached out to take Louisa's hands. "What happened?"

She pulled in a breath. I could tell she was trying hard to remain dignified and in command of herself, even though she must have wanted to dissolve into tears like her sisters. The weight of her new mantle as *prima* had to weigh so very heavy.

"We don't know," she said, speaking in an undertone that I had to strain to follow. "She was in the sitting room with Marco's mother and

Cousin Geraldo, and then—then she just collapsed. Dad went running to her, and at first we all thought that the stress had gotten to her and she'd fainted, but—" Louisa paused there, pressing her lips together. Even from a few feet away, I saw how her slender body in its black dress was shivering, as though she'd been taken by a chill.

Well, I could understand that. If I somehow lost my own mother so horribly and unexpectedly, I'd probably be trembling from reaction, too.

Rafe nodded, handsome features still and cold. "Where is she?"

"In her bedroom. We laid her down on the bed. We—we didn't know what else to do. Dad's with her."

"But the *prima* powers passed to you?"

"Yes." Louisa pulled in a hiccupy little breath. "I have them, but Rafe, I don't know what to do with them!"

"You don't have to *do* anything," he told her, his voice almost too calm, as if he knew he had to be the one to hold things together until Louisa could calm herself. "Except be *prima*." He glanced over at me. For one horrible moment, I worried that he was going to excuse himself, say that he and his sisters needed time alone with their mother, and I'd have to wait out here.

I should have known better.

"Please come with me, Miranda," he said quietly. "All of us—the immediate family—need to talk in private."

He reached out a hand and I took it, let him lead me through the house, past the ranks of sorrowful Castillos, all of whom looked more bewildered than anything else. I could tell they were all wondering how in the world this could have happened.

And I didn't know whether I could ever begin to explain how this evil had reached out and taken their *prima* from them. Guilt tore at me, even though I knew this was not my fault. No, this crime could be laid directly at Simon Escobar's feet.

We climbed the stairs to the second floor, Rafe and me in the lead, his sisters immediately behind us. That felt strange to me; I thought that Louisa, as the new *prima,* should have been at the head of our sad little procession. But even though Rafe and I had reconciled, I still felt very much the outsider here, and so I didn't make any protest, didn't say anything as we walked down the upstairs hall to the master suite.

I had never been up here before. My previous visits to this house had been confined to the more public areas downstairs—the living room, the dining room. This level of the house had the same dark beams overhead, the same white plaster walls.

Those walls were nearly a foot thick, heavy and unyielding. I didn't know for sure when this house had been built, but I thought it must be at least two hundred years old, possibly more. And, like the ground floor, this upper level felt just as weighty, just as dark and ponderous. The air was chilly, and I shivered in my thin sweater.

A pair of doors made of age-darkened oak stood at the end of the hallway. Rafe went up to them and knocked softly. "Dad? It's Rafe. We'd all like to come in."

No reply, but after a moment, one of the doors opened, and Rafe's father Eduardo looked out at us. His dark eyes were reddened from sorrow, although he now appeared composed enough, his handsome, patrician features calm and still. Without speaking, he pulled his son into a quick, fierce embrace, then stepped out of the way so we all could enter.

Now I almost wished Rafe had left me downstairs, although that would have been awkward, considering that I'd been among the missing for most of the past week, hidden away at the estate Simon had borrowed...or stolen...I still wasn't sure. The last thing I would have wanted to do was launch into an explanation for my absence, especially when I still didn't know what Simon was up to. That was a matter which should be discussed with Louisa, now that she was *prima,* and anyone else she wanted to take into her confidence—most likely Rafe and her sisters, and their father.

Well, we were all here now.

The room was large, the ceiling white plaster with dark beams—what they called *vigas*—overhead, the walls painted a surprising deep red. At the far end of the space was a large oak four-poster bed, simple in construction, the wood pale in contrast to the blood-hued walls. On that bed lay Genoveva Castillo.

Or rather, her body. I really didn't want to go any closer, but I knew I couldn't hang back while the rest of the family approached that bed, ranged themselves around it. Rafe held me by the hand, some warmth now returning to his fingers. Maybe now that he'd confronted the worst of it—had actually seen his mother lying dead on her bed—he felt as though he was in a better position to handle whatever might come next.

She looked like she was asleep. That was a relief, because my mind had conjured several horrible images of a gruesome death, even though Louisa had said that everyone thought she had fainted at first. Her eyes were shut, profile still proud and elegant, even in death. Someone had folded her hands on her breast, and the large diamond on the ring finger of her left hand sparkled in the sunlight coming through the window off to one side.

Sunlight. It was hard to believe it was still only the middle of the day, that Rafe's battle with Simon had taken place only an hour or so earlier. With everything that had happened, I thought we should now be buried in the deepest darkness.

That image sent a shiver through me, and for a brief moment I closed my eyes and recalled the bubble of protection I had cast around Rafe's house less than an hour earlier. I cast that same spell of protection around the *prima's* house now. It would be so like Simon to try something else dreadful while everyone was gathered here to mourn, and I wasn't about to allow that.

Rafe spoke first. His voice was tight and strained, but calm enough. "Did Daniel tell you who Simon really is?"

Cat nodded, her face pale, fear showing in her dark eyes. "He did. He came and found me, showed me the information his assistant had sent him. I was about to go warn Mom when—when this happened. And afterward, I told Dad and Louisa and Malena."

"We know what we're up against," Louisa said. She also sounded calm, but I could tell she was scared—her hands shook slightly, and she looked pale under her olive skin.

"I'm not sure you do," I said, and they all

turned to look at me. Faced by those combined stares, I swallowed, and wondered whether I should have waited for a more opportune moment to speak. Well, since I'd already put my foot in it, I decided to forge ahead. "Simon is—well, he's the most powerful warlock I've ever encountered. We're not talking about someone who's confined to one particular talent. As far as I can tell, he can do pretty much whatever he wants."

"All magic has its limits," Louisa said, although something in her tone made me think she was only saying that because she wanted to believe it, not because she necessarily thought it was true.

"We don't know that for sure," I replied. "We have our traditions, and we know what witches and warlocks generally can do, but Simon... Simon is different."

As was I, but I didn't feel like going into all that right now. For one thing, Simon had helped to awaken my powers, had taught me how to use them, but I still didn't know exactly how far they extended. The exercises he'd had me perform appeared to prove that I could do just about anything I set my mind to, and yet that didn't necessarily mean a lot when contrasted with the magic Simon seemed to command. Already I'd bumped into several instances where he easily brushed my efforts aside. The last thing I wanted to do was allow the Castillos to think I might be the answer to their problems.

More like the cause of them, as far as I could tell.

"Different how?" Eduardo asked. His voice was rough with grief. Genoveva Castillo had been a difficult, prickly woman, but Eduardo had appeared to love her unreservedly. To lose her like this must have been as painful as it was shocking.

"Because of who he is," I said. "From everything I've heard, Joaquin Escobar was an insanely powerful warlock. And Simon's mother is the *prima* of the Santiago clan in Southern California. When you combine two strong strains of magic like that in one person, you get someone who isn't exactly your run-of-the-mill warlock. That's why he was able to do…this." It would have been rude to point at Genoveva's body, so I only inclined my head toward her before continuing. "I've cast a spell of protection around this house, but that's only going to help while the people inside it are actually here."

Grim comprehension dawned in Louisa's face. She wasn't quite as beautiful as her sisters, but I saw a strength in her features that reassured me. Right then, I could only hope that Genoveva hadn't made Louisa her heir to magic simply because she was her eldest daughter. I'd had my differences with Genoveva, but surely she would have had too much integrity and concern for her clan to show that kind of favoritism.

"We have people in the clan who are skilled with defensive magic, who also know how to cast spells of protection," Louisa said. "I will make sure that every person in this family is made safe, one way or another." She paused, gaze flickering toward the still form on the bed for a moment. Then she went on, "Simon Escobar was able to do this because we had our guard down. I can assure you that it will not happen again."

Malena, who had been silent up until that point, asked, "You really think we can protect every single Castillo?"

"We can, because we must," Louisa replied. She looked over at her father, who stood near the head of the bed. "Dad, can you help get the word out?"

"Of course," he said. In a way, he appeared almost relieved to be given something concrete to do. "But we must also make plans for your mother's funeral."

"I'm not sure that's a good idea," Rafe cut in. Before his gathered family members could protest, he went on, "What if Simon is just waiting for another opportunity to have us all together in one place? Bad enough that so many of us were here for Marco's wake. You know that even more

Castillos are going to show up for their *prima's* funeral."

He was right. I still didn't know what kind of dark spell Simon had employed to strike at Genoveva, but I thought it was the sort of thing that must have required a lot of energy. It was entirely possible that he needed to rest up before he tried anything else, in which case the people assembled downstairs might be safe…for now. But whenever the funeral took place, a day from now, or two, by that time, Simon would probably be strong enough to attempt another attack.

"Are you saying we can't bury my Genoveva?" Eduardo demanded, shock and anger clear on his handsome features.

"No, Dad, that's not what I'm saying." Since he stood so close to me, I could feel the tension in Rafe's body, the way he strained to keep himself from sounding too harsh. "A private, quiet funeral, one with just the immediate family members. No big service at the cathedral. No notice in the local newspaper. We need to pay our respects, but in a way that won't attract atten- tion…especially Simon Escobar's attention. Later, after all this is handled and it's safe, we can have a memorial service for the entire clan. "

An uneasy silence fell. I could tell that Eduardo and Malena both wanted to argue with Rafe but realized he was only pointing out a hard truth. Louisa nodded, still with that aura of strained calm. For the first time, I wondered where her husband was, and Malena's, for that matter. Probably looking after their very young children so their wives could handle this distressing bit of family business.

And Cat—poor Cat just looked as though she wanted to go somewhere and cry for a good long while, her model-pretty face pale and strained, makeup smudged around her almond-shaped dark eyes. She was a few years older than I, but she was still the baby of the family and, at least from what I'd seen, had gotten along fairly well with her mother. I had a feeling she was taking this even harder than her sisters, who at least were married and had families of their own that required their attention. But Cat didn't have a husband or a fiancé or even a boyfriend to watch over her, comfort her.

Right then, I thought I'd never hated anyone as much as I hated Simon Escobar. That hatred thrummed within me, hot, roiling. I knew I couldn't give in to hate, that doing so would make me no better than he was, but I was still pretty sure that if he'd appeared before me right then, I could have reached out and snapped his neck.

"Then we'll make sure to be as quiet about this as we can," Louisa said, since everyone else seemed reluctant to speak. "Dad, can you talk to the bishop, let him know what we want? She'll need some kind of service—"

"Because if she doesn't get a good Catholic funeral, she'll haunt us forever," Rafe put in.

Cat shot him a pained glance. Then again, as someone whose talent was speaking with ghosts, the specter—so to speak—of having her mother's spirit hanging around would have to be particularly daunting. However, I had to assume that Genoveva's soul had moved on to the next world, because otherwise Cat would have told us right away that she still lingered here.

Eduardo sent his son a narrow look, clearly letting him know that his last remark hadn't been appreciated. However, he only said to Louisa, "Yes, I will do that. But people will become suspicious as time passes and there is no service for Genoveva."

"Hopefully, by then we'll have all this sorted out," Louisa said. She let out a breath, and suddenly looked very tired. "Although I'll admit I'm not sure what we're supposed to do about Simon Escobar."

"Root him out from that estate where he's holed up and make sure he doesn't draw another breath," Rafe growled.

This bloodthirsty suggestion didn't seem to faze any of the people gathered around Genoveva's deathbed. Then again, I doubted any of her family were feeling exactly merciful, not with the way Simon had somehow reached out with his magic and extinguished her life the way someone might carelessly snuff out a candle.

"Do you think he's even still there?" Malena asked, doubt clear in her voice. "After all, he's done his worst. The smart thing would be for him to get far, far away from us Castillos. He has to know we'll be looking for revenge."

I thought of the terrible things I'd seen in the outbuilding on the property where Simon was staying—the book of dark spells, the black candles, the cruel, curved knife. He'd found a sanctuary of a sort out there on that estate in Tesuque, only twenty minutes or so from where we all now stood. When he'd thought he could seduce me, could bring me over to his way of thinking, he'd been openly scornful of the Castillos and their talents, even though the clan was a fairly strong one. I thought it was entirely possible that his arrogance would lead him to think he could take on all of us, especially after being so successful at murdering the clan's leader.

"He might believe that," I said, then paused as five sets of eyes suddenly fixed on me. Up until that moment, I'd remained quiet unless answering a question; this was their family's tragedy, and although I was engaged to Rafe, we weren't married yet. I hadn't felt it was my place to talk very much. Now, though, I thought I needed to tell them what I knew. "But I think he underestimates you. He thinks his powers are a match for all yours."

"Then he's crazy," Cat said, a frown pulling her fine brows together.

Oh, I was pretty sure Simon was insane, only not in the way Cat meant. For all I knew, he'd been born flawed, the original bad seed. If not, his poor treatment at the hands of the Santiagos, who'd regarded him as a cast-out, a pariah, and who had made him live on the fringes of their clan, certainly had forced him over the edge. Now his only goal was revenge—revenge against the Castillos, whose former *prima* had contributed to his father's death.

As to why Simon hadn't also gone after my parents, who were far more directly responsible for Joaquin Escobar's demise, well, I didn't have a clue as to the reason behind that oversight…or rather, there was a possible explanation, a terrible one I didn't want to acknowledge but which I guessed must be fairly close to the truth.

Simon had avoided hurting my parents because he wanted me. Their deaths at his hands would have turned me against him forever. But now that I had so clearly spurned him, had returned to Rafe, the man I truly loved, I didn't know what might happen.

A cold wave of fear washed over me. I had to call my parents, had to warn them somehow.

In a murmur, I said to Rafe, "I need to borrow your phone."

"Now?" he asked, clearly startled.

"Yes," I replied. "It's important."

Everyone else was staring at us, obviously somewhat offended that we'd be carrying on a separate conversation while Genoveva lay there in front of us. I knew it must look awful, but I also knew I didn't dare let another moment pass without reaching out to my parents, telling them that they might be in danger.

I cleared my throat. "I'm sorry," I said. "But I have a feeling that Simon might also try to do something to my parents. I need to call them."

At once Eduardo's expression softened. "Of course," he said. "There is a sitting area off the bathroom, if you need some privacy. Through there."

He pointed to a doorway I'd barely noticed. Through it, I could glimpse a chaise longue and a luxuriant ficus tree in a large terra-cotta pot.

Rafe handed me his phone. "Go ahead."

I shot him a grateful smile and then went into the sitting area Eduardo had mentioned. There was a small bookcase in addition to the chaise and the potted tree, although I didn't exactly have time to inspect the books on the shelves. After quickly entering the number for my mother's cell, I put Rafe's phone up to my ear and prayed that she'd pick up, that the call wouldn't go to voicemail. After all, my mother and I had talked less than an hour earlier. She might have thought everything was fine and that she and my father could go out, have a drink and relax or something.

To my relief, she answered on the second ring. "Miranda, is everything all right? I thought you were going to call tomorrow to check in."

"Mom, I don't have time to explain everything," I said, speaking quickly so I didn't waste a precious moment. "Genoveva Castillo is dead, and I'm almost positive Simon Escobar did it. I'm really worried that he's going to try something with you and Dad next. You need to make sure you're as shielded as you possibly can be."

"Genoveva is dead?" my mother asked, incredulity clear in her voice. "When?"

"Just a little while ago," I replied, impatient that I was wasting time with details when we had more pressing matters to deal with. "Just promise me that you and Dad will be careful. Have the elders cast whatever spells of protection they can."

"All right," she said. "We'll be careful. But Miranda—"

I didn't know what she'd intended to say next, because the phone's tiny speaker suddenly emitted a horrible screeching noise, one so loud that I had to pull it away from my ear before it did any permanent damage. As I stared down at it, the screen went blank.

What the hell?

I swiped my finger over the "redial" button, but nothing happened. The screen remained black.

Rafe came hurrying into the sitting area. "What was that noise?"

"I have a feeling it was Simon Escobar, trying to make sure I couldn't get the word out," I said, then held the phone out to Rafe. "I think your phone is fried."

He took it from me, consternation clear in his face. A few abortive swipes of his finger over the screen, and he shook his head. "You're right. The goddamn thing is totally bricked. How could Escobar even do something like that?"

"I don't know," I said, fear running cold through me. Had Simon gone to Arizona, despite my belief that he wouldn't directly attack my parents? My voice shook as I added, "I still know so little about what he can and can't do. At least I was able to warn my mother before he killed the phone."

Cat had left the group standing by the bed and now paused at the entry to the sitting area. Clearly, she'd heard something of our conversation, because she extended one hand, which held her own phone. "Try mine."

With some reluctance, I took it. If Simon had intervened directly with my parents, I didn't see what using Cat's phone would prove. On the other hand…. "I don't want to break it—"

"We need to know," she said, her voice firm.

With a mental sigh, I entered my parents' number into her phone. I'd barely begun to raise it to my ear when it made that same shrieking sound and the screen went black.

"That's a hell of a spell," Cat remarked as she stared down at her ruined phone.

Despite the wreck of her phone, relief coursed through me. If Cat's phone was being blocked as well, then that almost certainly meant the spell was working from our end here in New Mexico, and nowhere near my parents. "Sorry—" I began, but she shook her head.

"It's not your fault." She turned to her brother. "What now?"

"Well, it seems pretty obvious that Simon doesn't want us to reach out to the McAllisters," he said, looking very grim. "I have a feeling he's trying to prevent us from getting any outside help."

"Well, he can't block *all* of us," Cat protested.

I wished I could be as sure as she seemed to

be. Right then, I didn't know what to expect, what Simon might try next.

From the other room came a sudden flurry of whispered conversation. Rafe and Cat and I all looked at each other, and then hurried back to the bedroom. Although Malena and Eduardo still maintained their vigil at Genoveva's bedside, Louisa now stood at the door that opened onto the hallway. An older man stood there, having some kind of fierce but *sotto voce* convo with his new *prima*.

As Cat and Rafe and I approached, Louisa turned away from the man who stood at the door, her expression one of consternation. "Miguel just got a call from his daughter, who lives in Gallup. She was going to head over the border into Arizona, because she has a friend who lives in Window Rock. But she never got there."

"What happened?" I asked, cold beginning to run through me.

Miguel looked down at me. His hair was iron gray, and I guessed he must be in his mid-sixties, at least ten years older than the *prima* he had just lost. In his dark eyes, I saw the kind of fear I'd felt building in me ever since I'd stopped to wonder how far Simon Escobar's vengeance might go.

"They say it was a car accident, but no one knows what really happened," he said. "The front end of her car was smashed in, as though she had driven at full speed into a brick wall, but there was no wall, only the open freeway. They took her to the hospital. I am waiting to hear whether she needs surgery."

Louisa reached with a reassuring hand to touch Miguel's arm, but the gesture barely registered with me. I was too busy trying to push back a sense of growing horror.

No phone calls getting out. No vehicles driven by Castillos allowed to leave the state. I had no evidence to back up my suspicions, but I had a feeling that any McAllisters or Wilcoxes who'd attempt to come to the rescue from the Arizona side of the border would meet the same fate.

Simon wanted to make sure none of us had any outside help.

We would have to do this on our own…no matter what happened.

2

PLOTTING

AFTER LOUISA MURMURED SOME SOOTHING words to Miguel and told him to let everyone know that she'd be downstairs shortly, I reached for Rafe's hand. I desperately needed the reassurance of his touch, even though I knew his physical strength was only an illusion. Simon was so much stronger than he—so much stronger than anyone I'd ever heard of.

Yes, possibly stronger than his father as well, although I didn't want to face that possibility. Working together, my parents had just barely defeated Joaquin Escobar more than twenty years earlier, and only because Isabel Castillo had given up her own life to lend them her strength as well. If it turned out that Simon commanded powers which dwarfed even his father's, I didn't know what in the world we were supposed to do.

Especially now that I couldn't count on any help from my parents. I'd briefly considered teleporting myself to Arizona to let them know what was going on, but I realized the risk was far too great. If Simon's magical barrier was strong enough to crumple a car driven by a witch, I really didn't want to think about what it might do to someone using magic to try to get through it.

"Simon's walling us off," I said, speaking not just to Rafe, but to Cat and Malena and Eduardo and Louisa. Especially Louisa. As the new *prima,* she would be responsible for getting the word out to the rest of the clan. "He's doing everything he can to make sure we're on our own. I don't think anyone can dare leave the boundaries of the state, at least not until we can find out for sure whether what happened to Miguel's daughter was the direct effect of a dark spell, or whether it was just some kind of horrible coincidence."

Louisa's cheeks were pale, but she nodded. "I'll make sure everyone knows. And the phones?"

"It's probably okay to call each other," I said. "Simon's spell broke both Cat's and Rafe's phones because I was reaching out to my parents. Then again, he might not want you Castillos communicating with each other as well."

"That's easy enough to find out," Eduardo said. He reached into his jacket pocket and brought out a slim, gunmetal-gray phone. A few swipes over its screen, and I heard a faint chiming sound coming from somewhere near. As I watched, he went to the nightstand on the opposite side of the bed from where he stood and extracted a phone from the top drawer, one that appeared to be the mate of his. "Genoveva's," he said briefly. "She left it in here because she knew she would not need it during Marco's wake."

Well, that answered one question. It seemed as though calling one another should be safe enough for the members of the Castillo clan. I was fairly certain that if any of them tried to reach out to any of the Arizona witch families, their phones would immediately get nuked, but I didn't think that was going to be much of an issue. The New Mexico and the Arizona clans in general didn't have much to do with each other. Maybe the situation would begin to change once Rafe and I were married, but I sure as hell didn't know when that was going to happen. We might have committed to one another for real, but we needed to solve this problem with Simon—and allow the clan time to mourn the loss of their *prima*—before we could even think about having an actual wedding.

Louisa didn't attempt to hide her relief. "Well, thank God for that, anyway." She hesitated, then looked over at me. "We have so many members of our clan gathered here, and I can't help but think there's some strength in numbers. Should we encourage those who've come from out of town to stay, rather than go back home?"

The question made me uncomfortable, mostly because I wasn't sure how I should react to the Castillos' new *prima* asking me for advice. Then again, I'd had more experience with Simon than anyone else. I hated being the expert when it came to such a miserable excuse for a human being, but it seemed I was, for better or worse.

"I don't know for sure," I confessed. "But Simon was still able to strike at your mother, even when surrounded by so many other Castillo witches and warlocks. If everyone's spread out, gone back to their own homes, they'll make for a more diffuse target." I pulled in a breath and crossed my arms, wishing that Louisa hadn't put me on the spot. What if I gave the wrong advice? What if my suggestions led to more deaths? I didn't know whether I'd be able to handle the guilt.

Rafe put a hand on my shoulder, rubbing it gently. I could practically feel his concern flowing toward me, and it did help me feel a bit better. "I think Miranda might have a point," he said. "I mean, if Simon wanted to get rid of a whole bunch of Castillos at once, we'd only be helping him out by all staying in one place. I think it's better if we have everyone go home. But anyone who's capable of casting spells of protection needs to do that for the people in their towns back home."

"I can do it for the people here in Santa Fe," I said. "I've already cast one around this house." If only I'd been here to do it earlier. But then, I'd had no idea that Simon would reach out to attack Rafe's family. I'd thought he would come after me and Rafe, which was why I'd done what I could to protect us as soon as we got to Rafe's house.

"There are a great many of us here," Eduardo pointed out. His tone was gentle, but he shook his head and gave me a somewhat indulgent smile. "Far more than you could protect on your own, Miranda. There are those in the clan who know defensive magic, and they will lend their skills to this fight."

"I can do it," Malena said. "Mother taught me. Louisa's talent is knowing when magic has been used, and what kind, but I've always been able to block magic, in addition to my talent with growing things."

"Then you'll come home with me and cast the spells of protection on my house," Louisa told her. "And then you and Miranda and anyone else with that gift can work together to make sure we're all protected." Her voice was firm; I could tell she felt better now that we had a plan of action, even if it was still a somewhat nebulous one. Of course, it was important to make sure that no more

Castillos lost their lives because of Simon Escobar, but I also knew that at some point we'd need to take the fight to him. We couldn't live forever under siege.

"And I will contact the bishop," Eduardo said, gaze straying to Genoveva where she lay on the bed. "And José can take her to the funeral home. I think it is better if she does not remain here."

A shiver went through me. I'd never been around anyone who'd died before, but of course I knew that the body would need to be taken away to be prepared for burial or cremation. At the same time, I wondered whether Genoveva would be safe at the funeral home. Maybe it wasn't enough that Simon had murdered her. Maybe he also had designs on the body, wanted it for some horrible ritual that would bring him even more power.

I told myself not to be ridiculous, that Simon had already done his worst, but I didn't know that for certain. I'd seen the fevered glitter in his eyes as he pushed me down onto the couch at the house in Tesuque, told me that he needed me to be his completely. That had been the look of a man who was willing to do whatever it took to get what he desired. He didn't think about right or wrong. The evidence of dark magic I'd found in the shed on the back forty of the estate was all the evidence I needed as to his desperate state of mind. Someone who would go to those lengths, who would allow himself to delve into that kind of depravity, was capable of crimes I couldn't begin to comprehend.

More than anything, I wished I could talk to my parents. My father especially, because I would have begged him to tell me what he knew of his own brother's experiments with dark magic, even if that was a subject he'd avoided for as long as I'd been alive. We couldn't avoid the topic any longer, though, not if we wanted to prevail against Simon Escobar.

Unfortunately, Simon had been several steps ahead of me, just as he had been for the past week. He seemed to know what I'd try before I even thought of it myself.

Rafe nodded, that calm yet grim expression back on his face. Would he ever truly acknowledge the hurt of losing his mother? I couldn't begin to guess, not when I knew they'd been at each other's throats for more than twenty years. "Just remember...a *quiet* service. Not at the cathedral. Choose some other church. And I really think you should have someone other than the bishop officiate."

This suggestion didn't sit well with Eduardo, judging by the way his lips pressed together and his eyes narrowed slightly. I could tell it pained him that his wife—his consort—wouldn't be given the respectful send-off she deserved. But at least he didn't argue, only nodded. "I'll see to it."

Louisa fiddled with the silver cross she wore around her neck. Would she now inherit the large coral piece that her mother had worn every time I'd seen her? I thought so; it seemed to be a family heirloom, and should go to the eldest daughter. "Well, I suppose that's all we can do for now," she said. "I'll send everyone home, and then make sure we get started with casting the spells of protection."

"Starting with your house," Malena said, her tone not allowing any argument.

"Starting with my house…although I guess it won't be my house for much longer."

No, I figured that Louisa would have to bring her family to live in the mansion that was the *prima's* residence. That seemed to be a tradition with the Castillos, just as it was with my own McAllister clan. This house, though, was much older than the Victorian mansion that had gone to my mother when her Great-Aunt Ruby died. How old the Castillo home was, I wasn't completely certain, because, as with a lot of the old buildings in Santa Fe, it had been added to and remodeled as the years passed, and probably bore little resemblance to the original structure it had once been.

"We can worry about that later," Rafe said, shooting a quick glance at his father, who looked unnerved by Louisa's comment. Would he have to move out when his daughter's family came here to live, or would he stay, maybe out in the casita that had been my temporary residence when I first came to town? That didn't seem very fair, but I honestly didn't know how all this was supposed to work.

And then there was Cat. She still lived at home, mostly because her mother had been intractable on the topic, and didn't want her daughter moving out before she was married. I supposed she would get displaced, too. Or maybe not; the house was huge, and I still didn't quite know how many bedrooms it had, or how many square feet it encompassed.

But those were all worries for the future. I doubted anyone was going to be moving anywhere until we'd worked out our problem with Simon Escobar.

"Right," said Louisa, who tucked a strand of hair behind her ear and suddenly looked distressed, as if she'd just realized what a can of worms she was opening by discussing her eventual move here. "Of course. I just went on autopilot there for a minute."

"It's all right," Malena said. She laid a reassuring hand on her sister's shoulder. "We all know what we need to do, so we should go ahead with our plans." A glance over at me, and she added,

"We should probably divide up the city, just so we can concentrate on our own areas as we work on making sure everyone's home is protected."

"We'll take the south side," Rafe said promptly. As Malena looked at him in some surprise, he went on, "Well, it makes the most sense, just because that's where all the shopping is. Both Miranda and I need phones—"

"And so do I," Cat broke in.

Not letting this interruption put him off balance, Rafe nodded. "Right. And all of Miranda's belongings got left behind at that estate where Simon is holed up, so she's going to need to get a few essentials, too. Not like we're going on a shopping spree," he added, as Louisa sent him a warning glance, as though she was concerned that our shopping trip might take up too much valuable time, "but we can take care of the basics and take care of our people down in that part of town at the same time."

"Of which there aren't as many, thank God," Louisa said, in tones that seemed to infer she knew that was part of the reason why Rafe had chosen that section to cover. "We should be able to get everyone here in Santa Fe taken care of today." Her gaze moved to a small antique clock on the mantel, and she shook her head. "I can't believe it's not even two o'clock yet."

Neither could I. It felt as though roughly a

century had passed since I woke up that morning. Even Rafe's rescue of me—or maybe my rescue of him, since I was the one who'd teleported us out of the estate in Tesuque after he attacked Simon—seemed to have happened in another lifetime. And if it felt that way to me, I could only imagine how this horrible chain of events must seem to Rafe and his sisters.

After that, there were awkward hugs all around. I could tell the Castillos weren't a very demonstrative family, but they seemed to understand that they needed to embrace one another now. Louisa went downstairs first, while Eduardo got on the phone with the bishop. As Rafe, Cat, Malena, and I headed to the ground floor of the house, it seemed that word had spread fairly rapidly, because a large part of the crowd who'd assembled there had already begun to disperse. I saw Louisa pause to murmur something to a tall, thin man who looked around Eduardo's age, and he gave a sad nod and went toward the staircase, even as he pulled a phone from his jacket pocket. José, the owner of the funeral home? I supposed I'd have to ask Rafe later on.

Malena quietly excused herself to go over to the person I guessed was her husband, an attractive, athletic man in his early thirties. He was with a little girl, really just a toddler, probably no more than two at the most. She murmured something to her husband, who gave a grim nod.

Rafe appeared to be looking around for someone, and frowned. Cat sent him an inquiring glance, and he said, "I wanted to see if Daniel was still here."

"Daniel?" I asked.

"Our cousin," Cat supplied. "He's a private detective. He was the one who first dug up the dirt on Simon."

"Barely in time," Rafe said. "But it helped. A lot." His brows pulled together. "I don't see him, though."

"Well, you can talk later."

The doorbell rang, and the two of them exchanged a mystified look. I supposed it wasn't that strange for them to be puzzled; after all, everyone was leaving, not coming.

Rafe went to the door and opened it. Standing outside was a guy around my age, maybe a little older, in a long-sleeved chambray shirt with his name embroidered on the left breast. Adam.

"Is this the Castillo residence?" he asked.

"Yes," Rafe replied, sounding guarded. I couldn't really blame him, after everything that had happened today. For all any of us knew, it could be Simon in disguise. I knew firsthand how good he was at illusions, how he was able to block his magical nature so that no others of witch-kind could even recognize him for what he was. I tensed, and wondered if I would have to confront him much sooner than I'd anticipated.

"I'm with Ortiz Towing," Adam said. "A Catalina Castillo had her vehicle towed from 342 Griego Hill Road to this address."

"Oh, right," Cat said, sounding relieved. "I'd completely forgotten because…well." She stopped there, tears glittering in her dark eyes. She swallowed, then told the puzzled-looking tow truck driver, "I'm Cat Castillo."

"Can I get some I.D.?"

"Sure, just a minute. I left my purse in the other room." She hurried off to get it, then came back a minute later and handed over the card.

He scanned it into the tablet he held. "There wasn't a key fob—"

"It's okay," Rafe said hastily, producing the item in question from his jeans pocket. "I had it. Stupid mix-up."

"All right," said the tow truck driver, looking more confused than ever. I couldn't really blame him, considering the situation. "You all have a nice day."

He nodded at us, then turned and headed down the walk.

"Nice day," Cat repeated. "There's a joke." She pulled in a breath before adding, "Well, at least I have my car back. Do you mind if I change before we head out? I want to get out of this dress."

"No, go ahead," I told her, since Rafe had been temporarily distracted by an older woman who paused to give him a fierce hug on her way out the door. Cat shot me a grateful smile and fled upstairs, presumably to her bedroom.

"My Aunt Rosa," Rafe murmured as the woman squeezed his hand before heading down the front steps. "My father's oldest sister."

I nodded. The Castillos were such a big and complicated family, I hoped that one day I'd be able to keep most of them straight.

Of course, now they were one fewer.

We stood in the entryway, arms around each other's waists, and said goodbye as the last of the group who'd come to the house for Marco's wake went out to their cars. Finally, Malena and Louisa came up with their husbands and children, and once again awkwardly hugged Rafe and me.

"Be careful out there," Louisa said, her tone fierce.

"We will," Rafe replied. "You, too."

"We're going to Louisa's first," Malena told him. "Then we'll circle back and start working on the north and east parts of town."

About all I could do was nod, since I had no idea where Louisa lived. Or Malena, for that matter. I knew where Rafe's house was located, because of course I'd been there, and I knew Cat lived at home, and that was about all I knew of Rafe's sisters. He and I had had so little time to talk, *really* talk, even get to know one another. Simon's criminal meddling had ensured our separation, but there was no way I would ever let him get between us again. On that front at least, he'd lost. I knew I loved Rafe, couldn't deny the fire that had flared between us, whereas I'd be perfectly happy if a pit opened in the ground somewhere and swallowed Simon whole.

Unfortunately, I didn't think we'd be that lucky.

"As soon as I have a replacement phone and get it activated, I'll call you and let you know," Rafe said.

Louisa nodded. "Good. With everything that's going on, we can't afford not to be in contact with each other."

And then she waved, making her farewell, and she and Malena and the rest of the group went outside, leaving Rafe and me alone in the foyer.

We looked at each other. "Rafe, I—" I began, but he shook his head.

"We can talk later," he said. "I'm...I don't know if I'm okay, exactly, but I'm holding it together. I need to, because of them, and because of Cat."

"What because of me?" she asked, reappearing

at just that moment, looking a bit more at ease in some jeans and a black sweater and boots.

"Nothing," Rafe replied. "I'm just glad you have your car back. It would've sucked to have to take a Ryde everywhere. You okay to drive?"

I could see the way she swallowed, but then she nodded. "I'm fine. It'll be good to get out of here, actually."

There was an understatement. I'd always found this house oppressive, something about its atmosphere like an actual weight, but now, knowing that Genoveva had died within these walls—well, I'd be happy if I never had to come back here.

"I know the feeling," Rafe said. "Then let's go. We have work to do."

3

PROTECTION

Rafe Castillo

Even though Cat had said she was okay to drive, Rafe couldn't keep himself from watching her closely as she pulled away from the curb and engaged the auto-drive function, instructing her Mercedes SUV to head south toward the mall. But she seemed calm enough… maybe too calm, but there wasn't much he could do about that. He knew he was imposing the same sort of rigid control on himself, just because he feared he'd lose it otherwise.

My mother is dead.

Those words kept clanging around inside his head, reverberating like some sort of ghastly, tolling bell. He still didn't know how he was supposed to deal with that. Genoveva should have been around for at least another twenty-five or thirty years. God knows there were times when such a prospect would have only depressed him, considering the way they fought all the time, but now he could only think of how he'd do anything to have her back. Despite the way she'd treated him, she sure as hell hadn't deserved what Escobar had done to her. About the only comfort Rafe could take from the entire horrible situation was that at least Genoveva had passed away while surrounded by her family, hadn't seemed to have suffered at all. Cold comfort, sure, but better that than nothing.

He glanced in the rearview mirror, saw Miranda sitting quietly in the back seat. Her hands were folded in her lap, as though she didn't know quite what to do with them. Well, he couldn't blame her for that. She'd gotten away from Simon Escobar, only to be dropped into another ungodly mess. Her face was pale but composed, and he couldn't quite tell what she was thinking. Then again, why would he? Despite the kisses they'd shared, despite the way they'd acknowledged their feelings for one another back at his house, they still barely knew each other.

That would all come in time, he supposed…if they were given that time.

And even though Rafe knew they'd all agreed that these errands needed to be run, and that the four or five Castillo families who lived in this part of town needed to be protected, he couldn't quite avoid the wave of guilt that went over him at how they'd all left their father behind to maintain a lonely vigil next to Genoveva's body. True, he wasn't completely alone, because José would stay with him until the hearse arrived to take her to the funeral home, but still.

Rafe didn't know exactly how this sort of thing was supposed to be handled, because he'd only been a little boy when his grandmother Isabel died in California, fighting Joaquin Escobar. Everyone had been very solemn, and the house had been filled with people coming and going, all of them murmuring things he couldn't quite understand. And then he and Louisa and Malena and their parents had had to leave their cheerful house in the hills, so close to so many trails for hiking and exploring, and come to live in the gloomy hacienda near the center of town. But because Isabel had died so many miles away, they'd taken her straight to the funeral home. He'd never seen her body, except later at the funeral, where her overly painted face as she lay in the casket had only frightened him. That hadn't been his grandmother.

But Genoveva still looked like his mother. Whatever dark spell Escobar had sent to kill her, it had killed from within. There was no mark on her.

She truly had looked as though she was simply asleep.

She wasn't sleeping, though. Simon Escobar had murdered her, and for that he was going to pay…and for what he'd tried to do to Miranda. Not today, because protecting the family came first, but soon.

Very soon.

Cat's Mercedes SUV brought them to a shopping center filled with national chain stores, the kind of place that didn't really fit Santa Fe's public image, and so was banished to the south side of town, safely away from the picturesque plaza and the historic buildings at the city's center. They parked and went into the electronics store, where all three of them bought new phones, enrolled in plans, and were out the door in less than fifteen minutes, despite the salesman's best efforts to upsell them all kinds of accessories and extra minutes.

From there they went to the mall itself, where Cat took Miranda by the arm, saying, "I'll help you with all this, since I doubt you want Rafe haunting the lingerie department."

Miranda had laughed at the comment, although she had sounded a little forced, as if she wanted this all to be normal even though she knew it was anything but. Still, as much as he hated to be parted from her—and as much as he feared Simon might pounce from some lurking place in the dressing rooms—Rafe couldn't help being a little relieved that he wouldn't have to be included in the selection of every item in her new wardrobe.

He loitered in the center of the department store, near enough a display case filled with men's watches that no one would think it odd that he'd be lingering in that particular spot, although he did have to fend off a few over-zealous salesclerks. Eventually, though, Cat and Miranda reappeared, burdened with enough shopping bags that he guessed they'd given the lie to his comment to Louisa that they'd only be getting a few essentials.

Still, it was done, and had actually taken less time than he'd feared, especially considering how much Miranda had bought. Once they had piled all the shopping bags in the back of the SUV, Cat started the engine and asked, "Where first?"

"Probably Arthur and Casey's house," he replied. "I think they're closest."

She nodded, then gave the voice command to have the car take them to that address.

"Arthur and Casey?" Miranda asked from the back seat.

Rafe didn't like how she had to sit in the back by herself, but it also wouldn't have been fair to expect Cat to sit up front alone and play chauffeur. He half-turned so he could at least see part of

Miranda's face, then said, "They're cousins of ours. I mean, Arthur is our cousin. Casey is his wife. She's a civilian."

"Oh." A pause, and then Miranda inquired, "Do a lot of civilians marry into the Castillo clan?"

"Not as many as in most," he said. "Genoveva didn't really approve of it, even though she knew it was necessary."

There, he thought. *I said my mother's name out loud, and it almost sounded normal.*

Miranda nodded. "It gets tough, I suppose. I always wondered why more clans didn't inter-marry, why they kept themselves so separate from each other. I mean, we see a lot of it now in Arizona, but it wasn't like that before I was born."

"Mom told me it was about maintaining clan identity," Cat remarked. She was facing forward, keeping an eye on the controls even though the vehicle was handling the driving duties, so Rafe couldn't get a good read on her expression. "It was one thing to marry civilians to keep a clan from inbreeding, but when that happened, the civilians always became part of the clan. They left a lot of their identity behind. But when you have people from two separate witch clans marrying, then you run into the problem of trying to figure out which clan you identify with, where you place your loyalty."

That sounded like something Genoveva would have said. God knows her whole identity was wrapped up in being a Castillo, in being part of a witch family that could trace its roots back for more than four hundred years. Even the clans in New England couldn't quite claim that sort of lineage.

"I guess I can understand that," Miranda said, her tone musing. "I know my parents were always careful to make it clear that Ian and Emily and I were equally Wilcox and McAllister, even though Emily was the *prima*-in-waiting of the McAllisters, and it was pretty clear that everyone expected Ian to be my father's heir."

"What about you?" Rafe asked, genuinely curious. "Did you identify with one clan over another, despite what your parents said?"

Her mouth curved in a smile. God, she was gorgeous, with those dark green eyes, ever so slightly tilted at the outer corners, and those lusciously full lips. "Well, don't you dare ever tell them this, but I suppose I always thought of myself more as a McAllister. Not because I didn't love my Wilcox relatives, or like being in Flagstaff during the part of the year when we lived there, but because something about Jerome always felt more like home to me, like I could really feel my roots more there."

There was a wistfulness in her voice that awakened new misgivings in Rafe. Yes, Miranda had told him she loved him, and she'd given no sign that she wanted anything except to stay here in Santa Fe and make a life here together, but he could tell she loved that crazy little mountain town where she'd spent half her life. Was it too much to expect that she might someday love Santa Fe the same way?

Rafe pushed that worry aside as best he could. They had enough to trouble them as it was. He didn't need to make the situation worse.

"I wish I could see it," Cat said.

"You should go for a visit sometime," Miranda told her. "Maybe we can all go…after."

The sentence sort of hung there in the air, but Rafe knew exactly what she meant. There was no point in making any plans for the future until they dealt with Simon Escobar. And while Rafe guessed that his mother wouldn't have looked too favorably on a trip to Jerome, he realized that didn't matter anymore. Genoveva was gone, and could no longer attempt to control her children with her ridiculous demands and outrageous expectations.

An odd sort of relief stole over him, even though he wished he could ignore it. He shouldn't be feeling that way, not when his mother had died only a few hours earlier. But the thought wouldn't quite go away.

Now I am free.

They all fell into an uneasy silence as the SUV turned into the neighborhood where Arthur and Casey's home was located. Rafe had never even been here before; his cousins were too numerous for him to have personally visited all their houses, and besides, all his relatives flocked to his mother's house when they came there for the Castillo picnic that was held every July. That had always been more than enough family togetherness for him.

This part of Santa Fe was much, much newer than the area downtown, the houses no more than five years old. It was a neat, tidy neighborhood of Spanish-style homes on modest lots, just the sort of place where someone with a civilian wife would want to settle, since it looked like just about any other tract of stucco homes in the Southwest. Then again, there was something almost reassuring about the samey-ness of the houses here. It certainly looked like the last place where a dark warlock would attempt to coordinate an attack.

The SUV turned a corner into a cul-de-sac, and Cat took over the controls so she could pull up into the driveway of the house at the center of the little curved street. The place looked well cared for, the front yard a xeriscape with cacti and other native plants, although most of them seemed to have already gone dormant for the winter.

The three of them got out of the SUV. Miranda looked a little wary, but Rafe guessed that her expression was simply shyness at having to meet yet more Castillos. He went to her and took her hand. "It's going to be fine," he said in what he hoped were reassuring tones. "Arthur and Casey are around my age, and pretty laid-back. I know they're going to like you."

"I'm not worried about that," she responded. "I just hate being the bearer of bad news."

"Don't worry about that," Cat said, coming up behind them as they went down the front walk. "The word's already gone out to everyone. Our cousin Ned set up a text alert that goes to everyone's phone with important clan news. I know it sounds sort of impersonal, but there are so many of us that calling everyone directly would take hours."

And clearly the bad news had already circulated amongst the clan, because Arthur was opening the front door before Rafe even had a chance to ring the bell. Dark eyes sorrowful, he said, "Rafe…Cat…I'm so sorry."

"It's okay," he responded. Of course it really wasn't, but none of them had time to sit down and mourn. "We're actually here about something else. Can we come in?"

"Of course."

Arthur stepped out of the way so Rafe,

Miranda, and Cat could enter. The foyer was small, leading to a modest living room to one side and a dining room on the other. A little ways down was a family room, open to the kitchen.

It was to the family room that Arthur led them. Sitting on one of the couches there was his wife Casey, pretty and with startlingly red hair, which always made her stand out at Castillo gatherings. She was also hugely pregnant, and Rafe belatedly recalled that she was due just about any day now.

Good, he thought. *If she goes into labor, she'll be safely in the hospital, away from all this mess.*

Then again, Simon had attacked Marco while he was in intensive care at St. Vincent's, so maybe the hospital wasn't all that safe a place.

No, Casey probably wasn't a target. Simon had only gone after Marco because he'd been about to reveal where Miranda was hidden. He'd have no reason to attack Casey specifically. They were only here at Arthur and Casey's house because all the Castillos could be at risk.

"I'm so sorry about your mother," Casey said. She shifted on the couch, one hand against her distended belly. "And I'm sorry I can't get up, but—"

"But these days it basically takes a crane," Arthur finished for her, a smile touching his lips despite the gloomy reason for their visitors being there. Despite his sorrow at his *prima*'s passing, it was clear that he was thrilled about his and Casey's soon-to-be addition to the family.

"No worries," Rafe said. "Actually, we're here because we want to lay a spell of protection on the house."

From the way Arthur nodded grimly, it seemed clear enough that he'd gotten sufficient information about Genoveva's passing to know why such a precaution was necessary. "Thanks, Rafe. I didn't know you or Cat did that kind of thing."

"We don't," Cat said quickly, as if she wanted to make sure that Miranda would get all the credit here. "Miranda is going to do it."

A flash of surprise passed over Arthur's face before he did his best to conceal his shock. Rafe couldn't really blame him; most people in the clan still had no idea that his fiancée possessed any kind of magical powers at all, let alone ones so strong that they put the Castillos' resources to shame. Also, it was entirely possible that most of the people in the clan still thought Miranda was missing. Word traveled fast, but today had just been one shock after another.

"Oh, okay," Arthur said. He glanced over at Miranda. "Is there anything we need to do?"

"No," she replied, giving him a reassuring

smile. "You won't even know the spell is active. But it will be doing its job invisibly."

"How long will it last?" Casey asked.

A slight frown pulled at Miranda's brows. "I don't know for sure, but I think indefinitely. So far, when I've cast a spell, it just keeps working until I consciously shut it off."

Well, that piece of information was useful. Privately, Rafe had worried a bit about how much maintenance Miranda would have to perform to keep all these spells going at the same time, but it sounded as if that wouldn't be an issue. The amount of energy it required might still be a concern, though. He'd have to ask her about that once they were safely back in the privacy of Cat's Mercedes. All these spells of protection wouldn't do much good if they completely drained her to the point where she couldn't function.

"Nice," Arthur said. "Then, um…I guess just do what you need to do."

Miranda nodded, then shut her eyes, lashes thick, dark crescents against the fair skin of her cheeks. She stood there in the center of the room for a moment, giving no sign that she was doing anything except breathing slowly and deeply.

Rafe felt it, though. Maybe not even consciously, not quite, but something seemed to stir along the periphery of his senses, a trace of energy so faint, he doubted he would even be able to explain how he'd managed to feel it at all. That energy had a warmth to it, a sort of reassuring glow, and it seemed to surround them all, moving up and out so it encased the entire house.

After a long moment, Miranda opened her eyes. "There," she said. "I think that should do it. Even so, if you see or hear or even feel something that doesn't seem right, you need to reach out to one of us."

"I had to get a new phone," Rafe put in hastily. "Let me give you the number."

He had to call it up from the information screen of the phone he'd just bought, because of course he didn't have his new number memorized yet. Arthur entered the information into his own phone, then put it back in his pocket.

"Anything else?" he asked. "I mean, I already took time off work next week because that's when Casey is due, but—"

"No," Rafe replied. He glanced over at Miranda, and she gave a tiny, somehow helpless lift of her shoulders. Obviously, she didn't have any more idea of what to expect than he did. "Just —keep on with your regular life. Louisa's in charge of the clan now, but I don't think she'd tell you anything different."

"Do you know when the funeral is going to be?" Casey asked in her soft, light voice. "With my due date so close, we might not be able to make it, but—"

"No funeral," he cut in, then hated himself for how harsh he sounded. Casey's eyes widened, and Arthur began, sounding puzzled,

"No funeral? Why not?"

"Because we're not sure it's safe. Don't worry —my sisters and I will be able to say goodbye to her. But we're trying to avoid a big clan thing."

Sad comprehension dawned in Arthur's dark eyes. "Sorry, man. That's rough. I get it, though."

"Thanks." Since they'd done what they'd come here for—and because Rafe didn't think he could take much more of the sympathetic looks both Arthur and Casey kept giving him—he went on, "We need to get to the next house. Like Miranda said, if anything feels off to you, let me know. I think you'll be fine, but…."

"Better safe than sorry. I get it." Arthur laid a hand on Rafe's shoulder, but briefly, just enough to show he was there for him. "Take care of your-self—and you, too, Cat. And thanks, Miranda."

Cat offered him a quick flash of a smile but didn't say anything, while Miranda also smiled, looking almost embarrassed to be thanked for something she wasn't sure would be all that effec-tive. Something about Cat's expression seemed even more strained than it had been a few minutes ago, but Rafe couldn't think of what might have set his sister off. This house was way too new to be haunted; he knew for a fact that Arthur and Casey were its first and only occupants, since they'd bought it from the developer.

Well, he'd ask her what was going on once they got back in the car.

After making their goodbyes, the three of them went outside and climbed into the SUV. Cat rattled off the address for their cousin Trey, who lived in a condo less than a half mile from Arthur and Casey's place. They'd barely turned the corner out of the cul-de-sac before Rafe asked, "What's going on, Cat? You look like—" He broke off there, since he'd been about to say "you look like you've seen a ghost," which in her case was entirely possible.

"No ghosts," she said, still wearing that tight little smile, one that was more of a grimace than anything else. "Just…something feels weird."

"What kind of weird?" Miranda asked from the back seat. Her tone was sharp with worry… not that Rafe could blame her.

"It's hard to explain." Cat's hands rested on the steering wheel, although it was the vehicle that was doing the driving. Her fingers tightened against the leather. "It's sort of like…like when we were at the hospital with Marco. This weird kind of pressure."

Cold inched its way down Rafe's spine. He

recalled how Cat had experienced some kind of strange sensation while they were at St. Vincent's, but had felt better once she was outside. "You felt it at Arthur and Casey's house?"

"No," she replied immediately. "Now it's as though I can feel it *everywhere*. The air seems heavier somehow. It almost feels as though something's pressing down on my temples, like I'm about to get a migraine or something."

"You don't get headaches," Rafe pointed out.

"I know. But that's what it feels like."

Rafe glanced into the back seat so he could gauge Miranda's expression. She looked concerned, but also puzzled. "You don't feel it?" he asked.

"No."

Well, that was a relief…or was it?

"My magic's strong," Miranda said, "but I never said it lets me do anything and everything. Cat's ability to see and talk to ghosts probably makes her sensitive to vibrations the rest of us can't feel."

"That's great," Cat said. "Except I don't have any idea what this is supposed to mean. It feels like a thunderstorm coming on."

Rafe didn't like that description. They were well past the monsoon season of thunder and lightning, which meant his sister was talking about an entirely different kind of storm. But since there didn't seem to be much they could do about it, he said, "I guess tell us if anything changes. In the meantime, though…."

Cat nodded, even the tight smile she'd been wearing now gone. "In the meantime, we have work to do."

4

CONNECTION

Miranda

In all, we went to six houses on Santa Fe's south side. At every one of them, we were met with the same sympathy for Rafe and Cat…and some rather furtive speculative glances sent in my direction. I couldn't even blame Rafe's cousins for looking at me that way, because not even a week earlier, I'd disappeared into thin air right in front of hundreds of Castillos, teleporting myself away from that botched wedding ceremony. The Goddess only knew what kind of gossip had been circulating, and we didn't have time to go into lengthy explanations.

At every house, I cast the same spell of protection, and every time I did it, I hoped I was actually doing some good and not wasting all our time. True, Rafe and I hadn't been attacked when we were at his house, and there hadn't been an assault on the Castillo *prima's* home, either, at least not after I got there. But were the spells really that effective, or was Simon only biding his time, waiting to see where he should strike next? I didn't have any way of knowing for sure.

But everyone seemed grateful for what we were doing, and maybe that was almost as important as the spell itself…that we were offering some hope. At least Genoveva's powers had passed smoothly to Louisa; Simon hadn't been able to interfere with that ages-old process. Her ability as a clan leader was as yet untested, but what I'd seen so far seemed encouraging. She hadn't allowed grief to overwhelm her, had done a good job of coping with the situation.

I was worried about Rafe, though. He'd seemed calm enough as we went from house to house, had been friendly with everyone, and thankful for their words of condolence, but each time someone told him they were sorry, I could see the way he tensed up, as if he was being wound tighter and tighter. I worried that sooner or later he was going to give way, that at last the dam would have to burst.

About all I could do was hope the breakdown would wait until we were alone.

At last we were done, though. As Cat pointed

her car northward toward the hacienda, Rafe called Louisa to let her know we'd taken care of all the Castillos on the south side. From what I was able to overhear, it sounded as though our little protection operation had gone smoothly in the other parts of Santa Fe as well, and that now the clan was about as safe as we could all make it.

"Do you want to come to the house, or should I take you home?" Cat asked as she turned onto Paseo de Peralta.

Rafe hesitated. I could tell he wanted more than anything to go back to his own place and decompress, but family loyalty appeared to win out. "I can come to the house if you need me to."

"It's okay." She was facing straight forward, so from my position in the back seat, I couldn't really see her expression. "Dad texted me while we were at Trey's house—and he said José had stayed the whole time, and that Aunt Rosa was going to come over to be with him, too. And I'll be there. He won't be alone." A pause, and she added, "You've been separated from Miranda for days. I don't think anyone's going to hold it against you if you go home and have some down-time together."

She sounded reasonable, but I hoped she was right. Family could be a strange thing, and I could see how some people might resent Rafe for not spending this time with his father. I certainly didn't want to be blamed for keeping him away from his family at such a terrible time.

"Maybe," he said, and he sounded as dubious as I felt. "What about you? Still getting that thundery feeling?"

"No," she replied. "I mean, it was there for a while, but as we were driving from Trey's condo over to David and Lily's place, it went away."

"What do you think it means?"

A nervous laugh. "I have no idea. I guess I'm hoping that it doesn't mean anything at all."

That was probably a vain hope. I hadn't been at the hospital with Cat and Rafe when they'd gone to visit Marco—before Simon killed him outright to keep him from talking—and so I had no idea whether I might have experienced that terrible, thundery sensation if I'd been there to experience it for myself. Certainly today I hadn't felt anything, which seemed to indicate it was something my own witchy senses couldn't detect. But just because I couldn't feel it didn't mean it wasn't important.

Rafe seemed to be thinking about the same thing. "Maybe it would be better if we stayed together."

Cat made an impatient noise. "I'm fine, Rafe. Besides, weren't we all saying earlier that it was better not to be together, that it was better to make Simon have to spread his resources?"

"That was just a guess," I said. "I don't know for sure."

"None of us knows anything for sure," Cat replied. "But Louisa agreed with you, and since she's the *prima* now, I guess we need to do as she says. You've already cast a spell of protection on the house, so it'll be safe there. If Simon knows as much about us as you seem to think he does, then he's going to know that my gifts don't present any kind of threat, and neither do Dad's. There's no point in coming after us."

Well, except psychological warfare, I thought, but I didn't say anything out loud. It would definitely throw the clan off even further for Cat and her father to be attacked. Right then, I wouldn't put anything past Simon.

At the same time, I didn't want to go back to that big, gloomy house. I wanted to go with Rafe to his place, which still didn't feel like home but at least was his own, someplace where we could be alone to truly reconnect. I felt my need for him growing, and wanted him to hold me.

Actually, I wanted a lot more than that, wanted his kisses and his touch to erase every taint of Simon's assault on me, but I knew I couldn't ask for more than what Rafe was willing to give. He'd lost his mother today, under the worst possible circumstances. I couldn't expect him to be intimate when dealing with that kind of pain.

He glanced back at me, and all I could do was give a helpless shrug. This was his decision to make; I didn't want to force him one way or another.

A gust of a breath, and then he said, "I guess just take us home, then. We'll only be a couple of minutes away. But you call me the second something doesn't feel right."

"I will," Cat replied immediately. "I really don't think you have anything to worry about, though."

"Maybe."

They both fell silent after that, and I sat quietly in the back seat, watching as the tall old trees and older adobe houses passed by outside the car windows. We looped around downtown, then turned onto the street where Rafe's house was located. The sun had dropped low enough that I couldn't see it anymore, only a warm orange flush on the western horizon, and a shiver went over me.

Even though I would be with Rafe, I feared the approaching night. Black magic was strongest in the dark hours.

What are you up to, Simon? I thought as Cat pulled up into the driveway. *Are you just biding your time, waiting to see what the Castillos are going to do, or do you already have some terrible plan in the works?*

There was no answer. He and I weren't connected at all, even though he'd wanted us to be. In his black and shriveled heart, he'd imagined us as some sort of unholy *prima* and *primus,* a dark echo of my parents' joining, only he'd wanted us to use our powers to control others, to subjugate those he saw as less worthy.

Thank the Goddess Rafe had gotten there in time. I still didn't want to know what would have happened if—

My mind shied away from that horrible thought. I was safe for now. Simon hadn't gotten what he wanted.

Of course, that didn't mean he wouldn't try again.

Cat turned off the engine. "Do you mind if I don't get out? This day has been—" She stopped herself there. "What I meant was, I'm exhausted."

"It's fine," Rafe said hastily. "Just let Miranda and me get her stuff out of the back, and then you can go on home."

"'Home,'" she repeated, then shook her head. "It's going to feel so strange now that Mom is gone."

"I know." He reached over and touched Cat on the arm. "You sure you don't want us to go back there with you?"

"Yes, I'm sure. I'll be fine."

A long pause, during which I sat without

moving, worried that he was going to press the issue. But then he seemed to realize it was worse for him to keep insisting, because he said, "All right. Just call if—"

"If there's anything weird," Cat broke in. "I know. Now get going."

He finally unbuckled his seatbelt, and I undid mine as well and slid out of the SUV, grateful that it looked like Rafe and I would finally have a chance to be alone together. The only problem was, I had no idea what we would be doing with that time.

Whatever Rafe wants, I told myself as we retrieved my new purchases from the back of Cat's car. *You'll just have to roll with it.*

The house was very dark, but he flicked the switches in the hallway as soon as we were inside. It was hard not to let out a breath of relief once I saw that the place was empty. I didn't know what I'd been expecting—Simon standing there, waiting for our return so he could blast us with more dark magic?—but it seemed that the spell of protection I'd cast had held up just fine in my absence.

"We might as well take this stuff upstairs," Rafe said.

"Okay."

I followed him to the second floor. When we got to the upstairs hallway, he paused, looking uncomfortable. "There's a spare bedroom I don't really use. Did you want—?"

I wouldn't let him finish the question. "I want to stay with you, Rafe, in your room. If that's okay," I added hastily, because I realized almost as soon as I'd interrupted him that maybe he didn't want me to stay with him. Maybe he needed to be alone for a while to get things sorted out.

But he appeared to visibly relax, and even smiled a little. "I was hoping you'd say that, but I didn't want to presume anything."

"We're together now," I said, my voice firm. "And that means I shouldn't be sleeping in your extra bedroom."

"Good."

He took me into the master bedroom, which was large and spare, almost monastic in its simplicity. A king-size bed with a plain oak frame, a dresser in matching oak with a Mexican mirror of pierced tin hanging over it. A large picture, almost abstract, of what I guessed were supposed to be the Sangre de Christo mountains.

That was it. The bed had a dark red duvet on it, but everything was rumpled; clearly, he hadn't bothered to make the bed before he left the house this morning.

The room practically screamed for a woman's touch. I didn't voice that opinion aloud, though. Rafe had been through enough today, and the last thing he needed was to hear me making plans for redecorating.

"The closet's here," he said, opening a door.

Clearly, the home's architect had planned for a more extensive wardrobe than the meager single rack that Rafe's clothes appeared to take up. There was plenty of room for me to hang up my new purchases and still have two more racks to spare.

"Thanks."

We set the shopping bags on the floor, and I got to work placing my new clothes on hangers and then putting them on the rack. That left the jeans and the underwear and the socks. Rafe took a look at the pile of stuff I still had left to put away and said quickly, "I'll go clear a drawer in the dresser."

I almost protested, but I really did need a drawer—or several—to store the items that needed to be folded. Instead, I nodded, then watched him go hastily through several dresser drawers, removing what looked like old T-shirts and mismatched socks. Well, at least I didn't have to worry about him displacing anything important. Once he was done—and had gone to stash the things he'd removed from the drawers on a high shelf in the closet—I went ahead and put all the underwear in one drawer and the jeans and T-shirts in the other.

"Well, that's settled," I said after I'd finished

that task. There wasn't a clock in the room, and I thought it would be rude to pull out my phone and check the time, but I guessed it must be way after six. We might as well think about getting something to eat. "Are you hungry?"

A lift of his shoulders. "I don't know. Not really."

This response didn't surprise me all that much, but I knew he needed to eat. And, after my exertions of that afternoon, casting all those protection spells, I was starving. "You should have something, though. Who delivers around here?"

I was worried my question might have annoyed him. To my relief, he only looked thoughtful. "A bunch of places, since I'm so close to downtown. But I think I could have some pizza. Is that okay?"

A few days earlier, I'd shared a pizza with Simon. The idea of having another one didn't seem all that appetizing, but I told myself it was silly to deprive myself of one of my favorite foods just because I'd eaten it with a dark warlock. If I let him influence me that much, I was giving him too much power…and he already had way more than his fair share.

"Pizza sounds great," I said.

"Good. Does just pepperoni work for you? I don't feel like getting too adventurous today."

"Pepperoni is my favorite," I replied, which was only the truth.

Looking relieved, he got out his new phone and called up the website for the pizza place in question. A few swipes over the screen, a pause while he dug his credit card out of his wallet and passed it over the on-screen reader, and then he said, "All right, it's on its way. We might as well go downstairs."

I nodded. "Sure."

He led me into the kitchen, where he got a bottle of Sangiovese out of the wine rack, then plucked two glasses from the cupboard. "I don't know about you, but I need this."

Although a glass of wine sounded great right then, I wondered whether Rafe should be drinking, considering everything he'd been through that day. But no, he deserved to have the opportunity to relax. If that meant cracking open a bottle of sangio, so be it.

"Me, too," I told him. "Do you want me to set the table or anything?"

"I thought we'd eat in the living room. It's more comfortable in there."

This suggestion worked for me. It wasn't as though pizza was the sort of meal that required you to sit at a dining room table. "Sounds great."

We went into the living room, taking the bottle of wine and the glasses with us. Once he'd set the bottle down on the coffee table, Rafe waved a negligent hand toward the kiva fireplace in the corner. The gas logs within flared to life immediately, sending some warmth into the room, which had felt a little chilly. I realized that I could have easily done the same thing, whereas not even a week ago, I would have had to physically lay hands on the logs to get them to light. So much power, just lying there, coiled, waiting to be used. After all those years of living as a *nunca,* or a witch with no real talent, I wasn't quite sure how to deal with the idea of my magic. It still frightened me, not the least because it was Simon who'd awakened that power. He said it had been there all along, only asleep, but I hated knowing that I might have gone my whole life without tapping into my inborn talents...if it weren't for him.

I did my best to push those thoughts aside. Whatever Simon had done, it didn't affect what I felt for Rafe, the nearly overwhelming need that surged over me as we sat next to each other on the couch. He was so very close, so close that his knee brushed against mine when he shifted to reach for his glass of wine.

Maybe he felt it, too...or maybe not. His expression, which was closed off and calm again, didn't tell me very much. And while there were so many things I wanted to say to him, now that we were together, I didn't know where to start. It was quite possible he wasn't even ready to have a serious discussion about our future together. We'd started a little ways down that road earlier in the day, when we'd kissed and he'd told me he still wanted to get married. However, that was before Simon had attacked again, before he'd murdered Genoveva. Now everything was back up in the air.

So, instead of trying to broach a more intimate topic, I thought I should ask something more innocuous. "Rosa and José? Who are they again?" I remembered that Rafe had said Rosa was his aunt, but I figured it couldn't hurt to bring it up once more.

"Rosa is my father's oldest sister," Rafe replied, then took a swallow of wine. "He's the youngest of four kids—the only son, just like me. José is Rosa's husband. He also owns the funeral home all we Castillos use."

Ouch. So much for an innocuous topic. I recalled how earlier Louisa had talked about calling José to take Genoveva's body to the funeral home, but José was such a common name, I hadn't realized they were both the same person. Doing my best to deflect from that delicate topic, I said, "That's why Rosa and José are staying with your father tonight? Because she's his big sister?"

"Yes. I guess sisters never outgrow being protective. Also, Rosa lives here in Santa Fe. My other two aunts and their families still live down in Belen, which is where he's from."

"Is that far?"

Rafe shook his head. "About a half hour south of Albuquerque. But they hadn't come up for Marco's for funeral, so they weren't here when... well, when it happened."

And there we'd circled right back to his mother's death. Luckily, I was saved from having to make a reply by someone ringing the doorbell. Rafe excused himself and went to answer it. I almost followed, just because I had a sudden stab of worry that it wouldn't be the pizza delivery person out there at all, but Simon. However, I stayed put and told myself not to be so paranoid. It wasn't that I didn't think Simon capable of a sneak attack, only that I didn't think he was monitoring us so closely that he'd be able to intercept a pizza delivery.

My fears were clearly groundless, because Rafe came back a moment later, pizza box in hand. I hurriedly shuffled our glasses and the bottle of wine off to one side so he could set the box down on the coffee table.

"I'll get some plates."

As much as I wanted to offer to help, I knew it was probably better for me to stay where I was. Rafe wanted to act as if everything was normal, and if that was what he needed, then I'd do my best to go along. Everyone grieved in their own way, and I didn't want to interfere with his process.

He returned to the living room, plates in hand, and set them down next to the pizza box. There was already a stack of napkins that had come with the pizza, so he hadn't bothered to fetch any from the kitchen.

When he lifted the lid, the most amazing aroma wafted out. I knew I was hungry, but I hadn't appreciated exactly how hungry until the scent of that pizza woke up my needy stomach.

Rafe put two pieces on a plate and handed it to me, then did the same for himself. For a minute, neither of us said anything. We just sat next to each other, eating pizza, pausing from time to time to take a sip of our wine. After Rafe had consumed nearly a whole piece, he said, "I guess I did need to eat something."

"So did I," I replied. I hadn't eaten quite as quickly as he had, but I'd still made a big dent in my slice in a very short amount of time.

"I just—" he began, then stopped himself. "I guess I'm just not sure how I'm supposed to handle all this."

Thank the Goddess he was finally opening up, if even just a little bit. I set down my mostly eaten slice of pizza. "I'm here, if you want to talk," I said. "And if you don't want to talk, well, I'm here for that, too."

He wiped his fingers on a napkin, then laid a hand on my leg. Not in a suggestive way, but more as though he needed to reassure himself that I was there, that I was real. Even so, that single touch was enough to practically set me on fire. Heat surged through my body, although I told myself that I needed to keep it together and be there for him, no matter what that might mean.

"You're amazing, you know that?" Before I could begin to reply, he went on, "And don't try to sit there and tell me you're not. It's not just the magic, either—it's that you've been through the wringer yourself, and yet you're ready to be here to support me, to help me through all this."

"Isn't that what you're supposed to do when you love someone?"

In response, he leaned over and kissed me on the cheek. "Yes, but I'm still getting used to the idea that you do love me, even though I was such an asshole to you in the beginning."

"Yes, you were," I agreed, smiling a little so he could see I wasn't entirely serious. "But you got over it. And I know exactly why you were being an asshole. It wasn't as though you didn't have a pretty good reason."

"Maybe," he allowed. "Maybe that's part of what I'm trying to deal with now. I spent so much time butting heads with my mother that I never stopped to think about what it would be like after you were here, what our lives might be. I never even stopped to consider that maybe I'd end up falling in love with you, that you'd be everything I ever wanted…and more."

Warmth filled me at those words. Yes, I knew that Rafe loved me, but I certainly wasn't tired of hearing it yet.

Before I could say anything, he continued. "I guess the really hard thing is that after all the time we spent fighting with each other, all the years I spent resenting my mother, resenting the situation she'd put me in, now she's gone…and I won't ever have the chance to tell her that she was right."

No hesitation this time. I turned toward him, just as he moved toward me. His mouth touched mine, and suddenly we were kissing each other, tongues meeting, my entire body aching for him, aching for more.

He pushed me down into the cushions, his weight on me. I loved the feel of him, the way our bodies touched. True, Simon had done nearly the same thing this morning, but this was different… so very, very different.

I wanted Rafe. Wanted all of him, wanted to seal our love in the best way I knew how.

It seemed he felt the same way, because his hands moved under my sweater, slipping up to unhook my bra. In the next moment, his fingers had closed on my bare breasts, gliding skillfully over my nipples. I gasped, for even that light touch was enough to make me throb with need for him, the ache between my legs growing stronger and stronger.

The next moment, both of us were struggling with the zipper on the other's jeans. In no time, those bulky, confining garments were tossed to the floor, followed by my sweater and his shirt.

Were we really going to do this like a couple of horny teenagers, right there on the couch?

Apparently, the answer to that question was yes, because I knew neither one of us wanted to waste even the few minutes it would take to get upstairs. Better to ease down the dark briefs he wore, better for him to slide off my panties and add them to the pile somewhere beyond the coffee table.

I could feel him pressing against my leg, hard, big. Maybe his size should have frightened me a little, just because this would be my first time, but right then I didn't care. I slipped my hand over his shaft, stroking him, as his fingers slid into me, deft and skilled, finding the exact right spot to caress me so I gasped aloud at the sensation, then shut my eyes and moaned.

He was breathing heavily as well, shifting so he was positioned between my legs. I could feel his tip touch me, and I let out another moan, wanting him, wanting it all.

For a moment, though, he hesitated. "Are you sure?" he whispered. "We can wait—"

"No," I said. "I don't want to wait. I want you. I want this. Do it, Rafe. Please."

A shuddering breath, and then it wasn't just the tip of his cock touching me, but all of him, sliding inside. A twinge of pain followed immediately afterward. I'd been expecting that, though, knew it wouldn't last. And it didn't. Almost at once he began to move in and out, slowly, deliberately, going deeper as I opened to him.

It was the most amazing sensation I'd ever experienced. Not just the sensation of Rafe filling me, but the way I now felt closer to him than ever before. We weren't two people anymore, but an amazing whole, breathing together, moving together…loving together.

A warm glow began to build in my core. I knew what that meant, knew my body was building toward the inevitable climax. Rafe's fingers locked with mine, holding on to me, strengthening our bond.

Yes, that's what it was. We were bonding, physically, spiritually, emotionally. I was Rafe, and he was I. Our bodies seemed to know exactly what to do, and the universe spun around me as the climax hit at last, shivering through every limb, my legs locked around his waist as he came as well, his moans blending with mine so it was hard to know where one began and the other ended.

Perfection. Utter, soul-searing perfection.

As I breathed in and began to return to myself, I remembered to mentally recite the charm of the McAllister witches, the one that would prevent a pregnancy from occurring. *Blessed Brigid, now is not the time. Bestow your blessings elsewhere.*

It wasn't that I didn't want to have children with Rafe—I hoped one day we'd have a whole house full of them—but now, as the charm itself said, was not the time. We had to get this situation with Simon resolved before we could even begin to start making those sorts of life-changing decisions.

Rafe shifted, easing his way out of me. I let out a small breath, not quite a gasp. It felt so strange to have been one being, and now to be separate again. He must have been experiencing more or less the same sensation, because he bent down and kissed me on the forehead, then on the mouth, softly, with a sort of wonder in his warm brown eyes.

"I love you, Miranda."

I smiled up at him. "I love you, too, Rafe."

5

A NEW DAY

Rafe

SHE WAS A MIRACLE. THAT WAS TRULY THE only way he could think of Miranda, this girl—this woman—who had once seemed as though she would be the one to end life as he knew it, but who instead had turned out to be the only person who could lead him forward into forging a new existence.

There hadn't been any awkwardness afterward, even though they'd had sex right there on the couch rather than going upstairs to the master bedroom. Once they'd disentangled themselves, they'd gotten dressed, kissed one another, returned to their neglected pizza. Neither one of them had talked about what had happened earlier that day, even though very soon decisions would need to be made about how to proceed with handling Simon Escobar. For the moment, it had been enough to simply be Rafe and Miranda, two people who'd made one another whole.

He'd always thought that was a trite expression, maybe even a self-defeating one. After all, you should be whole on your own and not rely on anyone else to make you the person you were meant to be. But now, Rafe thought, as he gazed down at Miranda, asleep next to him in his bed, now he understood. She was the person he'd been waiting for his entire life. He just hadn't realized it until tonight.

They'd come upstairs and fallen into bed, made love again, a little more slowly this time, savoring each other's bodies. He'd been somewhat surprised by her ardor, then realized that just because Miranda had been a virgin, it didn't mean that her blood couldn't run as hot as his. And God only knew that the internet provided plenty of how-to information for the sex act itself, even for someone who'd had to hold back her entire adult life.

Well, she sure wasn't holding back now. Rafe had had enough girlfriends to know that he'd never been with anyone like Miranda, had never experienced lovemaking the way it was with her. This was more than two bodies coming together, more than mere momentary pleasure. They'd connected in a way he hadn't expected. In fact, the experience had been so intense, he wondered if it was anything like a *prima* bonding with her consort. It felt that way, even though of course Miranda wasn't a *prima*. The most powerful witch he'd ever met, sure, but that still wasn't the same thing. Then again, she was the daughter of a *prima*. Maybe they still bonded more strongly than most witches. For a brief second he contemplated asking Malena, since Louisa would have experienced that bond as *prima*-in-waiting and Cat wasn't married yet, but he dismissed that idea almost immediately. He didn't think he could handle the embarrassment of asking his older sister whether she'd had absolutely mind-blowing sex the first time she and her husband had made love.

Rafe eased himself down onto his pillow, making sure not to disturb the sleeping woman at his side. She shifted slightly, but her eyes remained shut, her breathing regular and even. Good. It had to have been taxing for her to go from house to house, casting spells of protection, even though she'd said it was fine and didn't really require that much of her energy. Rafe hadn't been entirely sure about that—by the end of the afternoon, she'd begun to look pale and drained—but he'd also known that he couldn't stop her from doing what needed to be done.

The pain of his mother's loss lay somewhere below the afterglow of the evening's lovemaking, along with his concern over the very real and present danger Simon Escobar presented. Maybe at some point Rafe would allow himself to grieve properly, but he knew now wasn't the right time. Instead, he would take that pain and grief and channel it into revenge. What form that vengeance would take, he didn't know yet. On the surface, it didn't seem as though he had a very good chance of prevailing against Escobar, since the other warlock was so much stronger. But Rafe had gotten the drop on him this morning, and if he'd done it once, he could do it again.

Now, though, it was time to sleep, to get the rest he knew he needed. No matter what happened the next day, at least he knew he would face it with Miranda at his side.

Rafe awoke to Miranda pressing the lightest of kisses against his temple. When he stirred, she started slightly, then looked almost guilty.

"Sorry," she said. "You just looked so amazing lying there, I had to kiss you."

"It's all right," he replied, thinking it was more than all right. Really, was there a better way to wake up than to have the most beautiful witch in the world bending down and kissing you? He pushed himself up to a sitting position, was somewhat pleased to see the way Miranda's gaze moved over the muscles of his bare arms and chest. "What time is it?"

"A little past seven-thirty."

"No phone calls?"

She shook her head. With her hair tumbling down in a tousled mass over the tank top she wore and her face bare of makeup, she looked subtly different, but no less beautiful. More, actually. Or maybe that was just the afterglow from the previous night's lovemaking. "Nothing on my phone." The faint smile she'd been wearing disappeared. "Then again, no one except Cat even has that number. It's not like my parents can get through, thanks to Simon hexing all the cell towers in Santa Fe, or whatever it is that he's done to block my calls."

Right. It took Miranda's words to remind him that the Castillos were effectively cut off from the outside world. Most of the time, they kept themselves separate anyway, but that was their choice. He hated the way Simon had managed to isolate them even further, thus ensuring that there wouldn't be any help coming from the McAllisters or the Wilcoxes. No, the Castillos would have to manage this crisis on their own.

Rafe reached for the phone on his bedside

table, swiped his thumb over the biometric reader, and checked the home screen. No missed calls or texts. In a way, he supposed the absence of any communication should have been a relief, but he wished someone had reached out to him to check in, even if things had remained quiet overnight.

"I guess no news is good news," he said, doing his best to keep his tone light. Better to think that the radio silence only meant everyone was resting and doing their best to conserve their resources, rather than imagine Simon Escobar had come up with a new way to block contact between clan members. "Once we're up and dressed, I'll check in with Cat, see how Dad is doing. In the meantime, I guess we'd better order in some breakfast. I don't have much food in the house."

He really didn't, partly because he tended to go out most of the time anyway, and he'd been anticipating that he and Miranda would be in Taos for a week for their honeymoon and hadn't bothered to restock the freezer. All those plans had gone sideways, thanks to Simon Escobar, and in the chaotic days that followed, he hadn't had much of a chance to go to the store.

"You can order in breakfast?" Miranda asked, looking genuinely surprised.

"Sure," Rafe replied. "I do it all the time. There's a café not too far away that delivers. Smart, really—they kind of cater to all the government workers downtown. State capital, remember."

She nodded. "Right. I guess I hadn't thought about that." Her demeanor changed subtly, and she looked almost shy. "Do you want to shower first, or should I?"

What he wanted to do was take her in the shower and make love to her all over again, with the hot water cascading down on them both, but he knew that would have to wait. They'd made love twice the night before, after all, and even though it seemed as if everything was quiet enough this morning, he guessed it was better for the two of them to be up and dressed and ready to face whatever the world—or Simon Escobar—might throw at them.

"You go ahead," Rafe told her. "I'll go down-stairs and make some coffee, have it ready for you when you get out."

"That sounds great." She kissed him on the cheek, as though worried that anything less innocuous might lead into something more, then slid out from under the covers. Damn. He'd known her body was beautiful, but looking at her long, slim legs and the bikini panties that barely covered her firm little ass, Rafe could feel himself start to harden again. Good thing she was focused on getting some underwear from the dresser and wasn't looking at him.

Then she was safely in the bathroom. The water started to run a minute or so later, and he let out a relieved breath, even as his erection started to back off. His body needed to get its act together; maybe he'd never been with a woman who had this kind of an effect on him before, but he had to focus, no matter how enticing Miranda had turned out to be.

He got out of bed as well, dug out a pair of sweat pants from the dresser, and went downstairs. The day was bright and sunny, cheerful despite the bare branches of the trees outside in the yard. Looking at those blue skies as he filled the coffeemaker, Rafe found it difficult to believe that his clan had been visited by such tragedy just the day before.

Unfortunately, bright blue skies couldn't erase the reality of his mother's death.

It still didn't feel quite real, though. He'd seen her lying there in death, knew she was gone forever, and yet his mind didn't want to accept the fact, wanted to tell him that if he just drove over to the big house, he'd find her there, probably out in the gardens, since she'd always made it her business to make sure the gardeners kept up with the fallen leaves and other debris.

But she wouldn't be there. The only people who now lived in the house where he'd grown up were his father and Cat.

Poor Cat. He hoped she hadn't had too tough a time of it last night, with Uncle José and Aunt Rosa over to make sure their father wasn't alone. Rosa had the world's biggest heart, but she tended to harp on Cat's continuing unattached state even worse than their mother ever had. It was very possible that she might have revisited that particular topic in an attempt to keep the conversation away from other, much more difficult subjects.

The coffee was done. Rafe got out two mugs and set them on the counter, marveling at how natural it felt to be fetching a mug for Miranda. They'd get to wake up next to each other every morning, share their morning coffee, talk about their plans for the day.

Well, at least he hoped that was how things would go. With Simon Escobar hovering in the background, who knew how all this would turn out? Sure, Miranda's parents had managed to defeat his father more than two decades ago, but circumstances were different now. That particular piece of history might not repeat itself.

Scowling, Rafe poured himself some coffee but left Miranda's mug empty, since he didn't know how long it would take her to shower and get dressed, and he didn't want her coffee to get cold. After he'd poured a minute amount of milk and just a sprinkle of sugar into his own mug, he leaned against the counter and took a sip, inwardly thanking God for caffeine. It wasn't that they'd stayed up particularly late, but yesterday's events still hung with him, making him feel more tired than he otherwise should.

Sooner than he'd expected, Miranda appeared at the entrance to the kitchen. Her hair was brushed and in much better shape than it had been a short time ago, and he guessed she hadn't washed it today. It had been a while since he'd lived under the same roof as his sister, but he remembered how long it used to take her to wash and blow-dry her hair, even if she wasn't messing around with a curling iron or whatever else she used to beat it into submission.

Miranda's face was still mostly bare, although it looked as though she'd put on a bit of lip gloss. Rafe had to hold back a smile at noticing the tint on her lips; it seemed obvious to him that she hadn't wanted to come downstairs with absolutely no makeup on at all. In her new clothes—dark closely-fitting jeans and a simple V-neck sweater in a deep shade of purple that made her green eyes look that much greener—she appeared relaxed and yet ready to face the day.

"The coffee smells great," she said.

"Let me pour you some." He set up the mug for her, then handed it over, adding, "There's milk in the fridge if you want any. And the sugar's in that orange bowl over there."

"Thanks." She flashed him a quick smile, then went to the refrigerator and got out the milk, adding about twice what he'd used to her mug. A spoonful of sugar, and she was leaning against the counter, the mug clutched in both hands. "Everything still quiet?"

"Looks that way." Rafe pointed to his phone, which he'd brought with him and set down on the countertop close to the coffeemaker. "No texts, no phone calls."

Rather than looking reassured, Miranda frowned suddenly. "Maybe Simon's decided to block *all* our calls and texts."

An echo of the same worry he'd had just a few minutes earlier. Still, it was an easy enough hypothesis to test. "I'll text Cat. It's pretty early, but she should be up."

"That sounds like a good idea."

As Miranda took her first cautious sip of coffee, Rafe typed out a quick text to his sister. *I just wanted to check in and make sure you're all okay. I hope Rosa didn't bug you too much.* Then he touched the little arrow to send the message before putting the phone back down on the counter so he could retrieve his coffee.

He'd barely taken a sip before the phone pinged at him. With one hand, he reached out to retrieve it, then looked down at the screen. Sure enough, there was Cat's reply.

I'm okay. Dad's holding up. But Rosa's driving me nuts. Please tell me you'll be over soon.

Holding back a smile, Rafe replied, *I still have to get in the shower and we need to eat, but we should be there around 9:30.*

Make it 9:00, came the response, and again Rafe had to smother a smile.

That should be doable. See you soon.

He put the phone down. "Communications seem to be fine. I guess it really was just quiet."

Miranda nodded, her expression considering. "Maybe. Yesterday I was thinking about whether the kind of magic Simon used to—well, what he used on your mother—whether it's a lot more taxing than when witches and warlocks use their regular powers. My dad didn't talk much about his brother and the dark stuff he was dabbling in, but I remember one time he said that using those sorts of magic could really take a toll, like there's a spiritual and physical cost for all of it."

"So even though Simon wanted to do more harm to my clan, he really didn't have enough juice left to do much about it?" Rafe hated to sound so cool and impersonal when discussing the magic that had killed his mother, but there was no point in getting emotional, not when they had to look at the situation logically and decide on their next course of action.

"Something like that." She sipped her coffee,

still obviously pondering the matter. "I honestly don't know that much about it, because it's not exactly a field of study that's encouraged in my clan...or anyone else's that I know of."

"But it's safe to say that it's not a matter of if Simon does something else, but when." Rafe ran a hand through his hair—no doubt making it stick out everywhere, if the sudden look of amusement he noticed on Miranda's face was any indication. "And what." As much as it pained him to have to ask the question, he knew this wasn't the time to dance around the issue. "You were with him for a week—what do you think he's going to do next?"

Her lips pursed, and she stared down into her half-drunk mug of coffee. "I can't say for sure, because he spent the whole time being all friendly and helpful, just trying to help me access my magic and work with it. I had absolutely no idea he wasn't what he said he was, except at the very last there, right before you showed up to rescue me. Then he let his true colors show, but it still wasn't enough to give me any real idea of what he might be capable of." Her eyes closed briefly, then opened again to meet Rafe's, worried and full of concern for his pain. "I couldn't have begun to guess that he would kill a woman in cold blood."

"I doubt that he cared whether Genoveva was a woman or not. She was an obstacle, or possibly a tool for stirring up chaos in the clan. Because no matter how smoothly the transition might be from *prima* to *prima*-in-waiting, it's still something that shakes up the dynamic in a witch family. It's the best thing he could do to make us all off-balance."

"You're right, of course." Miranda was silent for a moment, turning the coffee mug around in her hands, even though she didn't seem inclined to drink from it. When she glanced up at Rafe again, that worried look was back in her eyes. "Rafe, how strong is your sister Louisa? I mean, I know she was the *prima*-in-waiting, but…."

This was something that had worried him ever since he was old enough to fully analyze the situation. Did he dare tell Miranda about his concerns, though? It felt disloyal—not just to his sister, but to the clan as a whole.

Miranda is part of the Castillos now, he told himself. *No, there wasn't a big wedding in the cathedral, but we're now just as bonded together as though there had been. She needs to know the truth.*

"She's a strong witch," Rafe said slowly. "Her ability to track magic has always been powerful— and it began to manifest early, according to my parents. Usually you don't start to see our powers develop until we're around ten or eleven, but Louisa's showed up when she was around nine, I guess. But…."

"But?" Miranda asked, her tone very gentle.

"But I don't know if she's the *strongest* witch in our clan," he said. "I always got the feeling that my mother wanted Louisa to be the *prima*-in-waiting because that's just how she thought it should work."

"Power doesn't always pass from mother to daughter," Miranda pointed out.

"I know. I mean, my grandmother became *prima* after her aunt passed away, because Great-Aunt Teresa only had boys. But my mother wanted her daughter to follow her. And since it's the *prima* who determines who the *prima*-in-waiting is…." Rafe let the sentence trail off there. From the way she nodded, her mouth tightening slightly, Miranda knew exactly what he meant; he didn't have to go into excruciating detail. And while he didn't want to make excuses for his mother, he still found himself adding, "She must have thought that Louisa's powers would be strong enough for her to manage the clan. After all, with Joaquin Escobar gone, there weren't any enemies to worry about. The witch world was at peace."

"So she made her daughter the *prima*-in-waiting, even though there were probably better candidates out there."

Still feeling intensely disloyal, Rafe simply replied, "Yes."

Miranda set down her coffee cup, then turned

toward the window over the sink, her hands resting on the edge of the countertop. Gaze fixed on the bare trees and the blue skies beyond that window, she said, "Which means we could be in some serious shit, Rafe."

"I thought we already were."

She let out a breath that wasn't exactly a sigh and continued to stare out the window. With an uneasy feeling in the pit of his stomach, Rafe realized that the window faced northeast, roughly in the direction where Simon's hideout was located. Was Miranda reaching out toward him, doing her best to see what he might be doing at this very moment?

He didn't know. Her powers had expanded at an almost frightening pace under Escobar's tutelage, but Rafe didn't have much idea what she was and wasn't capable of.

"Well, yes, things are pretty bad right now," she said, finally shifting so she faced toward him again. "But that doesn't mean they couldn't get much, much worse."

Her words had the effect of a gut punch. Because he'd known deep down that his mother's murder, horrible as the crime might have been, might only be the first warning shot fired over the Castillo clan's bow. Someone like Simon Escobar didn't care about right or wrong, who he hurt, which lives he ruined. As far as Rafe could tell, the dark warlock wanted only two things.

Power…and Miranda McAllister.

She seemed to have been thinking much the same thing, since some of the pretty color in her cheeks had faded a bit. "He scares the crap out of me, Rafe," she said, her voice not much more than a whisper. "I don't know what he can do, what other hurt and suffering he's willing to cause. I suppose he'll do what he can to avoid using any magic that would attract attention from the civilian population, especially civilian authorities, but I'm not sure we can even count on that. Not really."

He hated the hopeless tone in her voice. It was far too early to give up, especially since they'd dealt Escobar a painful blow the day before. Yes, he'd retaliated by striking out against Genoveva, but even so, the way Rafe had managed to get into the house where Simon was holed up and help get Miranda away seemed to indicate that the dark warlock wasn't invincible.

"Well, he's had some time to recover, but we're all still fine, and there don't seem to be any new attacks," Rafe said. "That tells me your spells of protection are working, which means it's very possible that he's had to rethink some of his strategies. I have a feeling he wasn't expecting you to step in and provide that kind of help right away."

"Maybe." Her shoulders lifted, and then she came to him and wrapped her arms around his waist. Her sweater was very soft—cashmere, maybe—and felt good against his bare skin. So did her hair, brushing against his arms. At once a wave of arousal washed through him, but he did what he could to push it away. *Not now,* he told his body, which didn't seem inclined to cooperate at first. After a few seconds, though, his burgeoning erection calmed down enough to allow him to focus.

"Anyway," he went on, "like I said, we all seem to be safe for now. Let's order some breakfast, and then I'll shower and we'll head over to the house before Cat loses her shit with my Aunt Rosa. Okay?"

"Okay," Miranda said, then smiled.

Watching that expression take over her face was like watching the sun rise over warm desert sands. Rafe could only hope nothing would ever happen to take that smile away from her.

6

UNDERCURRENTS

Miranda

We headed over to the Castillo house after we finished devouring some of the best breakfast burritos I'd ever had. Funny how a decent meal could make you feel so much better about the world.

Or maybe it was the man sitting in the Jeep next to me, the clear morning sunshine outlining his fine profile. Just looking at him was enough to make my body ache for his touch all over again. I knew he'd wanted to make love this morning but had pushed the impulse aside, since we had so much else we needed to attend to. The Goddess only knew I wanted him just as badly. I'd always hoped I would connect with him on this level, but

I hadn't known for sure until last night. Then I realized that, despite our rocky beginnings, our bond was one that would be just as strong as any shared by a witch and a warlock.

When we got to the *prima's* house, there was a silver Subaru Outback parked on the street next to the driveway. I had to assume it belonged to Uncle José and Aunt Rosa. Had they stayed in the casita, or one of the house's spare bedrooms? The place definitely seemed big enough to hold at least two or three overnight guests; I knew I'd only been put up in the casita because Genoveva had wanted to create a little space between me and my new family until Rafe and I were married.

Well, now we'd done the one thing she'd basically forbidden…and on the same day she'd died. Maybe that realization should have made me feel guilty, but it didn't, not when I knew that it was right for Rafe and me to be together like this. A few words from a priest or a piece of paper from City Hall wouldn't make any difference. Of course I wanted to get married—*really* married—at some point, but I couldn't think about that just yet, not when we needed to figure out our strategy for handling Simon.

Simon. My mind wanted to shudder away from the way he'd forced me down on the couch, from what I knew he'd wanted to do to me, and yet I knew I needed to face the reality of that horrible experience as squarely as I could. If anything, I needed to take strength from the encounter. He'd been so sure he would prevail, but Rafe and I had managed to overpower him long enough to get away. Then again, we'd escaped because we'd gotten the drop on him, not because we'd won some kind of magical duel. I couldn't really expect to catch Simon off guard a second time.

And some part of me hoped that he wouldn't want me anymore, now that I'd been with Rafe, now that I was no longer "pure." Maybe it was crazy to think in such terms—after all, this was the twenty-first century—but I had to try to think like Simon would. He'd had a crazy upbringing, and yet I guessed he'd still been raised Catholic, was still probably old-fashioned about certain things.

Or maybe I was just trying to fool myself into hoping he wouldn't want me now, because that would make me a little less afraid of him.

Rafe took my hand as we walked up to the front door of the house. His fingers were warm, reassuringly strong. Still, I didn't know whether he'd reached out to offer me comfort…or whether he was seeking the same thing from me. It couldn't be easy to walk back into the house where his mother died.

Possibly out of respect for what had happened

here—or maybe because he knew his father and Cat had guests—Rafe rang the doorbell, rather than walk right in. Cat opened the door so quickly, I wondered whether she'd been lurking in the foyer, waiting for us to arrive.

"Thank God," she said in an undertone, then much louder and falsely cheery, "Hi, Rafe, Miranda."

"That good?" Rafe commented as we came inside and she shut the door behind us.

"You have no idea." Except for some redness to her eyelids, indicating she'd probably cried sometime during the night, Cat looked astonishingly put together, makeup done, wearing a slim black skirt and a black sweater, very different from her usual casual attire. I had a feeling the clothes and the makeup were an effort to mollify her Aunt Rosa.

"Well, we're here now." Rafe glanced past her into the living room, which appeared unoccupied. "Where is everyone?"

"Dad and Uncle José and Aunt Rosa went over to Our Lady of Guadalupe. I think they're going to have the service there. I said I'd wait here until you two showed up."

"I thought we agreed Mom's service would be small and quiet," Rafe said, a warning note in his voice.

"It will be," Cat replied. She reached up to rub

her temple; possibly, she had a headache. Not all that surprising, considering everything she'd been through during the past twenty-four hours. "It's just that obviously Uncle José has to know the details, since they have to make arrangements with his funeral home to bring—well, to bring the casket over."

"Right."

This time, I was the one who reached for Rafe's hand, twining my fingers with his. I couldn't begin to imagine how difficult all this must be for him, especially when he obviously wouldn't allow himself the time to truly grieve. "I'm so sorry you have to go through this. I feel like it's partly my fault."

"No, it's not," both Cat and Rafe said, almost in unison. Then she shook her head and went on, "It's not your fault that some nutcase decided to be obsessed with you. This is all on Simon Escobar's head."

"Exactly," Rafe said. "And we need to bring the fight to him before he tries anything else."

I looked at Rafe in some alarm. We hadn't discussed anything of the sort, so I didn't know why he thought it a good idea to suddenly be so aggressive. "I'm not so sure that will work—" I began, even as Cat broke in.

"Rafe, this isn't an action movie. This guy is

dangerous. We've already lost Mom. I'd rather not lose my brother, too."

His jaw set, but I could tell that Cat's words had helped to check him, if only a little. "Well, I'm not suggesting doing anything impulsive, but I also don't think we can afford to sit on our hands forever."

Probably not. The thing was, there didn't seem to be much middle ground between charging in after Simon, or waiting here in Santa Fe for him to make his next move.

Something occurred to me, though. "Maybe we can check with the property management company to see if he's even still at the estate in Tesuque. For all we know, things have been quiet because he changed his base of operations, thinking we were sure to come after him."

Relief shone in Cat's dark eyes. It was fairly obvious that she'd feared she wouldn't be able to stop her brother if he really did decide to go rushing after Simon Escobar. "You know which company handles that property?"

"Yes," I replied. "I was there when they called the house one time. Casas del Sol was the name."

Rafe nodded. "They're one of the biggest management companies here in Santa Fe. Makes sense that the owner of a place that high-end would be working with them. Let me call and see what I can find out."

As Cat and I watched, he got his cell phone out of his pocket and surfed around a bit to locate the number, then made the call. A brief pause, and then he said, "Hi—I was calling about the property in Tesuque, on Griego Hill Road. A friend of mine, Simon Gutierrez, was overseeing it for you. I haven't been able to reach him and was wondering—" A pause, during which Rafe was clearly listening to the person on the other end. Then, "You're sure? No, that's fine. Thanks for letting me know."

"What is it?" I asked.

Rafe returned the phone to his pocket. "Just like we thought. He bailed yesterday afternoon. Told the management company that he'd had a family emergency come up and that he couldn't stay through the end of his contract. The woman at Casas del Sol didn't sound too happy with him."

"She can get in line," Cat remarked, and I couldn't help but smile a little.

"True," Rafe said. "Mr. Escobar has a lot of people pretty pissed off at him. So now we know he's not still in Tesuque, but he can't have gone too far. He still needs to be close enough to make our lives difficult."

"But how close?" Cat asked. "I mean, he can't be *right* in Santa Fe, can he? Louisa would be able to tell if he was around."

"Not necessarily," I told her. "Simon can block his powers so other witches and warlocks can't tell what he really is. I'm not saying he could move in next door to her, because at least then she'd recognize him—well, unless he cast an illusion to change his appearance—but he still can pretty much move around inside the city limits without anyone knowing."

"Well, that's just great." Off in the depths of the house, a phone rang, and Cat startled slightly. "I'd better go get that," she said before hurrying toward the kitchen.

"You have a landline?" I asked, a little surprised.

"It's a very old house," Rafe replied, one corner of his mouth quirking upward. I gave him a pained look, and he added, "And I have some very old relatives. We've had the same number here longer than I've been alive, so it just made sense to keep it all going. Maybe Louisa will get rid of it, although I doubt it. Anyway, if someone's calling that number, it's one of the relatives. Dad would call Cat's cell. But let's go see."

He led me out of the foyer, then down the open hallway that divided the bottom floor of the house, passing the living room and dining room, and a smaller, more intimate space that I guessed was some kind of sitting room. The phone in question hung from one wall in the kitchen; Cat stood there now, wrapping the overstretched cord around her fingers as she spoke.

"No, we haven't decided yet," she said. "It was all so sudden—no, I don't think so. I really don't know much, Aunt Lucilla. I'm waiting to hear what my father has to say, and Louisa. It's really their decision." A long pause, during which she clearly was doing her best to hold back her mounting impatience. "No, not yet. I think he's talking to the bishop. Maybe you should call him directly. Mm-hmm. Okay. Right. I'll let him know as soon as he gets home."

She hung up then, and Rafe said, "I'm surprised you could get through that conversation without having your eyes roll out of your head."

Cat gave both of us a weary grin. "Believe me, I had to fight the temptation." Obviously, I must have looked puzzled, because she went on to explain, "Aunt Lucilla is really a cousin, but everyone just calls her 'aunt.' Anyway, she's eighty-five and a sweet old lady, but she feels left out if she's not in the center of everything. I know she didn't like hearing that nothing's been decided about Mom's funeral."

"She's going to like it even less when she finds out no one was invited, but we'll deal with that later." Rafe looked over at me, then asked, abruptly changing the subject, "Do you have any idea where Simon could have gone?"

I shook my head. "None at all. Your guess is as good as mine—probably better, because you'd know more than me which areas might appeal to him the most. If the Tesuque estate is any indication of the sort of property he wants, then I'd say it would be something on a big plot of land, kind of isolated. Not in the center of town, that's for sure."

Cat and Rafe exchanged a glance. She shrugged, while he said, "That describes a lot of properties in Santa Fe County. Once you get outside the city itself, it's normal to have houses on three, four, even five or more acres."

Great. "Well, another thing about the estate was that it felt private because of all the trees around the house and on the property line. I haven't gotten out much, but I noticed when I was taking the Railrunner up from Albuquerque that most of the land around here is pretty open."

"That's for sure." Rafe went quiet for a moment, clearly pondering the problem at hand. Right then he looked very dark and brooding, and handsomer than ever. Or was I just watching him with sex-afterglow goggles on?

Not that it mattered. Despite everything, I had to fight the overwhelming urge to tell Cat we had important business to attend to so I could drag him back to the house and into bed once more.

"What about La Cienega?" Cat asked.

Rafe considered that suggestion for a moment, then slowly nodded. "Maybe. There's a spur of the Rio Grande down there—Cienega Creek. That means it's a lot greener than the land around it, lots of trees. There are properties down there that are pretty isolated, so one of them could work as Simon's backup hideout…especially since there aren't many Castillos in that part of Santa Fe County."

That sounded promising. At this time of year, the cottonwood and sycamore trees would be mostly bare, but Santa Fe and its environs had lots of evergreens, too, mostly juniper and piñon pine. If there were enough of them down in La Cienega, then they'd still provide plenty of shelter. "How far is that from Santa Fe proper?"

"Not too far," Rafe replied. "About fifteen, twenty minutes from the center of town."

"If that's even where he went," Cat said. "He could have gone up into Pojoaque, or out to Glorieta or Pecos."

Rafe looked dubious. "Those are all a lot farther out, though. I don't care how powerful Simon is—if he's suddenly having to send his spells fifteen or twenty miles, they're going to be weaker. I don't think he'd compromise himself that way."

I had a feeling Rafe was probably right. It

seemed clear enough that Simon wanted to inflict whatever damage he could on the Castillo clan, and intentionally weakening the effectiveness of his spells didn't line up with his plans for vengeance. This La Cienega place sounded promising, but we couldn't count on that, especially since it wasn't as though we could go out and conduct a house-to-house search for him. With the powers he had at his command, he could make us walk right past the place where he was holed up, and we'd never even know.

Then Cat winced, and put her hand to her temple again. "Are you okay?" I asked.

She shook her head. "I don't know. I've been feeling that weird pressure off and on all morning. It was okay last night, but…."

Damn. The last thing I wanted to believe was that Simon might be hurting her in some way. I glanced over at Rafe, who frowned. "Do you think you might somehow be feeling Simon working his magic?"

"I don't know." She shot a nervous glance at both of us and added, "I kind of hope not. That would be creepy."

"It's possible, though."

"I guess."

Why Cat would be able to feel that kind of a manifestation when I couldn't, I had no idea. Magic was such a slippery thing in so many ways.

No two people's experience of it were exactly alike; we all had to come to it in our own ways, with our own sets of beliefs and prejudices. However, an idea was beginning to form in my mind. "What if it's more that you can tell he's doing something, but it's mostly blocked because of the protective spell on the house?"

Rafe said, "That would make a lot of sense."

A bit of hope showed in Cat's face, but then she shook her head. "I don't think that's it, though. The first time I felt this pressure, we were at the hospital, visiting Marco. There was no spell of protection there, that's for sure."

Damn. And there I'd thought I was on to something. Still, it wasn't as though these weird sensations Cat was experiencing could be explained away as simply migraines or something with a purely physical cause. Deep in my gut, I knew they had to be connected to Simon's magic, even if I couldn't trace that connection at the moment.

From the disappointment in Rafe's expression, I could tell he was really hoping it would be a simple explanation like that. Although I knew he loved Cat fiercely and would never want to see any harm come to her, it would have been helpful to know for sure that she experienced those twinges whenever Simon was up to something, like an early warning system or our own personal magical barometer.

Before either of us could reply to her, however, I heard the sound of voices coming from the front of the house, and guessed that Eduardo and Uncle José and Aunt Rosa must have returned from their trip to the chapel. Sure enough, a moment later all three of them appeared, looking somewhat surprised that we'd congregated in the kitchen.

"Ah, there you are, Cat," Aunt Rosa said. Looking at her, I could see some resemblance to her younger brother Eduardo—the same long, aristocratic nose and finely molded mouth—but she was short and much more rounded, almost plump, while Eduardo was tall and well-built. Immediately, she turned toward me. "And here is Miranda. José and I are so glad you could be with the family in their hour of need. What a dreadful business, all of it."

I opened my mouth to make some kind of reply, possibly a few words of condolence, but she didn't give me the chance. Instead she turned to Rafe.

"You need a haircut," she pronounced, looking at him with a critical eye. From the way his mouth twitched, I guessed this wasn't the first time she'd made a comment along those lines. "But ah, the chapel will be lovely, although I still think it's a tragedy that Genoveva won't have her service at the cathedral."

"The whole thing is a tragedy, Rosa," Eduardo murmured.

At once she stopped, then gave a large sigh. "That it is, of course. A tragedy for you, and for the entire clan. I am just saying that it is also sad that Genoveva could not be given the respect she deserves when she is laid to rest."

"The respect is in our hearts, my dear, not in how many people attend Genoveva's funeral," José said, clearly used to these sorts of pronouncements from his wife.

Once again Rosa sighed. "I suppose you are right, José, but still—"

"Aunt Lucilla called while you were out," Cat cut in, her voice strained. "She was not happy when I wouldn't tell her anything about the funeral."

"No, I suppose she wouldn't be," Eduardo said, and offered his daughter a gentle smile. Grief had given him shadows under his eyes, and lines in his face I could have sworn weren't there when I'd first met him less than two weeks earlier, but the love for his family still shone in his handsome features. "I'll call her later, once I've figured out what I can safely tell her."

"I can call—" Rosa began, but her brother shook his head.

"No, if you call, she'll know I'm trying to avoid her. Sooner or later, everyone will know that we've gone ahead and had Genoveva's service without the rest of the clan present. I hope by that point I'll be able to explain why we had to do such a thing."

"When will the service be, Dad?" Cat asked.

"Tomorrow, at eleven in the morning. At least we were able to get that much planned." Another weary smile, and he went on, "That means we won't have to hold off the inquiries for too much longer."

Rafe shifted his weight as he stood next to me, then said, "Simon's left the estate where he was hiding."

Eduardo's brows pulled together, but he didn't look all that surprised. "I suppose that was inevitable, since he knows we know where he was living. But I also suppose it's no use hoping that he's left entirely."

"We don't want him to have left the area," Rafe returned, arms crossed and a martial light in his dark eyes. "We want to make sure he gets what's coming to him."

"If that's even possible." Eduardo's gaze moved to me, now faintly speculative. "I've heard that your powers are now quite formidable, Miranda, but the last thing I want is for you to be dragged into this thing."

I still didn't know Eduardo well, but I already felt the first stirrings of affection for the man who would one day be my father-in-law. He was so kindly and gentle, such a foil for the imperious Genoveva. Once again, I wondered how they could have gotten along so well, but I supposed theirs was the ultimate case of opposites attracting. And now she was gone. I'd heard that often consorts didn't live very long after their *primas* had passed, although I had to hope Eduardo would be the exception to that rule. He certainly was far too young to fade away, and the world would be worse off for his absence.

Since he was watching me with that air of gentle concern, I could only smile at him and say, "It looks like Simon's dragged me into it already. About all I can do is help keep everyone safe— and fight by Rafe's side, if it comes to that."

"A little thing like you?" Rosa asked, clearly not impressed by my comment. "I'm not quite sure what you think you could do in a fight."

Well, I wasn't entirely sure, either, but it wasn't as if I planned to get into a mixed martial arts brawl with Simon Escobar. Even as Rafe opened his mouth to protest, Cat rushed to my defense.

"Miranda is a very powerful witch, Aunt Rosa. I have a feeling if Simon tried to take her on, he'd be regretting it pretty quickly."

I could only hope so. The day before, I'd

managed to hold him off...but just barely. If he was waiting for me, had planned ahead for exactly that sort of confrontation, then I had a feeling he'd beat me, and badly. There was just so much about wielding magic that he knew, and I still didn't. He'd been my only teacher, but I wouldn't be able to get any further guidance from him, that was for sure.

Rosa sniffed, which made me think that was her standard response when she'd been outmaneuvered but didn't want to admit defeat. Something about her stubbornness reminded me of Genoveva. Maybe that was why Eduardo had been able to handle his wife so well—he'd already had years and years of dealing with that same sort of temperament in his sister.

"We don't know it will even come to that," I said. Even though I might have to face that eventuality one day, I really didn't want to think about having to go head-to-head with Simon. "I mean, just the fact that he's left Tesuque tells me he's a little afraid of what we might do to him. Otherwise, it would have been easier for him to stay put."

"Possibly," Rafe allowed. However, from the way he frowned slightly, I guessed he didn't think that was very likely. "Unless he's left because he found an even more defensible place."

Rafe had a point. I hoped he was wrong, though. The estate in Tesuque had seemed ideal, but for all its isolation, it did have acres of open land around it, land that could be used to sneak up behind him if you weren't too concerned about crossing someone's property lines. I wouldn't know La Cienega if you dropped me in the middle of it. However, I hadn't forgotten Rafe mentioning a creek there, an offshoot from the Rio Grande. If that creek was big enough, it could create a natural barrier...assuming Simon had been able to find someplace that backed up to it. Then all he'd have to worry about was a frontal assault.

I was about to say as much when Rafe's cell phone rang. He got it out of his pocket, checked the screen briefly to see who was calling, then put the phone up to his ear. "Hi, John. What's —?" That was as far as he got. The blood drained from his face, and he stood there, face like a stone, as he listened to the person on the other end of the line. I didn't know who John was. The name sounded vaguely familiar, but there were so many Castillos....

Everyone else clearly knew who was calling, though. The strain in Eduardo's face was almost painful to see, as though he knew this had to be yet more terrible news, yet another blow for the Castillo clan to suffer. Cat was just as pale as her brother, while Rosa quietly reached for her husband José's hand.

At last Rafe said, "Okay. We'll be right over." He touched the screen to end the call, then looked up at his watching family. I'd seen that terrible look in his eyes before...right after he found out his mother was dead.

"That was John," he said, quite unnecessarily. "Malena has collapsed."

7

TARGETS

Rafe

Malena's house was out in Las Campanas, not far from Louisa's place. Rafe had always suspected that they'd both settled in that area west of downtown Santa Fe because it gave them a healthy amount of space from their mother, while not being quite so far away that she'd have any real cause for complaint. Also, that area was so upscale, no one could really question why they'd want to live there. His two sisters had always been close, maybe even closer than he was with Cat.

And now one of them was….

His mind skittered away from that thought. Out of the corner of his eye, he saw Miranda watching him worriedly, her face pale and strained. Well, no wonder. What with the way family members were dropping like flies....

Again, he made himself avoid following that line of thinking. Better to focus on the road ahead, the long, winding route that led them away from the 599 and into the heart of Las Campanas. Past the golf course, past several gated communities, and then into the neighborhood where both Malena's and Louisa's homes were located. Behind him was his parents' dark gray S-Class, with José riding shotgun and Cat and Rosa in the back seat. Thank God there'd been too many of them to fit into one vehicle; Rafe knew he would have gone crazy if he'd had to ride along with everyone else, rather than taking his Jeep Wrangler. He needed to be able to drive so he could focus on the road rather than the horrors that seemed to be unfolding around him.

They turned down onto a long gravel driveway, then pulled up next to the white Volvo crossover SUV parked in front of the garage. Louisa and Oscar's car—Malena's and John's vehicles were probably safely inside.

Rafe had barely cut the engine when the gate in the low wall that fronted the house opened, and Oscar came hurrying toward them. That made sense. John would have wanted to stay with Malena.

The Mercedes came down the driveway next,

parking behind Louisa and Oscar's Volvo. Everyone climbed out, even as Oscar stopped a few feet away from Rafe and Miranda. "Thank God," he said. "Louisa's nearly in hysterics, and John has his hands full trying to keep Elisa away—"

"What happened?" Rafe asked.

"We—we don't really know," Oscar replied. He'd always been an outdoorsy-looking guy, his normally olive skin almost always tanned to a dark brown, hair cut short, usually in jeans and a khaki shirt—about the last person you'd ever suspect was a warlock. Now, though, he seemed just about as pale as everyone else, brown eyes haunted. He paused for a moment, waiting for everyone else to get close enough to hear what he was saying. "Louisa and I came over because none of us really wanted to be alone, you know? Also, Malena and Louisa were going to plan the flowers for Genoveva's service. We were all in the living room, having coffee and talking. Then Malena put her hands to her throat and whispered, 'I can't,' and just sort of stopped for a second before she slumped over. John caught her before she fell off the couch, but…."

"But…?" Rafe probed gently, even though he really hadn't wanted to ask. He didn't want to know what was going to come next, not after what had happened to his mother. *None of us are safe,* echoed in his mind.

"But we couldn't get her to wake up, no matter what we did. We called Yesenia, and she's on her way. John and I put Malena in bed, since we didn't know what else to do."

Eduardo's face was tight with pain. "But she is alive."

"Yes…barely," Oscar said. He made a helpless gesture with one hand, as though he wanted to reach out to offer comfort but didn't quite know the best way how. "I guess all we can do now is wait for Yesenia, see what she has to say."

Aunt Rosa's eyes were glittering with tears, and José put a comforting arm around her. Right then, Rafe felt Miranda's hand slip into his own, clutch it tightly. He looked down at her, saw tears shining in her big green eyes as well. Thank God for her. Thank God for the way they'd made love the night before, such an offering of life in what appeared to be a season of death. No, Malena wasn't gone, was still with them, but from what Oscar had just said, it didn't sound good.

Rafe wouldn't allow Malena to be taken from them. Malena, who'd always been a bit bossy, had wanted to keep her obnoxious little brother properly in his place. Louisa had never been like that, had always seemed more distant, probably because she was focused on her role as the *prima*-in-waiting and thought she had more important uses for her energy than to scold her annoying younger brother. But Malena had been much more involved with him, and he couldn't imagine the kind of hole she'd make in his life if…well, *if.*

"Let's go inside," he said, and everyone sort of fell into place behind Oscar, who led them into the house.

They went past the living room, where a leather couch and love seat formed what should have been a cozy group in front of a gas kiva-style fireplace, and down the hall into the master bedroom. Malena lay in bed, face still and white, while John sat in a chair he'd pulled up to her bedside, and Louisa stood a few feet away, staring down at her sister's unmoving form, her face nearly as white as Malena's.

John looked up as everyone came in. Rafe hoped he would never see that expression on anyone else's face—hopeless, and yet angry and confused at the same time. "Why didn't it work?" he demanded, one hand clutching his wife's where it flopped over the edge of the bed.

"Why didn't what work?" Cat asked, very gently, as though she was afraid the wrong tone of voice would cause John to shatter like over-stressed glass.

"The spell of protection Malena cast on this house! She was sure it would work. And *she* said it should be enough," he added, accusing dark glare shifting toward Miranda.

Although Rafe felt her fingers tighten on his, she didn't flinch or shrink away. Voice calm, she said, "I hoped it would work. All I had to go on was that Rafe and I hadn't been attacked once I cast the protection spell on Rafe's house, since I'd assumed we would be Simon's first targets. And everything was fine at your father-in-law's house, too."

"So you're saying Malena didn't cast it correctly?"

"No, that's not what I'm saying." Miranda's tone was still even enough, but Rafe could sense the tension in her slender form, the way she was keeping herself from biting out an angry retort. Obviously, she didn't want to get in an argument with John, belligerent as he was being.

Not that Rafe could blame him. It was easier to retreat into anger than into sorrow. He knew that all too well.

"Then what are you saying?"

"It could be anything. Maybe Simon's powers are expanding, and he tested them here first. I just don't know."

She looked from John up at Rafe, as though she needed some reassurance from him before she continued. He held her hand, keeping his fingers twined around hers, all the while hoping she could feel some of the strength and love he was attempting to send to her.

It seemed to work, because she pulled in a breath and went on, "For all I know, Simon could breach the spells I set up, too, and didn't because he wanted me to think we were all safe. It's just the sort of twisted maneuver he would pull. And —and I'm very sorry if he attacked Malena because of anything I've done. I'm really...sorry about everything. I know Simon is doing all this to get back at me."

John's eyes blazed with dark fire. Normally, Rafe would have described him as easygoing, friendly, the sort of person you could always rely on to show up with his truck when you needed something moved. He'd made a good life here with Malena and their daughter. Now, though, Rafe thought his brother-in-law was almost unrecognizable, his pleasant good looks twisted with grief and anger. "Then maybe you should leave. Go back to Arizona and take your curses and this Simon bastard with you before he does anything worse."

"John!" Cat burst out, then put her hand to her mouth, as though she wanted to prevent herself from saying anything further.

Eduardo stepped forward. Rafe thought he had never seen his father look so tired. Before he could speak, though, Louisa got up from the couch, tears still glimmering on her cheeks.

"That is very unfair, John," she said. Her voice trembled slightly, and Rafe could tell how much it was costing her to stay relatively calm while looking down at the limp form of her beloved sister, lost in some sort of magic-induced coma. "Miranda has done everything she could to help out. None of this is her fault. She's not responsible for Simon Escobar's actions."

John's eyes narrowed, but he muttered, "Sorry," and shifted back in his chair, his gaze avoiding everyone else's…especially Miranda's.

Not exactly the most heartfelt of apologies, but that was probably all they were going to get. Rafe looked over at Louisa. "What next?" he asked.

"I—I don't know." She plucked at the sleeve of the dark sweater she wore. Very rarely had Rafe seen his sister appear so helpless, and he didn't like it one bit. "If it's possible that Malena's spell wasn't strong enough, that means all the people we thought she was protecting might be in danger." Her gaze shifted to Miranda. "I know we've already asked so much of you, but I would feel better if you would go and recast all those spells."

"It's fine," Miranda said at once. "I'll do it here first, then take care of everyone else."

"You're a little late to protect this house," John said, and Louisa frowned.

"There's still your daughter to worry about," she retorted. "And yourself."

At the mention of his child, John seemed to sag suddenly. Rafe wondered where she was. Maybe at a friend's house? He knew that Elisa had a lot of civilian friends in the neighborhood, and it was very possible she's been off playing somewhere else when Escobar's dark magic struck at their mother. Perversely, he thought that the little girl was probably safer at a neighbor's house than she would have been at home. Any incident or accident that occurred where the civilian authorities had to step in meant increased scrutiny, and Rafe doubted Simon Escobar wanted to deal with anything like that.

"It's all right," Miranda said gently. "I'll just go down the hall where it's a little quieter and cast the spell there."

"Thank you," Louisa said, gratitude clear in her voice and her expression. Although her eyes were bright with unshed tears, she appeared to be holding herself together, at least until the clan's healer could arrive and deliver her verdict.

Reluctantly, Rafe let go of Miranda's hand and watched as she left the living room and went a little ways down the long hallway that ran the length of the house. Since the layout curved somewhat to match the contours of the landscape—and to offer the best possible views on the east side of the house, which faced toward the Sangre de Cristo mountains—he couldn't see exactly where she stopped. And because their kind of magic was quiet, everything to do with internal focus for external effects, it wasn't as though he could hear her reciting the words of the spell.

"What next?" Rafe asked his sister.

"When Miranda is done here, go to the houses where Malena cast her spells and make sure that they're truly protected. As soon as I hear something from Yesenia, I'll call you." Louisa hesitated, fingers toying with the silver cross she wore around her neck. "I'm not sure there's much more any of us can do right now."

"I'll go with you," Cat said. "Maybe I can help a little."

"Thank you, Cat," Eduardo said. "I'm sure Miranda and Rafe would appreciate that."

Rafe didn't bother to argue, although he didn't know for sure what Cat could do. Casting spells of protection wasn't where her powers lay. But she wasn't needed here, either, for of course Louisa and Oscar and John would be with Malena until the healer arrived.

Miranda came back to the living room. "The protection spell is in place. I hope—I hope it will work."

"I'm sure it will," Rafe said. He extended a hand, and she came over and took it. Her fingers felt cold, and he wished he could take her back to his house and make love to her again. Maybe that would do something to fix this dead, hollow feeling at the center of his body, as though he wasn't quite himself, was watching all these tragedies strike his family without allowing any of them to really affect him. "And Cat and I will show you where we need to go to strengthen the protection spells Malena cast yesterday."

"All right." She glanced from him to Louisa. "I'm—I'm so sorry."

"I know," Louisa said. "But we mustn't give up hope. Malena is still alive, and Yesenia is a very powerful healer. She may very well be able to bring Malena back to us."

Rafe could only nod. After what Simon had done to their mother, he wasn't nearly as sanguine as his sister. More likely, this was a spell that had gone awry, one that had been intended to kill just like the one that had struck down Genoveva. Now that the house had a real spell of protection on it, maybe Malena had a chance, but he couldn't be sure of that.

None of them could. Not really. Never before in his life had Rafe felt so helpless—not even after Miranda had disappeared—and he knew he would do whatever it took to make sure he never felt this way again.

They all went out, John bringing up the rear so he could lock the door. Rafe and Miranda waited until Rosa and José and Eduardo all climbed into Eduardo's S-Class, and then they got in the Jeep, with Cat squeezing herself in back.

Dead silence as they followed the Mercedes out to the main road. It wasn't until Rafe turned the Jeep north on Fin Del Sendero, while the two other cars kept going straight to the highway and on into town, that anyone spoke.

"God," Cat said. One simple syllable, but her voice trembled with emotion.

"I know." Rafe glanced at the rearview mirror, catching a glimpse of his sister's pale face. "You okay, Cat?"

"I'm not sure. I know Louisa's right, that we shouldn't give up hope, but...I guess I'm just sort of shell-shocked right now."

That was a good phrase for it. Just...numb. Too many shocks, too much pain. If he let it in, he wouldn't be able to function.

"I'm so sorry," Miranda said again. She was huddled into her seat, looking very small and forlorn. Gone was the strong, vivid woman who'd made such fierce love to him the evening before.

He couldn't really blame her. But obviously

she was still blaming herself, and that needed to stop.

"It's not your fault," he told her.

"It isn't," Cat chimed in from the back seat. "You've done everything you could. Malena swore she could handle the protection spells. Obviously, she couldn't."

Maybe they should have challenged her more on that particular assertion. But they'd all been stressed and worried, and Malena had seemed confident enough about her abilities to take care of her own household and the other Castillo families in the area that there hadn't been much point in arguing with her. It had seemed like a good idea at the time, especially since the last thing Rafe had wanted to do was make Miranda go to every single witch-occupied house in Santa Fe and cast her spell. That would have taken hours and hours, and she would have been completely exhausted by the time she was done, especially considering she'd started the day being attacked by Simon Escobar.

Frowning, Rafe did his best to push that ugly image out of his mind. At least he hadn't gotten any more panicked phone calls from clan members. He didn't think he could take much more of that. Bad enough that they'd have to get out the news of Malena's collapse, her inexplicable coma. Well, all right, it wasn't that inexplicable.

He had a pretty good idea of where it had come from.

As he looked back to change lanes so he could turn onto Tano Road, he caught another glimpse of Cat. She was staring off into the distance, lips pressed firmly together as though that was the only way she could keep herself from crying.

If anything should happen to her....

Was it wrong to admit to himself that he loved Cat more than either of his other sisters? It had always been that way, ever since she was born. Oh, sure, at the time he'd scowled and declared he was sick of sisters and wished he'd had a little brother instead, but the truth was, they'd bonded almost immediately, were always close, co-conspirators against their mother and sometimes even their sisters, if Malena and Louisa were being particularly stuffy about something.

And now they all seemed so fragile, their lives something that Simon Escobar could apparently reach out and snuff the way an ordinary person might blow out a candle. No care, no thought except how such an act might affect the Castillo clan.

Why Malena, though? Trying to get into Escobar's thought processes was unpleasant at best, but you'd think if he was really trying to destroy the Castillos, he would have gone after Louisa rather than Malena.

Maybe he had. Maybe the combination of Malena's protection spell and the *prima* gifts that had just come to Louisa from their mother had been enough to repel that dark magic, prevent it from finding its true target. If that was the case, then he could see why the spell might have sought out Malena next. She was a strong witch, possibly stronger than Cat, although it was hard to say since their talents were so very different.

But she hadn't been strong enough to completely fight off Escobar's death spell.

"Should we go to Nina's house first?" Cat asked from the back seat.

That had been his plan, although there were several Castillo households out this way. Still, Nina's was probably closest, although "close" was a relative term in an area where almost all the lots were between three and five acres in size, and the roads wound everywhere and meandered in picturesque but not very speedy ways.

Miranda stirred in her seat, looking out her window at the dry brush and junipers passing by. "Another cousin?"

Cat replied, "Yes—she's an artist. She lives by herself."

Out of the corner of his eye, Rafe saw Miranda's brows lift. It wasn't very common among witch-folk to be unattached, especially for someone like Nina, who was in her late forties.

"Nina always did things her way," he said. "She has a daughter around my age—she's married and lives down in Rio Rancho. But Nina didn't want to get married, even though I heard my grandmother threw a fit about her having a child out of wedlock. That's ancient history, though."

He supposed that was a true enough statement, although part of the reason Lisa, Nina's daughter, had settled in Rio Rancho was to put a safe distance between her and Genoveva, who'd decided that disapproval of Nina's life choices needed to be an intergenerational thing.

"No one knows who Lisa's father is," Cat put in. Now she didn't look quite as strained and pale, as though she, just like Rafe himself, was desperately searching for a distraction that would allow her to focus on something other than the tragedy that had once again struck her family. True, Malena was only in a coma, and hopefully she should come out of it at some point, since otherwise she was a healthy and energetic woman, but…. "Everyone thinks he was a civilian, since if it had been a Castillo, he probably would have said something."

"That sounds like my Aunt Margot's situation," Miranda said. "Her father was some Italian painter that her mother had a fling with when he came to the Verde Valley to paint one summer.

Margot's mother didn't want to get married, either, so I guess it was a good way to have the child she wanted without having to get attached."

"I'm glad it's not too much of a trend," Rafe remarked. "Because that would leave a bunch of warlocks with no one to marry."

Miranda reached over and laid a hand on his leg. Gently, in a reassuring sort of way, but even that light touch was enough to get his blood racing again. God, he had never expected she would have this kind of an effect on him. "I doubt that's going to be a problem," she told him, "considering how irresistible the Castillo men are."

He couldn't help but chuckle a little. "Not according to Cat."

His sister made a sound of disgust. "Thanks for the support, Rafe. Like it wasn't bad enough to have Mom—" She broke off there, clearly realizing she shouldn't be speaking ill of their mother when they'd only lost her the day before.

While Rafe understood why she'd stopped, he didn't think Cat should be too hard on herself. It was all right to grieve and yet still recognize the shortcomings of the person they mourned. Genoveva had given Cat way too much grief about being single, and everyone knew it.

Miranda said, "He's out there, though. I think you'll stumble across him when you least expect it."

Since they were only going twenty-five miles an hour, Rafe thought it was safe to steal a quick glance at his fiancée. She had a faraway look in her big green eyes, as though focused on something that none of them could see. A weird little chill ran down his back. "What, are you a seer now, too?"

The question seemed to make her snap back to herself. "I—I don't think so," she said with a nervous laugh. "I'm not really sure where that came from."

"Well, I hope you're right," Cat said. She'd been leaning forward slightly, but now she settled against the seat back, fingers playing with the safety belt that stretched across her chest. "Maybe this means some gorgeous, rich Wilcox warlock will appear and sweep me off my feet."

"I have to say, there are several who match that description. I guess it's just a matter of coaxing them over here."

"Which isn't going to happen, unless we can figure out what to do with that barrier Simon's put in place," Rafe remarked, glad he could comment on something other than the apparently overwhelming attractiveness of Wilcox men.

At once the faint smile Miranda had been wearing disappeared. "Right. I'd almost forgotten about that."

"I hadn't. But Louisa got the word out over

the family grapevine, so I don't think we're going to have any more car accidents at least. Good thing we witches and warlocks don't tend to travel much."

Cat grumped, "No, we never go anywhere."

He refrained from mentioning that the two of them had just flown to San Antonio a few days earlier. It wasn't as though that had been a pleasure trip, however. Besides, he hadn't yet told Miranda about his and Cat's abortive trip, and didn't want to add to her guilt over this whole situation, a guilt she couldn't quite seem to shake.

They pulled up into Nina's driveway. Her house wasn't large, but it sat on a hill that commanded a striking view of all of Santa Fe, with the Sangre de Cristos looming off to the left.

A chill breeze had begun to blow, and although the day had started off clear enough, a cloud passed over the sun. Rafe felt another one of those strange little shivers move its way down his spine, although he told himself there was nothing here to be frightened of. What Simon had been doing was horrible, but it was also obvious that he was intent on striking at the heart of the Castillo clan, rather than random distant cousins. There was no reason to think anything was wrong here.

It seemed as if both Cat and Miranda had felt it, too, however, because Cat frowned as she got out of the car, and Miranda hugged her arms around herself, as though she was suddenly far colder than the brisk breeze would warrant. By instinct, the three of them clustered together as they went up the front walk, which Rafe knew was surrounded by flowers in the warmer months, although the beds on either side were now not much more than carefully raked dirt, waiting for the return of the summer sun.

Wind chimes sang mournfully from the over-hang that shielded the front door. Rafe stepped forward and pressed the button for the doorbell, heard it sound within the house. However, no one came to answer that bell.

"Maybe she has music on or something and can't hear the doorbell?" Miranda asked.

"No, she works in dead silence," Rafe replied, with Cat adding,

"She always says that music distracts her. Anyway, we all heard the doorbell, so we should have been able to hear music if it was playing." Biting her lip, she leaned forward and knocked on the door, then called out, "Nina? Are you home? It's Rafe and Cat."

Only silence. Now it was almost impossible to ignore the creepy crawlies moving up and down his spine. Rafe knocked again, then decided the hell with etiquette. He put his hand on the latch, which pressed down easily. "It's not locked."

"Should we go in?" Miranda didn't seem too

thrilled by her own suggestion—not that Rafe could blame her.

"I think we'd better," Cat replied. "Rafe, you go first."

"Thanks," he said, but went ahead and opened the front door.

He'd only been here a few times, but as far as he could tell, everything seemed to be in order in the small entryway. One of Nina's paintings—an impressionistic blur of warm-hued autumn aspens—hung on the wall that faced the front door, and on the low table beneath it sat the same slate fountain, water quietly playing into the silence.

"Nina?" he called out.

Still nothing.

The house had three bedrooms—the master, one that had been Lisa's before she moved out, and one that Nina had converted into her studio. Rafe headed that way, mostly because he hadn't heard any signs of life in the main part of the house. Miranda and Cat followed, neither of them speaking.

As they approached the open door to Nina's studio, he at last heard something, a quick, whispery sort of sound. He glanced back at Miranda, and she gave a small lift of her shoulders, even as her worried gaze met his. Clearly, she'd heard the same thing.

He peered around the corner of the doorway

and froze. Nina stood there, brush moving rapidly across the canvas. However, instead of one of her usual landscapes, it was a rectangle of solid black, the paint growing thicker and thicker as she kept adding more and more from the palette perched on a small stand next to her.

"Nina?" he asked, having to work to get even those two small syllables out.

She didn't move, gave no sign that she knew anyone was there at all. Her brush kept swiping across the canvas.

Then she spoke, her voice only a cracked murmur. "They're coming. They're coming. They're coming."

And behind him, Cat let out a gasp and fainted dead away.

8

ARMY OF DARKNESS

Miranda

I DIDN'T STOP TO THINK, ONLY DROPPED TO my knees, immediately reaching for Cat's wrist. Thank the Goddess—there was her pulse, too fast, but strong enough.

Rafe's stricken gaze met mine. "Is she…?"

"She's okay," I said. "She just passed out. We need to get her to a couch or something."

Nodding, he bent and picked her up, then left the muttering Nina behind and headed back the way we'd come, back to the living room. Once there, he set Cat down on the sofa. Her head lolled on the pillow, dark hair streaming over it almost to the floor.

Rafe straightened, staring down at his sister. His expression was a tortured combination of anger, fear, and confusion. "What the *fuck* is going on?"

I didn't have a clue. "A different kind of spell?" I suggested. "One that affected your cousin and your sister in different ways?"

"Maybe." He ran a hand through his hair, eyes never leaving Cat's pale face. "You're sure she's okay?"

"Well, I'm not a healer or anything, but she's breathing and her heartbeat sounds fine. Luckily, she just sort of slumped down instead of going over backward, or she could have cracked her head open on that tile floor."

"Shit, you're right." Rafe hesitated, then glanced down the hallway toward Nina's studio. "'They're coming.' Who's coming?"

Again, all I could do was lift my shoulders in mystification. "I don't know. Is Nina a seer?"

"No," Rafe replied. "At least, I never heard that she was. Her talent is color, I guess. That's why she became a painter. She can see a color once and always replicate it, always match it. She once joked that she probably should have been an interior decorator, because she would have made more money at it."

I thought of the rectangle of pure black that sat on Nina's easel and shuddered. No color matching going on there, that was for sure. But I could see evidence of what Rafe was talking about in the room around me—the shades of the throw pillows on the beige couch coordinated exactly with the colors of the paintings that hung on the walls. More of Nina's work, I guessed, if the painting in the entryway was hers as well. The styles were the same, a sort of impressionism that bordered on the abstract.

And I vaguely recalled Rafe saying once that they didn't have any seers in the Castillos, although I couldn't remember the context of the conversation. Not that seers were the end-all, be-all when it came to being forewarned. They were often helpful, but, if the experience of my cousin Caitlin was anything to go by, it was more like the visions controlled her rather than vice versa. Even if the Castillos had had a seer, it wasn't as though we could have gone to her—or him, although seers tended to be female—and asked for the exact location where Simon was holed up, or to clarify just what the hell Rafe's cousin Nina meant when she kept saying, *They're coming.*

It felt sort of horrible to have left her in that room, adding more and more black paint to her canvas. On the other hand, she appeared other-wise safe and unharmed, and Cat was our more immediate concern.

She blinked, then opened her eyes. At first, they didn't seem able to focus on anything in particular, but then she blinked again and frowned slightly at Rafe.

"Where am I?"

The question was such a cliché, I almost wanted to break into nervous laughter. Then again, I could see why she would be confused. Even though she'd been to this house before, I got the feeling that she didn't exactly hang out here.

"We're at Nina's house," Rafe said, relief clear in his expression. After what had happened to Malena, he was probably expecting the worst. "You passed out. Do you remember anything?"

Cat pushed herself up to a sitting position, then rubbed her forehead. "I think I was feeling that pressure again, although it was worse than before. It felt like I couldn't breathe. It's still not gone completely, but at least I don't feel like I'm going to faint again." She looked around the room. "Where's Nina?"

I glanced up at Rafe. His mouth tightened slightly, but since he didn't tell me not to say anything, I guessed it was all right to give a truthful answer to Cat's question. "She's in her study. She's…in a fugue state or something. You don't remember the black canvas, the way she said 'they're coming'?"

"No." Cat frowned, this time with her fingers pressed against her temple, as though her head still hurt. "Or...I kind of remember the canvas. I just don't remember what happened next."

"We're not really sure what's going on," Rafe said slowly. His gaze moved from Cat to me. "Miranda, could it be another spell?"

"Maybe," I replied, then added, "Probably. I don't know why or how, though. I guess the best thing to do is cast a protection spell and see if it stops?"

"Yes, try that."

I closed my eyes briefly, visualizing a protective bubble encasing the house and its occupants, driving away any negative energies and preventing new ones from penetrating the shield the spell created. Almost at once, I felt better, as though some faint, foul smell had been driven from the room, even though I really hadn't noticed it previously.

"That's better," Cat said, almost as soon as I opened my eyes. "It's gone completely now."

Despite this promising development, Rafe still looked troubled. "Well, I guess that proves that your protection spells work, and Malena's really didn't. Which means we still have a lot of work to do."

I nodded, and held back a sigh. The strain of the day was already getting to me, and we still had a lot of houses to visit. But I couldn't shirk my duty. About all I could do was hope that the protection spells cast by other members of the clan were more effective than Malena's. The Castillos had more than a hundred households here in the greater Santa Fe area. It would take me several days to get through them all…and I didn't know if we had that much time.

Just as Cat began to ease her legs over the side of the couch so she could stand up, Nina entered the room. The oversized chambray shirt she wore was smeared with black paint, and she wore an expression that was just about as confused as I felt. She blinked when she saw us gathered in the living room. "Rafe? Cat? What—?"

"It's okay, Nina," Rafe said quickly. "We brought Miranda over to place a protection spell on the house."

Nina's brows drew together. She was a pretty woman in her forties, slender and not very tall, her black hair pulled up into a messy knot on top of her head. "Malena did that yesterday."

"It's just a precaution," I said. "We weren't sure if her spell was strong enough."

"Oh." Nina blinked again, then looked down at her stained shirt. "Do any of you know what happened to my canvas? It's covered in black paint, but I don't remember how it got there."

"Um, no, we don't," Cat replied. She stood up and tugged at her sweater, then smoothed her skirt as best she could. I could tell she was annoyed at having to wear such proper attire, which I had to admit wasn't very well suited to collapsing in hallways. "Maybe you were experimenting?"

"Maybe," Nina said, still in that same bemused-sounding tone. Her gaze slowly wandered to me. "Did you cast the spell?"

"Yes. Everything should be fine now." I had no idea whether those words were true or not, but I had to believe it would be okay. After all, Rafe and I were fine, as were Eduardo and Cat. That is, Cat had fainted, but not when she was in her own home, which was already protected by one of my spells.

"And we have other houses to go to," Rafe added. "But maybe it would be a good idea if you took a break for a while, Nina. I think you've been in there painting for too long today."

"Possibly," she said absently. "I did start right after breakfast. Well, it was nice meeting you, Miranda."

And then she drifted out of the room, back down the hall toward her studio. So much for taking a break.

"Should we do anything?" Cat murmured in an undertone, although I guessed that Nina was already out of earshot.

Rafe gave a helpless shrug. "What can we do? She seems okay, just a little out of it. And maybe her disorientation will go away the longer she's protected by Miranda's spell and the more time she has for the dark magic to wear off."

Cat looked down the hallway where Nina had disappeared, then tucked a lock of hair behind one ear. "Maybe. I guess we can ask Yesenia to look in on her, too."

"That sounds like a good idea." Rafe took me by the hand. "Are you ready, Miranda? We'll need to do this a few more times."

"Hopefully not exactly like this," I replied, thinking again of that black canvas, the urgent murmur of *they're coming...they're coming....*

"Hopefully not," he agreed.

But of course there was only one way to find out.

To my relief, though, we didn't have any more uncanny encounters after that. Everyone seemed a little puzzled by my coming around to perform the same spell that Malena had done just the day before, but no one seemed inclined to argue. Also, by the time we got to the last few houses, it was obvious that the word had gone out about Malena's condition, because people stopped asking about why I was casting these spells, and instead told Cat and Rafe they hoped their sister would have a speedy recovery.

At last we were done and headed back into the heart of town to take Cat home. When we got there, I was relieved to see that José and Rosa's Subaru was nowhere in evidence. While José seemed like a kindly soul, Rosa would have been a bit much to handle after the afternoon I'd put in. I guessed that Eduardo had sent them home, since there wasn't much for anyone to do except wait for Genoveva's funeral services the following morning.

Actually, I didn't see Eduardo's Mercedes, either. When we went inside, Rafe found a note on the table in the foyer, saying that Eduardo and Louisa and Oscar were all at Malena's, keeping watch. Yesenia had determined that it was all right for Malena to remain at her house rather than be sent to the hospital, since she seemed stable enough.

"It's just like Dad to leave a note rather than send a text," Cat said, setting the piece of paper back down on the table. "But I'm glad they didn't have to take Malena to the hospital."

"Well, we all know how well that worked the last time we tried it," Rafe replied darkly. "They probably didn't want to risk having her there."

I thought of how Simon's magic had killed their cousin Marco, even though he'd been in the intensive care ward at St. Vincent's. All those doctors and nurses hadn't been enough to save him. That realization only made the tension knot itself more tightly somewhere in the pit of my stomach, and I swallowed.

Cat nodded, arms wrapped tight around herself. She looked very cold, although the house itself was actually fairly warm. "I guess you two will be going home, then."

The words weren't exactly a plea, but I read between the lines. Cat didn't want to stay in this big gloomy place by herself, and I couldn't blame her.

Rafe had obviously also picked up on the subtext, because he said, "I think it's better if we stay with you until Dad comes home. We'll order some takeout."

"And have some wine?" she asked hopefully.

"Absolutely," I replied. I couldn't speak for the other two, but I definitely needed a drink.

"Perfect," Cat said.

After a bit of back and forth, we decided on Thai, since none of us had had it for a while. Rafe placed the order, and Cat and I set the big table in the dining room. As she laid down the last plate, she shook her head.

"It's going to be weird eating in here without Mom, even though we haven't had a lot of sit-down dinners lately."

I wished I knew her better, because Cat looked like she needed a hug right then. Maybe she would have been okay with an outward gesture of affection, maybe not. Even the brief time I'd spent around them had told me that the Castillos weren't the most demonstrative family in the world.

"It's hard, I know," I said. The words sounded horribly inadequate.

She shrugged. "What's bothering me is that it's not as hard as I thought it would be. Maybe it's just all this other craziness going on. I mean, I'm sad about my mother, and angry at Simon Escobar, but...." She let the words trail off, then looked up at me, a rueful smile tugging at her lips. "Maybe it just means I didn't love her as much as I thought I did."

This time I did go over and give her a quick hug. She looked startled, but I only said, "I'm not sure that's it at all. I mean, your mother was a difficult person, so I can see why your feelings would be complicated."

"'Difficult.' There's an understatement." Cat went over to the sideboard and got out some silverware, setting it down next to the plates. That silver was heavy and ornate, obviously a family heirloom. Possibly a bit much to go with Thai takeout, but then, maybe it was Cat's way of feeling connected to her Castillo heritage. "She and Rafe fought more. I mostly tried to stay out of the way."

"Well, I just think you shouldn't be too tough on yourself."

This time she smiled a little, dark eyes crinkling in amusement. "I could say the same thing about you."

"Which is what?" Rafe asked, coming into the room as he tucked his phone into his pocket.

"That we all need to be a little nicer to ourselves, especially now," Cat told him. "Food ordered?"

"It'll be here in about ten minutes."

Thank the Goddess for delivery. While we were waiting for the food to show up, we went and checked out the wine cabinet, deciding on a pinot noir. We chatted about wine, about Chinese food versus Thai, about anything except the way Malena lay in a coma at her house, or how we'd all be attending Genoveva's funeral the next morning.

Maybe it was wrong to pretend everything was normal, but I could tell we all desperately needed to feel that way, even if we understood that we were putting on a façade and nothing more.

And even after the food arrived and we were all sitting down, eating cashew chicken and pad thai and chicken fried rice, we focused more on the oddities of the day—that weird pressure Cat kept feeling, Nina's strange behavior, the possible reasons why my protection spells worked when Malena's didn't—than on Rafe and Cat's losses. It felt better trying to solve puzzles than come up with platitudes for something we couldn't fix or change.

Eventually, Eduardo came home, looking weary but pleased to see us all gathered there—and, most likely, relieved that none of us had come to any harm. We all went into the living room to hear his news. Malena was stable for now, really more in a deep sleep than a coma, albeit a sleep she couldn't seem to wake from. And Louisa and Oscar had gone home, satisfied that Malena wasn't in any immediate danger.

"And we should go home, too," Rafe said. The table had been cleared, the leftovers put away. I didn't know about him and Cat, but I had a faint wine buzz going, just enough to smooth down the sharp edges of an extremely rough day. He looked over at his father and sister, who occupied the pair of matching chairs opposite the couch where we sat. "It'll be another hard day tomorrow."

Yes, there was still the funeral to get through. At least it would be a quiet ceremony, just the four of us, plus Louisa and Oscar and maybe José and Rosa, although I hadn't heard for certain whether they would be attending or not. John wouldn't leave Malena's side, which I supposed was the right thing to do. All of

Genoveva's other children would be there, after all.

We said our goodbyes and headed back to Rafe's place. He'd barely shut the door behind us before he was pulling me to him, kissing me. I knew part of his urgent need was only his desire to reassure himself that I was safe, that we were both still okay. I welcomed his touch, because I was feeling the same thing. We needed to be together, to make sure our bond was as strong as it could be.

Upstairs then, to the bedroom we now shared. Our clothing fell to the ground piece by piece, and then we were on the bed, skin to skin, lips locked together even as our bodies joined in furious intercourse. No foreplay this time; no, this was raw animal need, an affirmation of our life forces, the strange bond that connected us even though we weren't husband and wife yet. That didn't matter, though. The only thing that mattered was the man who held me, whose body was locked together with mine.

And afterward, we slept entwined in one another's arms, knowing that here, together, we were safe.

Part of the reason my shopping at Dillard's had

taken a little longer than planned was that Cat and I had both realized I needed to get something to wear to her mother's funeral, in addition to the everyday stuff required to replace the clothing I'd left behind at the Tesuque estate. I stood in front of the bathroom mirror in the master suite at Rafe's house and scrutinized my appearance, hoping that no one would find fault with the modest black dress and matching sweater I wore, or the pumps with the low kitten heels. Growing up in Jerome, I'd worn flats all the time—the streets there were way too uneven to even think about stilettos—and so I'd never learned to walk in anything higher than about an inch heel.

At least I'd been wearing my jewelry when I fled Simon's hideout, so I still had my tourmaline earrings and silver bracelet and ring. I supposed if I'd had nothing, I could have asked to borrow a few pieces from Cat, but I was glad I could wear my own jewelry.

"You look fine," Rafe said, giving me a quick glance. "No one's going to be paying much attention to what we're wearing, anyway."

He didn't add, *Since it was always Genoveva who worried about that sort of stuff,* but I got the vibe anyway. True, Eduardo and Louisa would probably be too occupied with their grief to notice much. Even so, I wanted to make sure it looked as though I was paying the proper respect to their late mother, that I understood the customs and rituals of this old, old clan.

Rafe looked pretty proper himself, in a charcoal gray suit and subdued tie in shades of gray and slate blue. In fact, the whole ensemble was so out of character that I guessed his mother must have chosen it for him, or maybe his father. I went over and straightened his tie, then went on my tiptoes to give him a quick kiss.

"You're looking pretty fine yourself," I replied. "I like a man in a suit."

He shot me a pained glance. "Don't get too used to it."

Pure Rafe. However, considering we were just about to leave for his mother's funeral, I decided it was probably better to hold back any retorts. Instead, I shrugged, then said, "We should probably get going."

A huff of breath, followed by a reluctant nod. "I wish we didn't have to."

"It sounds as though it's going to be pretty quiet."

"I know, but even a quiet Catholic funeral is still long. And…." The words drifted into silence, and he jammed his hands into his pants pockets, his gaze avoiding mine.

"It's so final. I know." I touched his arm, hoping he could feel how much I loved him, how much I hated to see him going through this.

"'Final.' Yeah, that's a good word for it." He paused for a few seconds, gaze moving around the room even though I really didn't know what he was looking for. "Okay, let's go."

We headed downstairs, then out to the garage so we could get in his Jeep. Neither of us spoke on our way over to the church. It was a pretty Spanish-style building, much less grand than the chapel where Rafe and I were supposed to get married, but also much friendlier in feel. There were only a few cars in the parking lot—Eduardo's Mercedes sedan, the Volvo I recognized as Louisa and Oscar's. I didn't see any sign of Rosa and José's Subaru, so I assumed they weren't coming after all. Possibly José wanted to make sure everything was ready at the funeral home once the service was over.

Soft organ music was playing as we entered the church. Even though the place wasn't all that large, the ranks of empty pews were somehow intimidating, as if they served to point out how many Castillos should have been here to honor the passing of their *prima*. Only the very front pew off to the left was occupied, everyone apparently wishing to cluster together rather than scattering amongst all those open benches.

There was just enough room for us to squeeze in to one side, next to Oscar, who sat at the end, shoulder touching Louisa's, while Cat was on her right, sitting beside Eduardo. He turned his head and gave us a small, sad smile before looking forward again, at the lily-draped coffin that stood on the altar.

That coffin looked far too small to hold someone as formidable as Genoveva Castillo. Still, I remembered that she really hadn't been all that tall a woman—she just made everyone think she was.

The priest, a slim man of middle height and middle age, came out then, and walked over to Eduardo and murmured something to him I couldn't quite hear. Maybe he was only getting confirmation that there would be no other mourners. Whatever the content of their exchange, the priest gave a nod at the end and went back up to the altar, then said, "We have come to honor the memory of Genoveva Anna Lorena Castillo, who was taken from us far too soon."

Even though I certainly hadn't been a fan of Genoveva Castillo when she was alive, I could feel tears begin to burn in my eyes. Because she was taken far too soon, and all because of Simon Escobar's spite. It wasn't fair, and neither was Malena lying in a coma several miles from where we now sat, or Nina going into some weird kind of fugue state and destroying one of her canvases.

Or, come to think of it, Cat experiencing

some kind of otherworldly mental pressure so bad that it actually caused her to black out.

As Rafe had said, the ceremony was long. At certain points, Eduardo and Oscar got up to read passages from the Bible. I hadn't been raised in that tradition, so the words were unfamiliar to me. However, there was a certain beauty in those passages, in words laid down by men who had long since gone into dust.

At last, though, the time to say the final prayer had arrived—the Lord's Prayer, as we all stood there and began to murmur the words, even me, who had picked them up purely through reading and watching television and movies, not because the prayer was anything I'd been taught in my parents' house. According to Rafe, this part was usually done at the grave site, but they'd decided it would be safer to have the entire ceremony here now, and quietly bury Genoveva the next day.

"*For Thine is the Kingdom,*" we said in unison…

…and then all hell broke loose.

Cat gave a wailing cry and clutched her head as she sank to the floor, writhing. Eduardo began to bend toward her, even as the rest of us leapt up from the pew to offer our own assistance. In the next moment, though, her wails weren't the only thing tearing at the still air of the church.

From nowhere, dark, hideous winged shapes

dove toward us. I saw the reddish glare of their eyes, the obsidian gleam of their talons. Nina's words echoed in my mind...*they're coming... they're coming...they're coming...*and cold realization swept over me. I knew what these creatures must be, even though of course I'd never seen one, had only heard about the way they'd tried to attack my hometown so many years before.

Demons.

They came so quickly, I barely had time to raise my hands in the same protective gesture I'd used only the day before on Simon Escobar. The magic burned through me, moving outward in a shockwave of shimmering power.

It hit the first group of demons, blowing them backward so they tumbled over and over in the air, yet somehow managed to stay aloft. However, a second wave of the nightmarish creatures roared past them, claws outstretched, screaming toward the pew where we'd all been sitting.

Not at me, though.

At Louisa.

Oscar obviously saw that she was their target, because he pushed her to the ground, covering her with his body. Screeching in frustration, two of the demons dug their claws into his suit jacket and flung him aside like a rag doll. He hit the side of the altar and groaned, but apparently the blow wasn't strong enough to knock him out, because at once he was on his hands and knees, crawling toward his wife.

Beside me, Rafe growled. I let myself glance over at him, saw his eyes beginning to glow with red fire.

Which meant he was probably getting ready to shift into wolf form.

I didn't know what a wolf could do against these hellish creatures. Again I sent a shockwave spinning toward the demons, but although it stopped them from moving forward for a moment or two, it obviously wasn't doing much except making them angrier and more agitated. It certainly didn't seem to hurt them much, and I had to push back my fear as best I could, even while cold worry flooded through me. What if my magic wasn't enough to defeat them?

All this had happened in the space of a second or two. The horrified priest stepped forward, raising both his hands in an unconscious imitation of the same gesture I had used to drive the demons back, although his intent was very different.

"Stop!" he cried out, and lifted the large cross he wore around his neck. "This is a house of God!"

They're not that kind of demons, I thought, but I didn't have time to warn him. Several of the demons made a screeching noise that might have been laughter, and then the priest was grasped by his cassock and thrown backward, slamming into the wall with a thud that made me wince. For one horrible second, I thought they'd killed him, but then I saw one arm move, painfully beginning to push himself up to a sitting position.

Why the hell hadn't I cast a spell of protection as Rafe and I entered the church? We'd been in a hurry, the last to arrive, but still—

After that thought flitted though my mind, I didn't have any more time to spare, because the demons circled back, heading again for Louisa, although one of them split off and grabbed Oscar again, this time hurling him with such force that when he hit the ground, he remained still and unmoving. I wasn't sure why the demons had made Louisa their target, since clearly I was more of a threat to them; her powers as *prima* weren't necessarily the kind that could help her here.

Cursing, I once again sent a shockwave toward the demons. It seemed the most I could do—I didn't know how to dispel demons, and it wasn't as though I had a sword I could use to chop off their heads…not that I would have known what to do with a sword even if I'd been holding one. Rafe seemed to realize the same thing, because he hurried toward his sister, then crouched down next to her prone body, teeth bared in a snarl, although he still held to his human form for now.

And then it was as though an invisible hand slammed into my chest, knocking me backward so I fell into the center aisle of the church. The demons made that screeching laugh again, a sound that tore at my ears. As I struggled to push myself upright, a tall form materialized on the altar, standing in front of the lectern.

Simon Escobar, although he looked subtly different now, his usual T-shirt and jeans traded for a black shirt and black pants. Maybe he thought it was time to start dressing like a dark warlock, since we all knew now what he was.

He smiled at me, a mocking smile. His eyes shifted toward the left, over to where Rafe knelt next to his sister's limp form. One hand lifted.

I didn't know what he intended to do, but it couldn't be good. "Simon, stop!" I cried.

His gaze traveled back toward me, and one eyebrow lifted slightly. "You want me to stop, Miranda?"

"Yes," I said, my voice trembling. Sharp little pains from hitting the floor with so much force had begun to spring up all over my body, but I did my best to ignore them as I staggered to my feet. "Please, Simon. None of these people have done anything to you."

For a moment, he didn't reply. Then he descended the stairs from the altar, each step slow, deliberate. The entire time, his eyes remained fixed on me. Off to one side, Rafe made one of those rumbling growling noises in his throat again, but I didn't know if he still intended to shift into animal form or whether he was waiting to see what Simon would do.

"They are Castillos," he said, his voice careless, although the angry glint in his black eyes gave the lie to his casual tone. "That means they have done plenty to me. Are you their spokesperson? Going to bargain for their lives?"

"This is my family," Eduardo said, stepping forward. During the fray, he seemed to have escaped the demons' attention, possibly because of the magical gift that always sent him the best possible fortune. "I will speak for them."

Simon gave him a contemptuous look. "I don't care what you have to say, old man. Be quiet, or you'll suffer the same fate as your wife." He glanced over at the coffin with its covering of lilies and roses, which miraculously seemed to have survived the fray unscathed.

I ignored the rude words. Rudeness was the least of our problems right now. "What do you want, Simon?"

Again he smiled. I hated that smile…as well as the glance that accompanied it, one which seemed to travel up and down my form, taking in the slim-fitting black dress and thin sweater, the kitten heels I wore. "I think you know exactly what I want, Miranda. Since you seem to care so much about these people, I'll offer you a bargain. I'll leave them alone…if you come with me."

"No!" Rafe pushed himself to his feet, then took a step toward us. "Miranda, you can't agree to that."

"Shut up, wolf boy." A casual swipe of his hand, and Rafe was flung backward, landing several feet from where Louisa lay. "This is Miranda's decision to make."

I saw the murderous glitter in Rafe's eyes as he began to push himself up from the floor, but unfortunately, I knew it meant little. His power might have been a strong one in most cases. Now, though, when faced with an enemy as powerful as Simon Escobar, he didn't stand a chance.

And there was Louisa lying still and quiet on the floor, her husband a few yards away. Cat, too, although now that the demons had gone quiescent, standing off while their master traded words with me, she had begun to stir, to painfully push herself up to a sitting position.

They were my family now…and I couldn't bear to let Simon hurt them anymore. The pain of what I knew I must do burned inside me, but I pushed it aside, just as I blinked away the tears that had begun to form in my eyes.

I stepped closer to him. "Swear," I said. "Swear that you'll leave them alone, that you won't touch anyone in the Castillo clan again. Swear it, and I'll come with you."

Triumph flashed in Simon's black eyes. "I do swear it, Miranda. As long as you're with me, I won't hurt a hair on their precious heads."

The ache I felt now wasn't from the demons' assault, but from the knowledge of everything I was giving up, Rafe's love most of all. How could I live without him, when I now knew what it was like to be with someone I cared for so passionately?

That didn't matter, though. My feelings weren't worth all the pain Simon was willing to cause Rafe and his family. I had to agree with this, or I could never live with myself.

"All right," I said, every syllable an agony, "I'll come."

Another step forward, and Simon's arm snaked around me, tightening on my waist. In a flash we were gone.

But Rafe's despairing cry echoed in my ears even as we disappeared.

"Miranda, *no!*"

9

LEFT BEHIND

Rafe

HE STAGGERED TOWARD THE SPOT WHERE Miranda and Simon Escobar had stood only a moment earlier, but it was too late. They were gone, vanished into the air itself; obviously, Escobar commanded the same powers of teleportation that Miranda did.

How could she have gone with him? Did she really think that a fiend like Simon Escobar would keep his word and leave the Castillos alone?

Apparently, she had. Rafe had seen the despair on her face, but also the sudden resolve, the way her lips had pressed together and her gaze had gone steady, unwavering. She'd made that pact with Escobar because she knew they were outnumbered and outmatched. The Castillos had strong witches and warlocks among their ranks, but they couldn't hope to fend off the dark warlock's powers, or the evil army of demons he'd summoned to assist him with his dirty work.

Cat laid a hand on his arm. "I'm sorry, Rafe," she said quietly. "We'll figure it out. We'll find her. But right now, Oscar and Louisa need us."

His hands clenched into fists, but Rafe made himself nod. Cat was right. They had no way of immediately following Simon and Miranda, and both Oscar and Louisa were hurt. And that didn't count Father Francis, who was still lying at the rear of the altar, moaning faintly, although Rafe didn't know for sure whether those sighs of pain he made were due to physical injury or because he'd just seen demons with his own eyes, and had had his personal reality turned on its head.

Eduardo was already kneeling next to Louisa and had his phone out—probably to summon Yesenia. Rafe glanced down at Cat.

"I'll go check Father Francis," she said. "You see if Oscar's okay."

He nodded, then went over to where his brother-in-law lay and knelt down next to him. Oscar still hadn't moved, and Rafe was almost afraid to reach out and feel for a pulse. However, when he laid his fingers against Oscar's throat, he was able to detect a heartbeat—thready and too fast, but at least it was there.

Up on the altar, Cat was bending down and asking the priest if he was okay, if he thought he'd suffered any serious injuries. Still looking nearly as pale as the white plaster walls of the church, Father Francis shook his head.

"Bumps and bruises, nothing more," he told her. "But what—what were those things?"

Cat sent a panicked look in Rafe's direction. Right then, he wished he had one of those pen-shaped gizmos from those old *Men in Black* movies, those devices that would erase troublesome memories of an otherworldly incident in the blink of an eye. But Rafe certainly didn't possess that power, and he didn't know anyone who did.

He gave the faintest shake of his head, and Cat said, all wide-eyed confusion, "What things?"

"Those—those creatures," the priest replied. With a groan, he got to his feet. "Winged demons."

She looked at him as if she didn't have a clue what he was talking about. Rafe had to admire her acting skill, especially her ability to summon it so soon after having another one of those fainting spells or attacks or whatever you wanted to call them. "I didn't see anything like that. My sister fainted, but that's not so strange, considering the strain she's been under. You did stumble and fall, but I thought you must have tripped on the microphone wire."

Father Francis looked down at the innocent black cord near his feet and frowned. "I—I don't think that's what happened. And what about your brother-in-law?"

Right—her story hadn't included the reason for Oscar lying on the floor, clearly as out cold as his wife. Luckily, though, he moved right then, one hand going to his head. "What happened?" he asked.

"Forgot his insulin," Rafe said loudly enough for the priest to hear. "Like Cat said, we've all been under a lot of strain. But it looks as though he's going to be okay."

Despite his recent injury, Oscar was staring at him as though he'd lost his mind. Rafe bent down toward him, pitching his voice low.

"You're going to be okay," he murmured. "We're just waiting for Yesenia to come."

"Why don't you go along home?" Cat asked, putting a hand under the priest's elbow and helping him to his feet. "The people from the funeral home will be here shortly, and we can lock up the church for you."

"I—" From the way Father Francis frowned, clearly he found some issues with this suggestion. However, it seemed that he was still fuzzy-headed enough to nod absently and say, "If you're sure."

"We are," Cat said firmly. "You took quite a

spill there. It's probably best if you go home and put your feet up."

"All right." The priest took one last glance at the survivors, brow puckering slightly. "Wasn't there one more of you?"

"She went to the ladies' room to get a damp paper towel for Louisa's forehead," Cat replied. "That usually helps snap her out of these spells."

Once again Father Francis looked down at Louisa. It seemed that he had run out of protests, though, because next he said, "It does seem as though you have the situation under control—"

"We do." Still with her hand on the priest's elbow, she guided him down off the altar and toward the exit closest to them, the one on the east side of the church, which opened on a side street rather than the parking lot. "You take care, Father Francis."

His frown didn't disappear, but at least he did go out through the exit as she'd suggested. Once he was gone, she let out an exaggerated sigh of relief.

"That was close."

Despite his overwhelming worry for Miranda, Rafe couldn't help but smile at his sister. "Pretty good acting there, Meryl Streep."

Cat shrugged. "Well, I couldn't tell him the truth." She came over and knelt down next to him. "How are you, Oscar?"

"Okay," Oscar replied. "I think that bastard broke a couple of ribs, though."

"Well, try not to move," Rafe said. "Yesenia'll get those ribs fixed as soon as she gets here."

Oscar's gaze moved toward his wife, who still lay without moving a few feet away, Eduardo next to her, smoothing her hair back from her brow. "Louisa?"

"She's breathing," Eduardo said. "But other than that…."

The words drifted into silence, and Oscar shut his eyes for a moment, then expelled a breath, wincing slightly as he did so. "She'll be all right," he said after a long pause. "She has to be."

Yes, she did. Rafe didn't want to think of what would happen to their clan if Louisa's injuries were serious enough to prevent her from functioning as their *prima*. This was always a difficult time, that short period when a *prima* took over a clan but hadn't yet chosen her successor. In general, the new *prima* usually had someone in mind, but if Louisa had already made her selection, she hadn't spoken of it. They'd been a little busy the past few days.

Cat went over and brushed the hair back from her sister's face. Louisa's eyes were shut, her face slack and pale. Rafe could just barely see the way her chest rose and fell, but how much did that mean? Malena was also breathing, but she was in a coma, completely unresponsive. Despair congealed somewhere in his center, cold and heavy and unrelenting.

But he had another sister he needed to look after.

"What about you?" Rafe asked Cat, and she blinked at him.

"I'm okay," she replied. "My head hurts a little, and I feel kind of woozy. But it's not a big deal."

"You collapsed, too," he pointed out.

"I know." She paused for a moment, gaze moving to the stained-glass windows on the wall beyond him, to the sunlight that streamed through them. "I think it was the demons."

"They're what made you faint?"

"I think so." Another hesitation, as though she had stopped to try to put the pieces together as best she could. "I'm not sure how, but I wonder if my sensing that weird pressure has something to do with my ability to see ghosts, to communicate with them. I know that ghosts and demons are two different things, but they're both not from this plane, if you know what I mean. There's a wrongness to the demons, though. Maybe they create some kind of weird feedback loop when they come into this world, and somehow I can sense it."

This all sounded plausible to Rafe. He wanted

to believe Cat's hypothesis, because at least then these weird episodes she experienced would have some meaning to them. "And so you actually fainted this time instead of just getting a headache because they were so close?"

"I think so. Maybe. I never experienced anything like this until Simon Escobar came to Santa Fe, so it makes sense."

Fucking Escobar. The anger still seethed deep within Rafe, overriding even the concern he felt for his sisters, for his wounded brother-in-law. "We have to find him, Cat."

She laid a hand on his arm. "We will. You found him the last time, right? And we know that Miranda has the ability to hold him off, because she did it before."

Rafe wished he could share his sister's confidence on that particular point. When he'd come on the scene at the estate in Tesuque, Miranda hadn't looked as though she was holding her own. No, she'd looked a couple of minutes away from being a rape victim.

Worry churned in his gut, sour, acid. He had to put that image out of his mind, because otherwise he'd convince himself that that was what was happening to Miranda right now, and he couldn't bear it.

"I hope so," he said, his voice tight.

The doors at the far end of the chapel opened,

and both Rafe and Cat got up from where they'd been kneeling next to Louisa. Yesenia came hurrying in, her hair, which she usually wore pulled back in a long ponytail, windblown and messy, her expression strained.

"I was at Malena's house when you called," she said. "I'm sorry I couldn't be quicker."

"It's all right," Eduardo replied. He'd been sitting in the front pew, listening to Cat and Rafe talk, watchful gaze never leaving his eldest daughter's slack face. "We know you came as fast as you could."

She nodded, then went and knelt next to Louisa, her expression growing grave as she ran her hands over the *prima's* body, sensing the energies deep within and how they might have been disrupted. "I can't feel anything intrinsically wrong with her," she said. "Her mind has been taken far away, just like Malena's. But she breathes, and her heart sounds strong. I think the best thing to do is take her home and put her in her own bed. Perhaps if she is given enough time to heal…."

Yesenia stopped there. While she didn't quite shake her head, Rafe could tell she was mystified by this strange malady, something that seemed to have no real source. From what she'd said, there didn't seem to be any real reason why Louisa should be in a coma…or Malena, for that matter.

But magic could be unpredictable, and none of them had any real idea what type of terrible spells Simon Escobar had been using. The very blackest kind, obviously, because no witch or warlock who walked in the path of light would stoop to summoning demons, or using magic to inflict harm on another.

And, thanks to more of that dark magic, Rafe couldn't even reach out to the one person who might know something about all this. Miranda's father, Connor Wilcox, had never used these sorts of foul spells, but his brother had delved into all kinds of forbidden magic. At least Connor might have been able to offer a few words of advice on how to deal with it, to counter it, even though he himself had avoided falling into those traps.

"All right," Rafe said, and let out a weary breath. "Go ahead and see what you can do for Oscar."

Yesenia nodded, then went over to Oscar and knelt at his side, running her hands over him just as she had with Louisa a moment earlier. When she was done, she nodded. "You have cracked two of your ribs and strained your back." With a faint smile, she went on, "All of which is easy enough to fix." She brought her hands down closer to the injured ribs, a warm, faint glow emanating from her palms as she used her power to send the healing energies forth into her patient. After a moment, she laid her hands against his back, again waiting for the magic to do its work. When she was done, she sat back on her heels. "How do you feel now, Oscar?"

Cautiously, he pushed himself to a sitting position, hands flat against the wooden floor. "I feel—well, I still feel as though someone used me for a punching bag, but the worst of the hurt is gone."

"You will probably be stiff and sore for a day or so," she told him. "But at least you won't have to worry about those ribs or your back."

"No," he said, gaze moving past her to Louisa, who still lay as quiet as though she was dead, although Rafe knew she breathed. "Now I can just worry about my wife."

Looking solemn, Yesenia got to her feet and went over to Eduardo, laid a hand on his shoulder. "And how are you, Eduardo?"

"Sore in heart but not in body," he replied. "The demons did not attack me, for whatever reason."

Because of his inborn luck, Rafe guessed, and also probably because that same magical talent offered no outward threat to them. He recalled how the demons had pushed back hard enough on Miranda that they'd sent her flying. Apparently, she hadn't been hurt by their attack, but he had to wonder whether Escobar would give his flying monkeys a chewing-out for daring to strike the woman he wanted.

The woman he wanted....

Once again, worry rose in Rafe, sick and foul in his mouth. The mere thought of Miranda in Simon Escobar's hands made him want to retch.

"Well, that is something," Yesenia said, bringing Rafe back to the moment. "Rafe, can you and Eduardo carry Louisa to her car? I don't think Oscar should be lifting her yet, not when he's so newly healed."

"Of course," Rafe said automatically. He might as well be of some use to his sister, since he'd certainly been no help to the woman he loved. During the demon attack, the beast had risen in him, wanting to be let out, wanting to go for Escobar's throat, but he'd hesitated just a moment too long. He still wasn't sure why exactly, although he knew deep down that his wolf form couldn't have prevailed against the dark warlock. The first time, he'd gotten lucky. That was all.

Eduardo got up from the pew where he'd been sitting, and the two of them went to Louisa and eased her up off the ground. She felt very heavy in Rafe's arms, even though she was slender enough. Maybe it was just that the life force within her seemed as though it had gone very far away, leaving behind only dead weight.

Despite that, Rafe and his father were able to

carry her outside without too much trouble, pausing for just a moment as Oscar unlocked the rear door of his car and opened it wide so they could lay her on the seat there.

"I'll follow you back to your house," Yesenia said. "Then we'll do what we can to get her comfortable."

"What if she stays in the coma for days and days?" Oscar asked, worry pulling at his brows. "Won't she need an IV or something?"

"Hopefully, she won't stay unconscious that long. But yes, if she's out for more than twenty-four hours, we'll have to take more drastic measures." She gave him a reassuring smile, laid her hand on his arm. "I am a healer, but I also have training in these things. I can take care of Louisa as long as her condition doesn't worsen."

"And Malena?" Eduardo asked. He'd stepped back out of the way once Louisa had been safely set down on the back seat.

"Her condition is the same. Actually, her coma isn't as deep as I feared, because when I squeezed some water into her mouth, she swallowed. Her reflexes are there."

"That's a good thing, right?" Cat asked. Her arms were crossed tightly, almost as if she hugged herself, although Rafe had a feeling she wasn't so much cold as trying to reassure herself that she was actually okay.

"It's a very good thing," Yesenia replied, offering a reassuring smile. "That's what I told John. If we can keep getting her to drink, then she runs less risk of becoming dehydrated, and we won't have to give her an I.V. Since Louisa's condition looks similar, I have to hope we can do the same for her." She turned toward Oscar, who was now hovering near the driver's door, the key fob to the Volvo in his hand. "We should get Louisa home. Even if she can't consciously feel it at the moment, she'll be more comfortable in her own bed."

Oscar nodded, then gave a half-hearted wave to everyone watching as he got in the car. Yesenia murmured a quick goodbye to Eduardo, Rafe, and Cat, then went over to her Ford SUV and climbed in.

"What now?" Cat asked.

Eduardo's gaze moved back toward the chapel. "I would like to say goodbye to Genoveva. José's people will be here soon to take the coffin away, and since we can't be there at her graveside when she's interred…."

Oh, God. Rafe had almost forgotten about that, thanks to all the tumult. He supposed he should be glad that the demon attack had left his mother's coffin undisturbed, since that would have made an already horrible situation truly dreadful. Deep down, he had a feeling that they would be perfectly safe going to the cemetery and being there as Genoveva's coffin was lowered into the ground, since Simon Escobar now had what he wanted—Miranda—but he kept his thoughts to himself. They'd already mentally prepared themselves to not be present, and he didn't see the point in changing their plans now.

Besides, even if he thought it might be safe, Rafe couldn't be absolutely sure. For all he knew, Escobar would go back on his promise to Miranda as soon as the opportunity presented itself. Better that they not make targets out of themselves.

"Sure, Dad," he said. "I think I'll wait out here, though."

Eduardo nodded, as though he wasn't too surprised that his only son would want to excuse himself from such a vigil. "Cat?"

"You go on inside," she said. "I've—I've made my goodbyes. And I really don't want to go back in there."

Although her reply clearly saddened their father, he didn't try to argue with her. "Of course. I'll only be a few minutes."

"Take as much time as you need," Cat told him, laying a hand on his arm and giving it a squeeze.

A resigned smile, and Eduardo went back into the church. Rafe watched him go, hating the slump of his shoulders, the way he didn't seem quite as tall as he had been a few days ago. Once he was gone, Cat looked up at Rafe.

"What now?"

"I don't have a frigging idea," he said. God, he hated this feeling of impotence, of knowing that the woman he loved was in Simon Escobar's hands and that there wasn't a goddamn thing he could do about it. "I guess we put our heads together and try to figure out where that son of a bitch is hiding."

She nodded, gaze moving past him to the street just beyond the church, where cars moved along placidly and people made their way along the sidewalk, pausing here and there to look in a storefront, or to consult their phones. Despite the brisk wind—or maybe because of it—the day was clear and bright, if cool. Santa Fe appeared completely serene.

Too bad Rafe knew that all kinds of ugliness lurked just under the surface.

"I think you should come stay with Dad and me," Cat said. "I don't like the idea of you being alone in that house."

"Miranda put a protection spell on it," he protested. While he knew that Cat had a point, he didn't want to go back to the big house where he'd grown up. He'd never liked it, and now, knowing that his mother had died there....

"I know," Cat replied calmly. "But there's also

one on our house. And I'd just feel safer if you were with us. Please?"

He stared down at her, saw the naked pleading in her face. None of this could have been easy for Cat—her mother dead, her two older sisters in strange, magically induced comas. And that didn't even include having a strange psychic reaction every time Escobar decided to deploy his demons for a new bit of nastiness.

Of course Cat would want her family around her. Really, it was selfish of him to remain on his own, especially when he knew she'd be worrying about him every single minute he was alone in his house.

"Okay," he said, doing his best to keep the reluctance out of his voice. "Just let me get back there and pack some stuff, and then I'll come over."

Some of the tension seemed to leave her face, and she gave him a relieved smile. "Thanks, Rafe. I really appreciate it."

"No problem. It'll make it easier for us to work on finding Miranda."

"That's what I was thinking."

She sounded almost hopeful. Rafe didn't want to discourage her or make her worry that much greater, but he had a feeling this search would be far from easy. However, as Cat had pointed out earlier, he had been able to track down Miranda before, although at least then he'd had a few leads, nebulous as they might be.

Now, he had nothing. Sooner or later, though, he'd find Simon Escobar. And when he did....

I'm going to kill him.

10

GILDED CAGE

Miranda

As soon as solid ground touched my feet again, I pulled away from Simon Escobar, leaving him clutching empty air.

However, he didn't seem angered by the immediate distance I'd put between us. Again he wore that almost lazy smile, as though he knew he had the upper hand here. "Welcome home," he said.

I took a quick glance around. As far as I could tell, his new hideout looked like a typical pueblo-style Santa Fe house, with high beamed ceilings and tile floors. We stood in the eating area off the kitchen, which was shiny and appeared to have been recently remodeled, all top-of-the-line stainless appliances and polished stone countertops.

"This isn't my home," I flung back at him, and he shrugged.

"It is now. You agreed to come with me. Remember what will happen if you change your mind."

I swallowed, recalling how Louisa lay on the floor of the church, not moving, how Cat also had appeared to be knocked out, or worse. As much as I hated the sight of Simon Escobar, the sound of his voice, I hated even more the thought of being responsible for the deaths of any more Castillos, especially Cat or Rafe.

God, Rafe.

His voice cracking as he called out to me, the utter despair on his face. The memory tore through me even now, reminding me that, no matter how much I loved him, I had to walk away if I wanted him to live.

"Fine," I said. "I'm not going anywhere. That doesn't mean I have to be nice to you."

One eyebrow lifted. "Really? You're going to play it that way, Miranda?"

"How else am I supposed to play it? Threatening to hurt or kill the people I care about isn't exactly the best way to endear yourself to me, you know."

For a moment, Simon didn't reply. He only stood there, watching me carefully. Then he gave the faintest hitch of his shoulders, as though he'd assessed my current mood and realized there was no real way to gain any ground with me. Not right away.

Not ever, I thought.

"I only wanted to point out that they weren't worthy of you, Miranda," he said. "The *prima* of the clan, your supposed fiancé, Genoveva's youngest daughter—none of them mounted any kind of a defense. You were the only one who stood up to my demons, who had any kind of an effect on them."

"That wasn't their fault." I crossed my arms, even though it wasn't that chilly in the house. Actually, the temperature inside was almost uncomfortably warm. I would have pushed up the sleeves of my sweater, but I didn't want Simon to think that I'd been put off balance by my new surroundings. "We're witches, not demon hunters." Narrowing my eyes at him, I added, "How were you able to summon those demons, anyway?"

A careless shrug. "It's a talent that runs in my family. Supposedly, my brother could perform the same kind of summonings. It's not so difficult, if you know what you're doing." He came closer, and I had to force myself not to flinch, even though he made no move to reach out and touch me. "I'm surprised no one told you about how he once sent demons to your little town in the mountains."

Actually, I had heard the story. Before I was born, when my parents and the three Arizona witch clans fought against Joaquin Escobar and the Santiago clan he controlled, demons had attacked on the border of Jerome. Levi, one of the elders—although he hadn't been one at the time—had driven them back, then done what he could to help ward the town against any further incursions. If it hadn't been for him, I really didn't know what could have happened. The McAllister witches and warlocks weren't known for the defensive magic, and could have been easily overcome. Possibly my parents working together might have succeeded, but they hadn't come into the fullness of their combined powers yet. At any rate, it had been a scary time, and when Matías Escobar died some-place in the otherworld, everyone had hoped that the ability to summon demons had died with him.

Apparently not.

"Ancient history," I said with a shrug, doing my best to hide the fear that sent icy tentacles to every limb. If Simon could summon demons with what amounted to the snap of a finger, what else could he do? "We didn't discuss it much because it didn't seem as though anyone else could call demons to this world."

"Short-sighted. Anyway, it's clear these Castillos aren't exactly as impressive as everyone thinks they are. You're wasting your talents on them...on *him*."

I didn't bother to ask who Simon meant by "him." "I think your opinion might be slightly biased."

"Probably. But just because it's biased doesn't mean it's not accurate." Once again he moved closer, and this time he took me by the elbow. More than anything I wanted to wrench my arm from his grasp, but I knew I walked a very thin line between attempting to keep my distance and provoking him into a reaction that might bring more harm to the Castillos. "You need to forget about Rafe, Miranda. You're here with me now." With his other hand, he reached out touch my hair, push it back over my shoulder.

This time, I couldn't quite hold back a shudder. However, I forced a casual note into my voice as I said, "Just so you know, Simon, Rafe and I have already had sex...multiple times. The last time was just last night, so you might want to hold off on making any moves if you don't want his sloppy seconds."

A dark, angry light kindled in Simon's eyes and his lip curled, although he didn't step away from me. "Didn't waste any time, did you?"

"Why would we? We're supposed to be together. Nothing you've done can change that."

Abruptly, he let go of my arm. Still sneering, he said, "'Supposed to be together'? According to whom? It's not like you're some *prima* bonding to her consort. The only reason you were with Rafe Castillo in the first place is because his bitch of a mother wouldn't let it go and insisted that you two get married."

I almost retorted that having sex with Rafe did feel like that kind of bonding, but refrained. For one thing, that particular detail was just a bit too intimate for me to want to share it with Simon Escobar. Also, his comment set me wondering about the times Rafe and I had made love. Sex with him had felt amazingly intense, to the point where I honestly couldn't imagine ever having sex with anyone else. Maybe there actually was some kind of bonding going on, something no one could have predicted. For all I knew, this was what Rafe's grandmother Isabel had seen before she died, why she had made it clear that her grandson needed to marry the daughter my mother had been carrying at the time.

However, there was no way in hell I was going to tell Simon that. Let him think what he wanted.

Ignoring my lack of response, he went on, "I will feel a little bad if anything's happened to Cat. She's pretty hot. But I sure as hell am not going to apologize for killing that bitch Genoveva Castillo. She deserved it. If she hadn't made sure you were sent here to marry her stupid son, I could have approached you back in Arizona, and none of this ugliness would have needed to happen."

"Nice deflection, Simon," I shot back. "Putting your predilection for murder aside, do you really think my parents would have let you get within ten feet of me? They would have sniffed out your dark magic and sent you packing."

"I wouldn't be so sure of that. I'm pretty good at hiding it when I need to."

Again I wanted to argue, but I knew he was at least partially right. He'd been able to hide his magical nature from me over a period of more than a week, had been able to conceal it from a couple of Castillo witches when they'd only been sitting a few feet away from us in a restaurant. There was no reason to think my parents would be able to detect his abilities when he was working so hard to keep them hidden. They probably would have thought he was a member of the de la Paz clan and would have welcomed him, especially if he'd been able to awaken my powers when no one else could.

He had paused and was watching me closely, clearly waiting for some kind of a response. Since I had none, except an exaggerated shrug, he smiled to himself, then said, "Yeah, that's what I thought you'd say. Come on upstairs so I can show you where you're going to be staying."

Since refusing to do as he asked didn't seem to be an option, I only followed him in silence, praying that he wasn't going to put me in his bedroom. It would be just like him to force the issue, and I honestly didn't know how I could react in a way that would tell him I had no intention of sharing his bed, and at the same time manage to keep the Castillos safe.

At the top of the stairs was a sort of landing, with a small sitting area outfitted with a love seat and low table, and a couple of those old-fashioned, rustic-looking lamps with the amber mica shades. We went past that and into the first doorway on the right. A bedroom, true, but definitely not the master; it wasn't large enough, and the bed was a small single, with a painted table serving as its nightstand.

To my surprise, the duffle bag I'd left behind at the house in Tesuque was sitting on that narrow bed. As I stared down at it, Simon said, "I brought this along. I figured you'd need some of your stuff."

I wasn't about to thank him. All I did was lift my shoulders and say, "I suppose it could come in handy."

He chuckled. "Yeah, that's my gracious Miranda. The bathroom is across the hall. And my bedroom is down at the end of the hall, if you should need me."

"I doubt that's ever going to happen."

The faintly amused expression he'd been wearing disappeared, to be replaced by an intense black stare I recognized all too well. "Oh, it's going to happen," he said. "Not today, or tomorrow, but someday you'll realize that we were meant to be together, that this infatuation with Rafe Castillo means nothing. In the meantime… go ahead and get settled in, then come downstairs."

I didn't bother to reply as he left the room, his footsteps sounding on the tile staircase a moment later. Instead, I stood there for a moment and pulled in a few breaths, willing myself to stay calm. If I allowed fear to overtake me, I wouldn't be able to deal with Simon in any kind of an effective way. What I needed to do now was wait and see what he had planned, and do my best to keep him at arm's length until I figured out how to extricate myself from this mess.

So I went over to the bed and unzipped the duffle, then began to methodically remove its contents and set them out in neat piles, depending on where they were going to be put away. Underwear here, jeans and T-shirts there, sweaters off to one side, toiletries in a pile that would eventually end up in the bathroom.

Everything seemed to be present and accounted for—everything except the wedding dress I'd been wearing when I'd first run to Simon, thinking he would be my refuge. I'd had it folded as tightly as I could and stuffed into one end of the duffle, without much regard for the silk fabric. At the time, I'd been so angry with Rafe that I hadn't cared how I treated that damn wedding gown. But now the dress was gone.

I wasn't sure I wanted to know what its absence meant.

Better to put that worry aside. I had far more important things to concern me at the moment. As it was, I decided to change into jeans and a different sweater, one not so close-fitting. The dress I was wearing had seemed modest enough when I put it on—it came down to just the tops of my knees—but I couldn't help remembering the way Simon had ogled my legs back at the church. Better to be as covered up as possible.

The bedroom didn't have a lock. Not that it mattered, because a regular lock wouldn't stop the least skilled witch or warlock, let alone someone like Simon Escobar. Hoping for the best, I quickly stripped out of my funeral attire and into the jeans and sweater I'd selected, then zipped up my boots.

There, that was better. At least I didn't feel as though I was quite as on display.

Since I hadn't been given a time limit for my "settling in," I took my time hanging up the clothes I'd been wearing, then went over to the window to do my best to get my bearings. It was still just early afternoon, even though the day felt as though it had already been a hundred years long. The sun shone brightly, the deep blue sky streaked here and there with wisps of high, thin clouds.

From what I could tell, the property here backed up to a creek, just as Rafe had surmised. *Cienega Creek,* I told myself. Like every other river or stream I'd seen in the southwest, this creek was lined with cottonwoods, now mostly bare, although a few brave yellow leaves still clung to some of their branches. On either side were more bare-limbed trees: aspens and sycamores and oaks. Unlike a lot of places in this part of the world, the backyard appeared to have a real lawn, even though it was now yellowed by frost. When everything was green, this was probably a beautiful spot. Now it just looked forlorn and a little sad, even with those bright skies overhead.

I wondered if this place was another property management job Simon had lied his way into, or whether it was simply a vacation rental he'd taken over. Early November wasn't exactly prime tourist season in these parts, so he'd probably gotten a deal. And this house, while nicely decorated and updated, certainly wasn't on a par with the estate where we'd been staying in Tesuque.

Unfortunately, even while bare, the trees provided enough cover that I couldn't tell how close the neighbors—if any—might be. Not that it really mattered. This wasn't the kind of situation where I could break out and go knock on their doors for help. No civilian could give me the kind of assistance I needed, and that realization made me feel even more trapped.

I'd just have to hang on until Rafe found me. While my magic had been getting stronger and stronger, and I might—*might* — have been able to put up a credible defense against Simon, I didn't quite dare to take action. If I failed, I knew he would be merciless. He'd already proven to me that he didn't give a damn about human life. I just couldn't allow any more members of the Castillo clan to be hurt.

I didn't even have my phone with me, because my purse had been sitting on the front pew in the church when the demons attacked. Presumably, it was still sitting there, unless Rafe or Eduardo had noticed it and taken it with them when they left.

Thinking about Rafe hurt too much. I didn't want to remember how wonderful it had felt to lie in his arms the night before, or how good it had been to share even the little moments, like teasing him about how good he looked in a suit. We were meant to be together, I just knew it, and yet I couldn't see how I was supposed to get from where I was now back to the place where I was supposed to be. But I wouldn't allow myself to despair. That would be letting Simon win.

One step at a time, just like everything else.

I took a breath, smoothed my hair as I looked into the pretty mirror of Mexican tin that hung over the dresser, then went to the door and opened it. There was no point in delaying any longer; I couldn't stay up here forever. Besides, the longer I lingered, the more risk I ran of annoying Simon.

Despite my resolve, I descended those stairs slowly, experiencing with each step a mounting tension that clenched my gut. I didn't know for sure why I was so much more tense now than I had been when Simon first brought me here less than a half hour earlier, but I guessed it was because we had already gotten the preliminaries out of the way. Now I would see exactly what he had planned for me…and to say I wasn't looking forward to learning the answer would have been a massive understatement.

He was there in the kitchen when I approached. Judging by the assortment of food on the polished stone counter, it appeared he'd been assembling some fairly complicated sandwiches.

Was he really expecting me to eat?

Apparently he was, because he paused and looked up at me, smiling. If he was disappointed that I'd changed out of my short dress and heels, he didn't show it.

"Mustard or mayo?" he asked.

"Neither," I said. Sometimes I didn't mind the tiniest bit of mustard, but right then, with my stomach churning away and clenched with tension, I knew even a small taste would make me want to vomit.

My response made him lift an eyebrow, but then he shrugged and put a piece of bread on top of one of the half-completed sandwiches, set it on a piece of cheerful hand-painted Mexican dishware, and pushed it across the counter toward me. "I thought you might be hungry."

"I'm not," I said. Well, that wasn't precisely the truth. Physically, I could tell I was hungry—it had been hours since the breakfast burritos Rafe and I had shared that morning—but I didn't know whether I'd be able to force anything down without wanting to throw it right back up afterward.

He didn't seem put off by my reply. "Even after expending all that energy fighting off demons?"

Damn it, he knew me too well. He'd seen the way I gobbled almost everything in sight after our magical practice sessions, and so he had to know that my body was craving some of the fuel it had used up.

Still, I hesitated.

"It's just a sandwich," he said. "Eating it isn't going to condemn your eternal soul to hellfire or anything."

"That's not what I was thinking."

"Really?" Simon smeared some Dijon on the piece of whole-grain bread he'd just picked up, then placed the slice of bread on his own sandwich. "Your expression says something different."

I crossed my arms. "My expression is probably saying that I can't believe you'd expect me to act as though all of this was normal, that I'd just accept food from you like it was no big deal."

"You're going to have to eat sometime, aren't you?" he said reasonably. "I mean, I suppose you could try to go on a hunger strike to guilt me into letting you go, but I'll tell you in advance that that's not going to work."

No, it probably wouldn't. Simon had enough tricks up his sleeve that he could probably come up with a way to force-feed me, or to use some kind of stratagem to fool me into eating his food.

"It's fine," he went on. "All this stuff just came straight out of the fridge. I haven't done anything to it. See?" And he took a big bite out of the sandwich he held.

Which still didn't prove very much. He could

have doctored one of the components of my sandwich while leaving everything that went into his alone. It wasn't as though he'd poured us both soup out of the same pot or something.

Shaking his head, he picked up the knife he'd just used to spread mustard on his bread, wiped it off on a paper towel, and then cut a corner off the sandwich he'd prepared for me. Making sure I was watching, he lifted it to his mouth, chewed, and swallowed.

"See? It's fine. Bread and cheese and sliced roast beef. It's not going to kill you."

That was a more convincing display. Still, I couldn't quite put my hand out to take the sandwich, even though my stomach gurgled a little, telling me that it was probably about to growl loudly if I didn't do something to shut it up.

Fine. While I knew Simon was capable of just about anything, I didn't think he'd poison me right off the bat. He wanted me here, wanted me to go along with his crazy schemes. Doing something outrageous this early in the game wouldn't be smart.

Holding back a sigh, I picked up the sandwich from the plate and took a bite. "Satisfied?" I asked after I'd stopped chewing.

"I don't know about satisfied," he said. "But at least it's a step in the right direction. Want something to drink? There's water, or Coke, or iced tea —the bottled kind."

"Tea," I replied. If it was bottled, it was probably safe. Anyway, I could use the kick of caffeine, and I didn't drink soda, so Coke wasn't an option.

"Got it." He went over to the fridge and got out a bottle of iced tea for me and a can of Coke for himself, then came back over and set them down on the counter. "We can go sit in the dining room, or the living room, if you want. We don't have to stand here."

"This is fine," I said firmly. The last thing I wanted was for him to think I was softening toward him, an impression that sitting down with him to eat like civilized people might too easily give.

That response earned me a sideways glance, as if he'd guessed exactly why I'd declined having our late lunch in a more comfortable place. But at least he didn't say anything, which meant I was able to eat my sandwich and drink my tea in relative peace—very relative, because although I hoped I looked calm enough on the outside, all I could do was keep thinking about what Rafe might be doing at that very moment, and whether Simon's attacking demons had really hurt Cat or whether she'd just passed out from all the psychic tumult.

And, as much as I hated to eat any food

Simon might give me, I really didn't have the choice to go on a hunger strike, partly because I doubted he'd even allow me to do such a thing, and partly because I knew I needed to keep my strength up so I could exploit any opportunities for escape, should they arise. The sandwich was tasty enough—the roast beef tasted like real deli meat, not something out of a package, and the bread was fresh—so it wasn't too much work to get it all down.

When I was done, I took a large swallow of tea. Simon was still chewing, but I found myself compelled to ask anyway. "What *is* your end game in all this, Simon? I mean, what exactly do you hope to achieve? You might have the upper hand right now, but you're only one person. Even a warlock as powerful as you really isn't capable of taking on an entire witch clan."

He didn't appear too troubled by my remarks. After finishing the last bite of his sandwich, he drank some Coke, then put the can back down on the countertop. "You so sure about that? After all, I just beat some of the Castillo clan's strongest witches and warlocks back there at the church. Who else are they going to throw against me?"

I really didn't have an answer to that question, mostly because I hadn't been acquainted with the Castillos long enough to even begin to know who they all were, what their individual talents and strengths might be. Despite that particular lack of knowledge, I couldn't believe that Simon thought he alone would be able to prevail against them, even with a bunch of demons under his control. They'd mounted a fairly serious attack, true, but Simon had only had seven or eight demons fighting on his side. It would take a lot more than that to beat a clan made up of hundreds of witches and warlocks.

"You tell me," I returned. "You're the one who's made such an in-depth study of the Castillo clan."

"They have a few powerful witches and warlocks," he allowed. "But not enough. Their new *prima* is a joke. And now that they can't bring in outside help—"

"Yeah, how did you manage to do that, anyway?" I cut in, genuinely curious. Just because I didn't approve of Simon's methods—to put it mildly—that didn't mean I wasn't eager to learn something of the spells he'd deployed.

His mouth curled slightly, as though he was amused by my question. A wicked light in his black eyes, he said, "Trade secret."

I should have known. No way was Simon going to tell me anything that might allow me to subvert his efforts—at least not until he was sure of my loyalty.

And that was never going to happen.

"But Miranda," he went on, moving closer to me. My entire body stiffened, although I refused to retreat. I didn't want to give him that power over me. "You want to know what I want out of all this? That's easy enough. I want you, of course, but you at my side, not some kind of hostage. Like I told you before, we're two of a kind. There are no other witches or warlocks like us in the world."

"That you know of," I said, my voice sounding shaky even to myself.

He didn't appear put off by my comment. Instead, his smile only returned, wider this time. "Oh, I'm pretty sure we would have heard of it, even as isolated as the clans tend to be. I know word about my father's exploits—"

"Crimes," I cut in.

"—went everywhere in America, maybe the world," Simon went on without missing a beat. "People knew, because he was so out of the ordinary. Which means if there was anyone else like him out there—or me, or you—then we would have heard about it, if only for word to get out in the clans that people needed to keep their guard up."

I supposed he had a point. However, since I really didn't want to admit that he might be right, I only shrugged and said in grudging tones, "Maybe."

"Anyway, it makes much more sense for us to work together, rather than being at odds. I have no idea why Isabel Castillo thought it was so important for you to be here with her grandson, because it's so obvious that you don't belong with him. You belong with me."

"No, I don't," I said. "If you think I would ever agree to go along with your horrible plans, you're crazy. And you're just as crazy if you think I'm going to suddenly switch off my feelings for Rafe and transfer them to you."

For a second, Simon's expression clouded. Then he shook his head, clearly doing what he could to shrug off my protests. "I don't think so. You'll figure it out soon enough. Rafe can do nothing for you."

"Except love me."

This time, the frown that twisted Simon's features lingered, and once again he moved toward me, this time so less than a foot separated us. More than anything, I wanted to turn and run away, although I knew that he could catch me easily. Besides, even teleporting out of here wouldn't do anything except make him so angry that he'd probably send his demons after me, or, worse, after the people I cared about—Rafe, Cat, Eduardo.

"You think I don't love you, Miranda?" Simon asked. Fear held me still, because I was worried that if I tried to move away, he would only reach out and grab me, pull me toward him. "Everything I've done has been for you."

There was no mistaking the intensity in his voice, his expression. He really did believe he loved me, which only made him that much more dangerous.

"No, Simon," I said carefully. "I think you're obsessed with me, which isn't the same thing. If you love someone, you don't want to hurt them, or the people who are important to them. But all you've done is prove how much you enjoy hurting the Castillos."

"Maybe it's more that they're so easy to hurt," he replied. Eyes still glittering, he reached out and took my hand. As much as I wanted to snatch it back, I knew I didn't quite dare. "Weak, all of them. Neither Malena nor Louisa should have fallen into comas like that, but their spirits weren't strong enough to handle the backlash from my demon-summoning spells. Is that my fault? A true *prima*—hell, even a true *prima's* daughter— shouldn't have succumbed that easily."

Was it true? I didn't know what to believe, and yet, strangely, I thought Simon was being honest with me here. "As opposed to the spell you sent against their mother," I said.

His mouth twisted. "Oh, yeah, I already told you I wanted that bitch dead. And I wanted her to drop dead in front of her family members. That was why I sent the spell when I did, rather than waiting until she was asleep, or at least alone in her house. I wanted all of them to know how vulnerable they were."

"But…why?" I asked, still wishing I had the courage to pull my arm from his grasp. "What twisted reason could you have for making them all afraid, when it was Genoveva you had a vendetta against?"

He let go of my arm, but I couldn't be all that relieved, not when he lifted the same hand and used it to brush a tendril of hair away from my face. Still wearing that twisted smirk of a smile, he replied, "I thought that should be obvious."

"Well, it's not."

His gaze moved from me toward the window. The Sangre de Cristos were much farther away from this vantage point but still recognizable, which was how I knew he was staring straight into the heart of Santa Fe.

"It's because I plan to take them over, just as my father took control of the Santiagos."

11

REACHING OUT

Rafe

HE HATED THIS. HE HATED HAVING TO BE here in his house, packing enough stuff for a time away of indeterminate length. He hated the thought of having to go stay in the home where his mother died.

Most of all, he hated the thought of Miranda in Simon's clutches, with absolutely no idea of what might be happening to her.

Unfortunately, Cat was probably right. It would be safer for them to be together. Rafe didn't really know what either his father or his sister could do to protect him, but he figured if he was in wolf form, he might be able to rip out the throats of a few of those miserable demons if they dared to show their ugly faces anywhere around here.

That is, if he didn't completely choke again. He still couldn't quite figure out what had prevented him from shifting into wolf or coyote form and going after Simon, despite the odds stacked against him. Was it some strange kind of worry about having Father Francis see him make such a transformation?

Possibly. Cat had been able to bald-face her way through an explanation of the demons, but watching the son of one of his most prominent parishioners turn into a wolf before his eyes would have needed a *lot* more explaining. Even Cat probably couldn't have convinced the priest that there was nothing strange about that kind of a display.

Whatever the reason, there wasn't much Rafe could do about it now, except vow that it would never happen again. Unfortunately, he very much feared he might not get a second chance to prove himself to Miranda.

Scowling, he went out to the garage, threw his two duffle bags in the back seat of the Wrangler, then opened the garage door and backed out. The house had come with a security system, but he never used it. Not much point, when pretty much everyone in Santa Fe knew to leave the properties that belonged to the Castillos severely alone.

Would Miranda's spell of protection keep out ordinary civilian burglars? For that matter, was the spell even still active? Since Rafe wasn't the one who'd cast it, he couldn't feel the thing, couldn't sense it working. Miranda had made it sound as though it was the sort of spell that would keep working until she nullified it, but he didn't know for sure. She could be so far away that the energy which kept it alive had been attenuated to the point of uselessness.

No, somehow he knew that wasn't the case. For whatever reason, Simon Escobar seemed compelled to hang around in the greater Santa Fe area. You'd think that now he had his prize, he would have taken off, but if he did that, he wouldn't be close enough to carry out his threats of revenge should Miranda get out of line. The dark warlock was holding her hostage with those threats, and that was yet another aspect to the situation that Rafe really hated. Simon wanted to hurt the Castillos, or else he could have just grabbed Miranda and taken off. She must know that as well, which was why Rafe feared she might bend to Simon's will, just to protect her new family.

By now it was mid-afternoon. Cat had texted him a few minutes ago that Genoveva had been interred without incident at Rosario Cemetery, the same place where generations of Castillos had been buried. Rafe couldn't even feel anything about that particular piece of news, except to experience a certain weary relief in knowing his mother's body was safely buried. There hadn't been any interference. No one had known who'd gone into that hole in the ground, because of course the headstone wouldn't be ready for several weeks. Eduardo had sent instructions to make sure the flowers that had rested on her casket were placed on her grave, but that would be the only marker to show that Genoveva Castillo, former *prima* of the Castillo clan, now rested there.

Rafe pulled up into the driveway of the big house and parked the Jeep; he no longer had a remote to open the garage door. No matter; even a Castillo might get a parking ticket if their vehicle remained on the street overnight, but the Santa Fe police couldn't ticket people for leaving their vehicles out in their driveways, even if the cops might want to.

After pulling his two bags out of the back seat, he locked the car and let himself in through the garden gate, following the path that led through the dry and dreary gardens to the door off the patio. As he went along, he tried not to think of how he had walked here with Miranda, how he had done his best to push her away. Thank God he hadn't been successful.

Then again, maybe that wasn't such a good

thing. If he hadn't allowed Miranda McAllister to enter his heart and soul, maybe he wouldn't be hurting so badly now.

A touch on the handle of the French door that opened onto the back patio, and he let himself into the living room. Voices came to him from the direction of the kitchen, so he turned that way, even though some part of him wanted to head upstairs and put his things away before he had to face his father and sister.

Cat and Eduardo were sitting at the kitchen table, both of them with mugs clutched in their hands. From the sweet-spice smell in the air, Rafe guessed they were drinking the strong cinnamon tea that Genoveva had liked so much. She'd drunk that tea all through his childhood and youth, and breathing in the aroma seemed to take him back years, to the time when the only thing he had to worry about was his next argument with his mother. He wished he could go back in time and apologize to her for being such an ass. Unfortunately, the time for such apologies was now past.

"Hey," he said as he came in.

"Hi," Cat replied.

Eduardo responded, "Rafe. I'm glad Cat convinced you to come stay here. Do you want some tea?"

"No, thanks." While he appreciated the scent of the tea, it was too sharp and spicy for him.

Right then, he thought what he could really use was a beer, although he knew better than to ask for one now. Maybe later, if he and Cat had the opportunity to talk alone.

Instead, he went and got a glass of water from the pitcher in the fridge—no one in the house had ever trusted the stuff that was piped through the refrigerator door—and then came over and sat down at the table, across from his father and next to Cat.

"You okay?" she asked.

"Not really," he replied tightly. Then he added, "Is everything else quiet so far?"

"So far," Eduardo replied. His fingers tapped against the creamy stoneware of the mug he held. "Yesenia made sure Louisa was home and safe. Her condition hasn't changed, but Yesenia is still hopeful that she'll wake up soon. In the meantime, their children are going to stay with Rosalie and Luis down in Corrales. They always enjoy visiting there, and it will be one less thing for Oscar to worry about."

"And Malena?"

"The same," Cat said. "Although John doesn't want to send Elenia to stay with relatives, even though Yesenia said she thought it might be a good idea. I guess if the situation continues for much longer, he'll have to decide if he really wants to keep running after a two-year-old while watching over his wife, but we've all decided to stay out of it for now."

Which was probably a good idea. John could be prickly, although he was a decent enough guy. Right now, it didn't seem as though Malena needed a lot of care, and John was probably more stressed at the idea of not being able to watch over his child than at the thought of having to keep up with her.

"But nothing else is going on."

"That we know of," Eduardo said. "The word has gone out, so everyone knows to get in touch with me if they encounter anything out of the ordinary, but so far all seems to be quiet enough."

Good. That meant Rafe and Eduardo and Cat could focus on tracking down Simon Escobar. He said as much, and Cat nodded.

"I already called Daniel and asked him to look into anything in the La Cienega area that might have been rented in the past few weeks, anything that could have been offered on Airbnb or one of the other vacation housing sites," she said, then sipped at her tea. "He's on it."

"Maybe more than that," Rafe replied. "I'd have him look into recent sales of property in the area, too."

"You think Simon would have bought a house there?" Eduardo inquired, looking vaguely surprised. "He's very young."

"I don't think that makes a difference if his money is good," Cat said dryly. "Knowing him, he could've stolen a chunk from somewhere and is using it to finance all his activities."

"Probably using faked identification and any other paperwork he needs to cover his tracks," Rafe added. "You know he'd make sure his real name didn't show up on anything that could leave a trail."

Eduardo frowned. "Which will make it harder to track him."

"Well, we knew this wouldn't be easy." Even as he spoke, however, Rafe sensed a glimmer of hope within himself. It felt good to have Cat approaching this so methodically, like a puzzle that needed to be solved, rather than being panicked and running off in all directions. That was what Rafe had felt like doing ever since Miranda disappeared with Simon, even though he knew such an approach wouldn't have helped at all.

"No," she said. "On the upside, I know Simon isn't going to hurt Miranda, Rafe. I saw how he was looking at her." Rafe winced, and she went on quickly, "I'm not saying that to pour salt in the wound or anything. But if he's trying to work on her, trying to convince her he isn't the bad guy—"

"Seems like a waste of time," Rafe cut in, annoyed. "Since we all know he's the bad guy."

"True, but…." She trailed off for a second, then said, "You know that old saying about how everyone's the hero of their own story? Well, I'm sure Simon feels the same way. He's probably trying to convince her that the world has wronged him somehow, and he's just trying to get his own back. I'm not saying Miranda is going to fall for it, but if that's his approach, it means we should have some time to figure all this out."

"And then we will catch up with him before anything can happen," Eduardo said.

That all sounded hopeful. Maybe too hopeful. Still, Rafe could see what Cat was driving at. Simon wanted Miranda to love him, and so he would be careful about what strategies he employed to bring her around to his side. The last thing he'd want to do was alienate her…although he'd already made a pretty good attempt at that, considering the demon attack in the church and its aftermath. Then again, Simon would probably be quick to explain that he hadn't killed anyone else, which was true enough. Cat was fine, and while Louisa and Malena definitely weren't, neither were they at death's door.

"You could be right," Rafe allowed. "That doesn't mean we should drag our feet on this. Besides, even though we're focused on La Cienega, there are other places that aren't too far away where he could have gone."

"Not a lot," Cat said. "I mean, there are plenty of isolated properties in Santa Fe County, but if you and Miranda thought he'd also be looking for a place that backed up to a river or a creek because it would be more defensible, then that narrows it down a good bit."

True. La Cienega sprang to mind first, but there was also tiny Cerrillos, where the Rio Galisteo wound its way through the old mining town. But no, that didn't make a lot of sense. In a place that small, the arrival of someone like Simon would be sure to attract attention. Maybe Pecos? It seemed a little too far out, but if they were going to start casting their net that wide, then they'd also have to consider possibly Española, or farther upstream, in one of the little hamlets that clustered along the banks of the Rio Grande as it wound its way down from Taos...Velarde, or Dixon, or Embudo.

No, none of those possibilities felt right to him. Maybe downstream, in Rio Rancho, or the northern semi-rural part of Albuquerque, where wineries had sprung up in the last few decades or so. He knew there were properties that backed up to the river in that part of the world. Problem was, once you started looking outside Santa Fe proper, there were just too many places where someone like Simon Escobar could have gone to ground.

He expelled a breath, then said, "Well, we'll stay focused on La Cienega for now, and if that doesn't turn up anything, we'll start looking at other options. It's probably best not to have Daniel scatter his resources too much anyway."

"True." Cat reached into her backpack purse, which had been hanging off the ladder-back chair where she was sitting, and pulled out her new phone. She went to the list of her recent messages, then typed out a rapid-fire message—to Daniel, Rafe presumed, to let him check the property records in La Cienega and environs for any recent sales.

It was probably a long shot. Even paying cash, you just didn't buy a house overnight, which was basically the timeframe they were working with. Unless Simon had been planning for a backup hideout all along, knowing that the situation in Tesuque wouldn't last forever. Although Rafe hadn't had a chance to ask Miranda all the questions he'd wanted to—so much had been going on, they'd barely had a spare moment to catch their breaths—he knew that Simon had been watching Miranda for a long time. The chances of him plotting all this out well beforehand were fairly high.

"Ask Daniel to check the records going back a year," he said, and although Cat arched an eyebrow at him, she didn't miss a beat, just kept on with her texting.

"Do you really think Simon Escobar might have been planning this for that long?" Eduardo inquired after taking a sip of his cinnamon tea.

Rafe shrugged. "At this point, I'm not willing to dismiss anything out of hand, just because I know that Simon has been obsessing over Miranda for a lot longer than I really want to think about." If he'd been speaking only to Cat, he might have added, "the fucker," but he knew the profanity wouldn't go over too well. Eduardo was far more patient and relaxed than anyone who'd been married to Genoveva Castillo for more than thirty years had any right to be, but even he had his limits.

"That's troubling."

There's an understatement, Rafe thought. "Yeah, it is. I guess he started thinking they were supposed to be together because they're both children of a *prima* and a *primus,* some weird kind of soul-mate situation. To someone with Simon Escobar's twisted logic, I suppose it makes some kind of sense. But of course Miranda doesn't feel that way—could never feel that way."

"You love her very much, don't you?"

The question made Rafe pause. He was uncomfortably aware of his sister sitting next to him. Yes, she appeared to be busy with her text convo with Daniel, but still. Although he knew that Cat must be aware of how he felt about Miranda, it was hard to come out and say it so baldly. They weren't a family that was comfortable with showing emotion. A lot of that had been due to Genoveva's iron rule, but still....

And she's not here anymore. You need to mourn her, but you also need to recognize that she doesn't control you anymore. You, or anyone else in this family.

"Yes," Rafe said, hands cupped around the glass of water in front of him. "I love her a lot. And that makes me an even bigger jerk, because I spent so much time trying to figure out how to get out of being married to her. Now all I want is for her to be my wife."

"She will be," Eduardo replied, his voice strong with conviction, his expression far more serene than it should be. "You will find her, and you will make a happy life together."

Rafe wished he could be that confident. At the moment, all he could think about was how it would be so easy to hide Miranda away some-where obscure, a place where none of them would ever bother to look. And they didn't have Marco anymore. There was no one else in the Castillo clan with the ability to find missing people.

Unless...unless they reached out to another clan. The McAllisters were completely off limits, thanks to the dark spell Simon had cast to keep them all penned in New Mexico's borders, but what about the Montoyas? After all, their *prima* had said to ask if they needed any help with their missing "cousin." And Miranda was still missing, even if this was a different circumstance than the one that had sent Rafe and Cat to San Antonio, looking for any leads that could help them find his vanished fiancée.

It would be taking a hell of a risk, though. He supposed someone from the clan could simply attempt to inch their way across the border—even if they crashed into a barrier, they wouldn't cause too much damage beyond a dented bumper at those low speeds. But....

He sat up suddenly, an idea racing its way across his brain. "Dad, are there any Castillos near the Texas border—maybe in Clovis—who have civilian spouses? I can't keep track of everyone."

Eduardo's head tilted to one side as he stared up at the ceiling, obviously pondering the question. After a moment, he nodded. "Yes, your cousin James's wife is a civilian. Lorena."

"Perfect. Can you call him and see if Lorena would mind driving over into Texas? Just across the border and back."

For a moment, Eduardo stared at him, mystified. Then he said, "Ah—you want to find out whether the barrier Simon put up will keep out civilians as well, or whether it's somehow keyed to our witch blood."

Even as Rafe nodded, Cat set down her phone and said, eyes shining, "And if Lorena can get across, then she can go into Texas and see if any of the Montoyas will help us."

"Exactly," Rafe replied.

"A good plan," Eduardo said, although he frowned almost immediately afterward. "But won't the barrier keep the Montoyas out?"

"That's what we need to test next, if it turns out that a civilian can get through. Maybe the spell is sort of like a membrane, permeable on one side but not the other."

"There's only one way to find out." Eduardo pushed back his chair and stood up. "All the contact information for the clan members is stored on Genoveva's computer." Sorrow flickered in his dark eyes, but his voice was firm enough as he continued, "Luckily, I have the password. Give me a moment to look up James's phone number and make the call."

He went out of the kitchen, leaving Cat and Rafe alone. She didn't exactly smile, but he could tell she was hopeful that maybe they'd come up with a way to make an end run around Simon Escobar.

"Do you really think the Montoyas will help?"

About all Rafe could do was lift his shoulders.

"I hope so. I mean, it's in their best interests to make sure that a dark warlock doesn't set up shop in the territory next to theirs. It's the same reason why we Castillos got involved in the fight more than twenty years ago."

"I hope this one will turn out a little better," Cat replied, suddenly looking much more subdued.

Considering that their mother was dead and their two sisters were currently in comas, Rafe wasn't sure how it could get much worse. But then, Cat was still all right, and so was Eduardo. It could get a lot worse if Simon took it into his head to go on a rampage. About all Rafe could do was hope that, whatever might be happening with Miranda and the dark warlock, she was cooperating enough that he would have no reason to lash out.

What if that cooperation includes sleeping with him? he thought suddenly, blood going cold. *Are you still going to think it was all worth it?*

He didn't know. He *couldn't* know. Having sex with someone you hated would be terrible, but it wasn't as horrible as murder…not by a long shot.

But he trusted Miranda. She was smart and strong and capable. If it came to that, she might capitulate, just to make sure no one else was sacrificed, but Rafe thought she would do everything she could to keep stringing Simon along, to make sure she never completely extinguished his hope but also never gave her body over to him. They just had to make damn sure they found her before the situation reached that boiling point.

"I hope so, too," he said, realizing that Cat was watching him, clearly waiting for him to reply. "Simon is strong, but his father had years to practice his craft, to hone it into a horrible weapon. Simon's not that experienced."

"True." She paused as Eduardo came back into the kitchen, looking relieved. "Well?"

"Lorena is heading out now. I told her that she had to go very slowly when she came to the border, and she assured me she'd be careful. It's about twenty miles from their house to the Texas border, so we should know within the half hour."

Eduardo wasn't the only one who was relieved. Not that Rafe really thought that James and Lorena would refuse to make the test, but still, this way they would know very soon whether they could count on the Montoyas to help out.

And in the meantime....

Cat shot him a curious glance. "What is it?"

"Oh, I was just thinking about the differences between our situation now and the one the Castillos faced back when Miranda's parents came here, asking for help."

"They must be good, judging by the expression on your face."

Rafe nodded. "I hope so. That is, I was thinking about how Simon isn't as experienced as his father. But that's not the only thing going for us."

"What is it, then?" Eduardo inquired, sitting back down and reaching for his tea.

"Miranda herself," Rafe replied. "I don't know everything her powers can do, and neither does she. I think Simon still underestimates her. And I think that makes her our secret weapon."

"Fingers crossed," Cat said, although, judging by the way her mouth pursed slightly, it looked as though she wasn't entirely sure whether Miranda's talents were up to the task.

They all went quiet for a moment, probably because there really wasn't much they could do right then except wait to hear back from James's wife Lorena as to whether she had been able to cross over into Texas, or whether she'd crashed into the same barrier that was working to trap all the witch-born Castillos in New Mexico.

"I'm going to go outside, get some fresh air while we wait," Rafe told Cat and Eduardo, then pushed his chair out from the table. They both nodded, and Cat had a look on her face that told him she'd thought about asking him whether she should come, too, but then thought better of it.

Good. Most of the time Rafe was perfectly happy to have Cat around, but right then he wanted to be alone.

He went out into the chilly afternoon air and walked aimlessly down one of the garden paths. It was too bad that everything was so dry and dead right now; he'd hoped that by going outdoors, he'd be able to regain some equilibrium, but there was little about the landscape around him to offer any solace. He'd always hated this time of year anyway, with the color and flash of autumn gone and the knowledge that more than six months of cold awaited before the land became green again. In other parts of the world, spring might come sooner than that, but winter always liked to keep northern New Mexico in its grip for as long as possible.

It felt strange to think that his mother would never see the return of her beloved flowers, would never see these lawns stretch green and smooth again under a canopy of fresh leaves. She'd always taken such care of these gardens, but now he supposed it would be Louisa's job—assuming she ever came out of her coma.

Rafe's mouth thinned to a flat line. Simon Escobar had a lot to answer for.

As he drew closer to the casita where Miranda had stayed so briefly, Rafe made himself turn away and head back in the direction from whence he'd come. He didn't want to look at the casita, didn't want to think about what could be happening to Miranda at this very moment. True, she was smart and resourceful, but was she really strong enough to hold off a warlock as powerful as Simon?

Hands jammed in his jeans pockets, Rafe came up the steps to the kitchen door, only to have Cat open it and say, "She got through!"

"What?" he asked, not quite able to track what she'd just said.

"Lorena! She went through the barrier like it wasn't even there, which means it doesn't affect civilians. Dad's talking to her now."

Oh, right. That had to be good news, didn't it? They could all use some good news about now, that was for sure.

Rafe followed Cat into the kitchen, where Eduardo was still seated at the kitchen table, cell phone held to his ear. "Yes," he was saying. "I need to get the information off Genoveva's computer, but I know that Lupita Montoya, the *prima* of the clan, lives in San Antonio. So it is a journey that will take some time." A pause as Eduardo apparently listened to Lorena's reply, and then he said, "It's urgent, but I understand if you need to make arrangements. And obviously we don't want you driving all through the night. Yes, that should work. Thank you, Lorena. I'll text you the address." Eduardo swiped his finger over the screen to end the call, then laid his phone down on the table.

"Well?" Cat said.

"She'll do it, of course, but she wants to leave in the morning. It's already past four, and so even if she left now, she wouldn't reach San Antonio until midnight. We are already asking a favor of her, and so I thought it better to tell her it was all right to start tomorrow."

"A favor that benefits the whole clan, including her," Rafe growled.

"True, but she has young children, and James can't take off work at such short notice without it causing problems, so she will have to arrange for someone else to watch them. But this way she can set out early in the morning—she hopes no later than seven-thirty—and get to San Antonio by mid-afternoon. We may have help as soon as tomorrow night."

The thought of so much delay made Rafe grind his teeth, but he managed to say levelly enough, "Only if the Montoyas can get in from their side."

"True." Eduardo fiddled with the handle of his now-empty mug and said, "I know this is not the kind of delay you wanted to have happen. But it will be all right. You must have faith."

Rafe wanted to ask his father how he could have faith when their enemy had already killed his mother and put two of his sisters in comas, but he realized that arguing with Eduardo wasn't going to change anything. His father was probably hurting even more than he was. And really, Lorena was doing them a huge favor. She might have married into the Castillo clan, but she wasn't a witch herself. She probably didn't fully understand what they were facing here.

"Okay," he said at last. "I get it. But I'm going to be climbing the walls until then."

"I know," Eduardo replied, his expression one of sympathy. "And I don't know what to say, except that we need to be patient."

"In the meantime," Cat said. "I'm going to make us all a big batch of chicken enchiladas for dinner. It'll destroy the kitchen, but it'll keep me busy."

In response to this suggestion, Rafe could only offer her a weak smile. Still, he understood her motivation. They all needed to do something to keep busy so they wouldn't go completely crazy. In fact—

"I'll help," he said.

12

A SUMMONING

Miranda

I SHOULD HAVE KNOWN THIS WOULD BE Simon's endgame—to use his insanely powerful magical talents to sweep away anyone who might challenge his authority, and to take over the clan whose *prima* had once given her own life to make sure his father died before his plans for domination could come to fruition. And who would stop him? Louisa had already shown that she really wasn't strong enough to be *prima*. Maybe during peacetime, when there wouldn't be anyone to contest her authority or question her powers, but going up against someone like Simon Escobar?

She didn't stand a chance.

And neither did anyone else in the Castillo clan, unless they were hiding some insanely powerful witches and warlocks in other parts of the state. Rafe had a fairly amazing—and rare—talent, but I didn't see how changing into a wolf, coyote, or even a bear would be enough to take down Simon.

After I'd stared at him in shock, not sure I'd heard him correctly, he'd smiled at me and said, "Give yourself some time to think about it, Miranda. Maybe get some air—it's a nice day."

He'd been flaunting his control over me, I was sure. Letting me know I would be free to walk the grounds, but that I didn't dare try to escape. I hated the whole charade, and yet I'd taken him up on the offer. At least that way I could get out of the house, away from him, and see if some fresh air might allow me to figure out a way to stop his terrible plan.

So here I was, walking the grounds, pretending to be looking at the trees and the bare flowerbeds and the clear blue sky overhead, but really doing my best to figure out how I could prevent him from taking control of the Castillos. It did feel good to be outside, although I'd had to stop and put on a jacket before I went out.

This property was more extensive than I'd thought. Maybe not quite as big as the Tesuque compound where we'd been holed up previously, but still at least four or five acres. Unfortunately, the trees kept me from seeing very far, and besides, I didn't know New Mexico nearly well enough to even start to guess at my location. I figured we were next to Cienega Creek, but that didn't tell me very much, since it could wind along for miles.

It was very quiet except for the sound of the wind shuffling some fallen leaves along, and the occasional cawing of a raven. I knew it had to be a raven, because the sound was hoarser, throatier than that of a crow.

Weren't ravens supposed to be harbingers of death? I couldn't remember, because I'd never studied up on that sort of thing, had sort of avoided some of the more woo-woo aspects of being a witch. I might have been born with magical blood in my veins, but it had taken its own sweet time manifesting itself, and I'd never wanted to compensate by playing with crystals or trying to pretend there were signs and symbols in the most ordinary, everyday things.

Even so, the sound of that raven croaking off in the distance made the skin at the back of my neck prickle.

I went down to the shore of the creek and stood there for a long time, watching the water move slowly past. At this time of year, after the monsoons but months before the snow melt would return, it was running low and languid. I could see the rocks in the bottom, saw a quicksilver flash that might have been a fish, or only my eyes tricked by the angle of the sun. Even at its current low point, the creek was still probably at least two feet deep, with a rocky, treacherous bottom. Despite that, I might have attempted to wade across, except that I knew I wouldn't have gotten very far. Simon would have been at my side in an instant, and I didn't want to think about the consequences such an escape attempt might invite.

Instead, I turned away from the water and walked back toward the house. From this vantage point, it appeared friendly enough, a large square structure in the traditional pueblo style, with a sizable covered patio that looked out over the garden, a built-in kiva fireplace, and some cast-iron furniture to complete the outdoor space. If I were here with anyone else, I might have enjoyed sitting out on that patio, even at this time of year —after all, that fireplace had been put there to allow the home's residents to be outside as long as the weather wasn't too cold. However, I certainly didn't want to participate in such cozy activities with Simon Escobar.

He came out through the French doors and stood there, watching as I approached. A brief squint up at the sun, which was now moving ever lower toward the west, and he said, "Beautiful day, isn't it?"

I made a noncommittal sound. Although I didn't want to directly contradict him, neither did I have any desire to agree that it was in fact a beautiful day. How could it be, after the scene in the church earlier, after he'd coerced me into coming here with him?

A brief tightening of his lips was the only sign that I'd gotten to him. Still in that friendly, casual tone, he said, "Come on. There's something I want to show you."

That was about the last thing I wanted to hear from him. I could feel myself tense, but I nodded, pretending that his comment hadn't sent alarm bells sounding through my entire body.

We went back inside the house, and he led me past the kitchen and into the garage, where his white BMW SUV was parked. I glanced at it for a moment, wondering if he planned to take me somewhere, but he ignored the vehicle and went over to a little alcove off the main part of the garage. It was the sort of place you might use for storage—and in fact there were metal shelves on all three walls filled with cans of paint and stucco patch and all the other detritus of a house that's been recently remodeled.

Then I noticed the trap door in the cement floor.

"This is part of the reason why I wanted this house," Simon said, kneeling down so he could grasp the latch and lift the piece of roughly painted plywood out of the way. "I guess the previous owner was going to build a wine cellar down here, but he never got past digging out the space and laying the cement slab. Still, that was all I really needed. Come on."

"You want me to go...down there?" I asked, gruesome images from every horror movie I'd ever seen replaying in my head. Not that I really expected Simon to be taking me down there for some sort of ritual human sacrifice, but....

He laughed, pausing on the top step. At least there were real stairs—unfinished plywood, but sturdy-looking enough—but even so, I had absolutely no desire to set foot on them.

"It's fine," he said, extending a hand. "Come on."

The last thing I wanted to do was have him holding my hand as I went down the stairs. Unfortunately, I had a feeling he would be annoyed with me if I refused him. I swallowed, then stepped forward, let him wrap his fingers around mine.

That weird sensation of wrongness I'd sensed from him was gone now. I had no idea whether it was because he'd figured out that I'd detected it somehow, and was now masking it the same way he could hide his magical nature, or whether some sort of terrible spell had been fresh on him previously, and that was the only reason why I'd felt something was off. Either way, rather than being reassured that he seemed better—for lack of a different word—I could only feel disquiet move through me once more. There were so many layers of deception in Simon, I had no true idea what about him was real.

If anything.

There was a light switch on the cement wall near the top of the stairs. Simon flicked it on, so at least we weren't descending into utter darkness. The air felt damp and cold, but it didn't have the kind of harsh mildew odor I'd been expecting. No, instead it smelled almost sweet.

I saw why soon enough. The area that had been carved out for the wine cellar was perfectly square, about twenty feet by twenty feet. Chalked on the cement floor were intricate symbols, similar to the ones I'd spied in the little shed on the back forty of the Tesuque property, but much, much more complicated. To one side was a low table draped with a black cloth, and the same tarnished silver candlesticks with black candles sat there, with the cruel curved knife in the center of the altar. Off to the other side was a small table—really, more like a plant stand—on top of which rested an ebony incense burner inlaid with what looked like mother-of-pearl. It was from the incense burner that the sickly sweet scent emanated, and I had to hold back a cough, even though no incense was burning now.

"So you got a replacement for your little shed," I remarked, still trying to sound casual, although being that close to the knife and the arcane sigils on the floor was enough to set creepy crawly sensations moving down my spine and every limb.

"Oh, it's more than that," Simon replied. He went over to the table and ran a finger along the hilt of the curved dagger, although, to my relief, he didn't pick it up. "There's a power in the earth, and power in this place being so close to water. Air we already have, and fire is easy enough." With a snap of his fingers, the black candles in their tarnished holders lit themselves, adding to the sickly illumination from the overhead fixture.

"'We'?" I repeated, unease stirring somewhere in the pit of my stomach. I knew I didn't want to be involved in anything that might take place in this dank little underground chamber.

"Yes, *we*." He turned back toward me, a strange light flickering in his black eyes. "I was able to summon the demons without any assistance, just like the brother your Levi murdered so many years ago."

As far as I could recall, Levi hadn't murdered anyone. He'd had to kill Matías Escobar in self-defense. Then again, I hadn't been there. I didn't know for sure exactly what had happened, except that Levi had sealed the portal which had allowed the demons to come through to our world.

"Then you don't need me, do you?" I asked. Even though I knew such an attempt would probably be futile, I still eyed the steps going up into the garage, wondering whether I'd be able to make it very far before Simon caught up with me. Or, better yet, if I teleported the hell out of here.

No, I couldn't do that. Too many lives were at stake.

"I do need you," Simon replied. He moved closer to me, a lot closer than I would have liked. I was barely able to keep myself from flinching as he reached out and took both my hands, wrapping his fingers tightly around mine. At least his skin was warm, but to me it felt like the unhealthy heat of a fever, not the reassuring warmth I experienced whenever Rafe had held my hand. "You see, to make sure no one tries to contest me, I need more than an army of mindless demons. Those I've summoned have only the crudest intelligence, and they can't be trusted to carry out all my plans. That requires a certain kind of demon."

"What kind?" I asked, barely able to get the words out past the growing tightness in my throat. While I wasn't worried about him trying to conjure Beelzebub or Asmodeus or the Devil himself—we weren't talking about the demons and devils of Christian mythology here, but a kind of creature that existed on a different plane entirely—there were still entities in other worlds we absolutely had no place messing with.

"He is a lord of demons, one who rules over those I've been summoning," Simon replied. For someone who was suggesting summoning beings of intense, alien power, he looked a bit too casual, despite the way his hands remained wrapped around mine. "But because he's so powerful, I need you to combine your gifts with mine, Miranda. I need us to join our powers to bring him to this plane."

"You're crazy," I whispered, and Simon immediately shook his head.

"No, I'm really not. The two of us together can do this. I know we can."

Without worrying about the consequences, I pulled my hands from his. "You can't seriously think I'd be okay with helping you summon a demon even more powerful than the ones you've already called here. It's too dangerous."

A frown creased his brow, but he still looked almost too relaxed, as if the outcome of our argument was a foregone conclusion, and he was only allowing me to make my protests because he knew he'd wear me down in the end. "You need to think about this, Miranda," he said softly. "Think about the Castillos, these people you claim to care about. I don't want to hurt any more of them… but I will if you won't help me."

I wasn't surprised by this threat; I'd been expecting it. "By helping you, I'd be putting them just as much at risk." *And the whole world,* I thought, but I doubted that argument would carry any weight with Simon. "You think that you'll be able to control this being you want to summon, but if he's as powerful as you say, I don't see how he would ever obey your commands."

"Because he would be bound to me," Simon said, his tone completely reasonable. Too bad I knew his arguments were basically the exact opposite of reasonable. "That's how these things work. I've studied how to do this—do you think I learned something like that in high school?"

He pointed at the complicated patterns and sigils on the floor, and I swallowed. No, he had to have delved into some pretty arcane materials to come up with all that. I remembered how he'd told me that he'd hidden his magical nature from the de la Paz clan, posing as a gardener or house cleaner or whatever else it took in order to get close to the books on magic and ritual they'd been collecting for generations. That they possessed these things wasn't any real secret, although no one talked about it much. They'd always been more interested in the knowledge behind magic rather than its actual practice.

What frightened me now was that I couldn't know for sure whether he'd actually drawn all these patterns correctly. One line off by a degree or two, the wrong symbol used in a critical spot, and all those fancy markings on the floor wouldn't be of any more use than a hopscotch grid. And when a summoning like this went wrong, it went horribly wrong.

He had trapped me neatly, that was for sure. I had to go along with his plans for this ritual, because if I didn't, I could be the cause of the spell backfiring...and I knew I didn't want to be anywhere around if something like that happened.

"You say that it's going to work that way," I told him. "But how do you know for sure? This isn't a simple demon we're talking about, right? Who is it?"

"I can't say his true name," Simon replied. "It's part of the summoning. But one nickname for him is the Lord of Chaos."

That epithet sounded vaguely familiar, as if I might have once heard someone mention it someplace within earshot. Or maybe I just wanted it to sound familiar, because I had to admit that "Lord of Chaos" didn't sound like a very friendly person. "I'd think chaos is the last thing you'd want," I remarked. "Considering you're so into making sure you have control of everyone and everything around you."

"You're missing the point," Simon said. "He's extremely powerful, and because he's chaotic, any attempts by the Castillos to bind him—even if they have someone with this kind of talent, which I seriously doubt—are going to fail."

None of this was reassuring in the least. I had no reason to believe Simon could control this being any more than I or one of the Castillos could. What would happen once it was let loose on the world?

"But you can control him," I said, not bothering to hide the skepticism in my voice.

"Together, we can control him," he corrected me. "That's what I was talking about you—you and me together, harnessing his energy. He'll be our servant, and the Castillos will have no chance of fighting back."

I didn't want anyone to be my servant, least of all a demon with the unappetizing name of "Lord of Chaos." Besides, I'd seen plenty of horror movies that involved demons and devils and what-have-you, and it never seemed to turn out well for the people who did the summoning. You'd think they would have learned.

"It sounds exhausting," I said. Although the last thing I wanted to do was seem at all friendly, I had to do something to get Simon off this tear. I moved closer and laid a hand on his arm. "Can we talk about this upstairs? It's cold and damp down here."

He hesitated for a moment, eyes searching my face. I didn't know what he was looking for, but I had to hope I looked as guileless as possible, that I was only asking him to go upstairs because I was getting chilled in the little underground chamber, and not because looking at all those diagrams and symbols on the cement floor had begun to make me feel almost physically ill.

"All right," he said at last. "We can't do the summoning until three in the morning anyway. I just wanted to show you."

I managed to smile. "Thanks, Simon." I let go of his arm, and he hung back while I began to climb the stairs, then followed a moment later. Soon enough we were back in the relative brightness of the garage, although I couldn't quite shake the sensation that something was now watching me, a cold intelligence not quite of this world.

No, that had to be just the heebie jeebies. Simon hadn't opened a portal yet, hadn't uttered any words of a spell. So much of our magic was done by sheer strength of will, by calling forth the powers hidden within us, but this kind of a summoning would require an incantation, a rigid ritual to ensure that the entity being summoned would be properly controlled when it emerged on this plane.

If such a thing was even possible. I'd seen Simon's powers at work myself, but even he was overreaching here. Whether I'd be able to convince him of that was uncertain at best. The thing he wanted above all else—yes, above even me—was to take control of the Castillos, to give himself the status in this clan that he'd been forever denied by the Santiagos. Obviously, he was willing to take enormous risks to achieve that goal.

For the moment, about all I could do was be relieved that we had some time before this supposed ritual was going to take place.

When we came into the kitchen, Simon took both our glasses and refilled them, then handed me mine. "Drink it all," he commanded me. "You'll need to drink at least eight glasses between now and the ritual, to purify yourself of any toxins you might be carrying with you. And we'll both have to fast until then."

"Do we really need to do this tonight?" I asked, although I took a few obedient sips of water once I was done speaking. "I mean, this doesn't sound like the sort of thing we should rush into."

"It's two nights past the full moon," Simon replied. "That's what I need—that waning power, the power of the dark, but one that's more powerful than a waning quarter moon, or a crescent moon. We can't afford to wait."

I hated how he kept saying "we," as though I'd already agreed to this insanity, rather than doing my best to talk him out of it. "I don't even know what to do—"

"You don't need to *do* anything," he cut in. "I'll be doing all the work. I just need to borrow your power to make sure the spell is strong enough. In the meantime, though, we'll both need to purify ourselves."

That sounded ominous. Our kind of witchcraft didn't require purification rituals, unless you counted quiet meditation to center one's mind as a kind of ritual. "Purify?"

He smiled at me, but that glitter was back in his eyes, the one that told me he was thinking of matters that were anything but pure. "We'll need to bathe—separately, if you were worried about that."

Of course I was, but I didn't want to come out and admit it. I settled for giving a noncommittal shrug, and he continued.

"I'll give you some incense to take to your room. For the rest of the day, once you've bathed and cleansed yourself"—he paused there, and I wondered if he was thinking about my boast about having sex with Rafe multiple times—"then you'll sit quietly and meditate, and keep drinking water. That's all. I need you to be focused, not distracted by inconsequential things."

I couldn't think of anything less likely to keep me from being distracted than asking me to meditate. Many of the witches in the McAllister clan were very good at it, but I'd never been able to count myself among their number, maybe because I'd never seen much need for focus because of my sad lack of any magical skills.

Well, all that was in the past. I'd do my best to get my brain to cooperate, not because I wanted to help Simon, but because I was scared shitless of what might happen if his spell backfired and this Lord of Chaos was set loose to go rampaging through this plane of existence.

"Got it," I said, my tone neutral.

He appeared pleased that I didn't want to argue anymore. "Drink up," he said, "and then I'll refill your glass and bring a pitcher by later on."

I didn't really feel like chugging the water in my glass, but I knew he wasn't giving me much of a choice. Without replying, I lifted the tumbler to my mouth and drank the water all down, then held the glass out to Simon. Still wearing that pleased expression, he refilled it.

"Good. Go on upstairs. Run a bath, and use the bath salts in the little canister on the shelf by the tub."

None of this sounded very reassuring—what if

he decided to walk in on me while I was naked in the bath?—but I didn't argue with him. I had to hope that he was serious about this whole purification thing. Trying to get down and dirty with me while I was in the bathtub didn't sound like a very good way to remain pure.

"Okay," I said, then took my glass of water with me and went upstairs. Since Simon didn't immediately follow, I supposed that meant he wanted me to go ahead and get started.

To my surprise, I found a dark hooded robe lying on the bed when I went into the room he'd given me for my use. The robe definitely hadn't been there when I'd left earlier, which meant Simon must have left it on the bed while I was out walking around the grounds. The message seemed clear enough, though; he wanted me to put on that garment after I was done in the bath.

Fine. But I sure as hell was wearing something under it.

I got out clean underwear and a T-shirt and some yoga pants, figuring that would be a simple enough ensemble to wear under the loose-fitting robe. It slithered over my hands when I picked it up, telling me the fabric was probably silk. He must have bought it online, or maybe commissioned a local seamstress to make it. Either possibility seemed equally plausible... although its presence told me he must have been plotting this ritual for a while, planning to have me assist him. Goosebumps lifted on my arms, but I told myself I needed to stay calm. Simon's scheme was crazy, and yet I knew my best chance for survival was to keep it together and pray that this summoning wouldn't go horribly wrong.

Carrying my change of clothes draped over one arm and my glass of water in one hand, I went across the hall to the bathroom. After I set everything down, I locked the door, and sent a little of my magic out toward it, telling it that it wasn't supposed to open for anyone except me. Whether that would really work, I didn't know, but it felt a little better to know there was more than just a flimsy interior door lock between Simon and me.

This bathroom was large, with a separate shower stall and sunken jetted tub. The window on the far wall had been redone with stained glass, a stylized rose. It sent an odd, bloody reflection into the room. Not all that reassuring, but at least the patterned glass made an effective visual barrier.

I turned on the taps, then located the little canister of bath salts Simon had told me to find. When I opened the lid and took a sniff, I found that the contents had a sharp, aromatic scent, not sweet at all. What it was, I couldn't be sure. It wasn't smooth and subtle enough for sandalwood, but it had that kind of a feel to it.

After waiting for a few minutes, I tipped some of the salts into the water, then trailed my hand through it. The temperature was just about right, and nothing about the feel of the water against my skin seemed any different than the times I'd taken a scented bath at home.

Moment of truth. I hesitated for a long moment before I reluctantly grasped the hem of my sweater and pulled it over my head, then laid it on top of the counter. Next with my boots and socks, then my jeans. I paused again, fingers closed around the front clasp of my bra. Even with the door locked and that extra spell laid on it, I couldn't keep myself from worrying that Simon had been waiting for precisely this moment to come walking in.

However, as the seconds passed, I realized I had to do this. Jaw clenched, I unfastened my bra, then stepped out of my panties and got into the tub. The water felt soothing, and the scent of the bath salts Simon had provided was curiously relaxing. If someone had told me I would have felt comfortable taking a bath under the same roof as Simon Escobar, I would have laughed in their face, but I couldn't deny that this felt better than I'd expected it to.

All right. Time to meditate.

I closed my eyes, let the warm water swirl around me. Problem was, all I could really think about was Rafe, about how I prayed with every fiber of my being that he'd somehow find a way to locate me before the clock struck three and Simon forced me to perform this terrible ritual with him. And also, my thoughts kept straying to how good it had felt to be in his arms, to have him make love to me. I would have liked to have him here in the bath, that was for sure.

None of this was exactly conducive to entering a purified state, but that was Simon's fault for expecting me to follow all these silly steps. After about ten minutes or so, I basically gave up on the meditation and reached for a washcloth, scrubbing myself down before I at last climbed out of the bath and dried myself off.

Then it was time to get dressed as quickly as possible. Once I was safely covered up, I went back to the bathtub and drained the water, then gathered my dirty clothes to take them back with me to the bedroom, where I'd spied a hamper just inside the closet door.

No sign of Simon during any of this. I disposed of the clothing in the hamper, then went and sat on the bed. Was I supposed to be in a lotus position? I didn't know about that, but I spotted the incense and a burner of carved soapstone sitting on the dresser, and realized I was supposed to be burning some while I meditated.

This incense had a fresh, clean scent, unlike the cloying stuff Simon had burned in his basement ritual room. It reminded me somewhat of a white sage incense my Great-Aunt Rachel used sometimes, although I couldn't be sure whether it was the same kind or not.

I did my best. I really did, because I knew the consequences of this summoning going wrong were even worse than what would happen if Simon actually managed to summon this demon lord and somehow get him under his control. But my thoughts kept skipping and jumping around, refusing to leave me alone. I thought of Rafe, and Cat, and Eduardo, and Rafe's two sisters in their comas. I thought of my parents, and how I wished I could somehow get a signal out to them that we needed help. So many things, none of which had much to do with the ritual that loomed ever closer.

While I was in the bath, Simon had put a pitcher of water in my room. From time to time I would refill the glass and drink, and then a while later have to go use the bathroom. During none of these excursions did I see any sign of him, although the door to the master suite stood slightly ajar, as though he kept it open so he could keep tabs on me.

Outside, dusk eventually fell, then night itself. My stomach began to complain about not getting any dinner, but there wasn't much I could do about that. I supposed we would eat later… assuming we both survived the summoning we were about to attempt.

More time passed, and I found myself fighting sleep, my eyelids drooping now that my stomach had apparently realized it wasn't going to get fed that evening. Several times my whole body would jerk as another wave of weariness passed over me. I wondered whether it really mattered if I slept or not, but some stubbornness forced me to stay awake. Possibly I did sleep for a few fitful periods, although I couldn't really recall whether I'd done so or not.

At last, though, Simon was at my door, a tall, looming figure in the black robe he wore. In fact, I could see very little of his face except the gleam of his eyes, thanks to the hood he'd pulled up to cover his head.

"Are you ready?" he asked quietly.

Of course I wasn't, but I nodded anyway and got down off the bed. My muscles were cramped from sitting crosslegged for so many hours, although I hoped the kinks would work them-selves out once I'd been moving around for a while.

"Come along," he said.

I followed him downstairs, then out to the garage, where I stood, trying not to shiver in the dead of night cold, as he lifted the trapdoor to the basement. At least he turned on the light, which allowed me to descend the stairs without tripping over the long robe I wore. When I got to the bottom, I moved to one side, giving the chalked symbols on the floor a wide berth.

Simon came down after me, then paused to wave his hand at the candles, bringing forth their flame once again. After he had done that, he moved to the wall next to the bottom step and touched his hand to the light switch, shutting off the overhead fixture.

I couldn't stop myself from letting out a gasp.

"It's all right," he said, even though I knew this was far from all right. "We can't have any artificial light during—well, during."

Dark deeds done in the dark, I thought, but I kept those words to myself. "I understand."

He seemed pleased that I hadn't protested. "Good. Come here."

I really didn't want to close up the small distance between us, but I knew I didn't have much of a choice. And while I was so scared of being down in that room, of what was going to happen next, I made myself think of everyone once again—Rafe and Cat and Eduardo and all the others—and how I needed to do whatever I must to make sure they were safe.

If that was the case, though, what was I doing here? Shouldn't I be doing anything I could to prevent Simon from carrying out his terrible plan, even if it meant sacrificing myself? I had to admit the idea wasn't very appealing, but sometimes you had to consider the greater good. Death wasn't really anything to fear, or so I'd been taught. It was only a portal to the next world. Still, I didn't think I was ready to step through that portal, not when I had so many reasons to live.

As I went to stand next to Simon, as he shifted our positions so we stood at the "north pole" of the terrible compass he'd drawn on the floor, a plan began to form in my head, one so audacious, I wasn't sure I'd have the strength to carry it out.

But I'd have to try. For all their sakes, I'd have to make the attempt.

"You'll need to stand very still," Simon said quietly in my ear. "Don't move or speak, no matter what happens. I'll be drawing on your energy. You're powerful enough that you probably won't notice, but if you do, all you should feel is a faint dizziness at the very most. Okay?"

I only nodded, since I didn't quite trust myself to speak. The last thing I wanted was to dwell on that "should" in his instructions. What if he was wrong, and I fainted, or worse? Beyond that, would this plan I'd begun to devise be successful if I were having some of my energy taken from me? I had no idea, but I guessed I was about to find out.

Simon's hands settled on my shoulders, heavy, warm even through the silk fabric of the hooded robe and the T-shirt I wore underneath. I experienced a small tingle, followed by a shiver running down my back, but I honestly didn't know whether that was only a reaction to his touch, or whether he'd begun to tap into my powers already.

Then he began to speak. The words weren't English; I didn't think they were Latin, either, but something utterly foreign, harsh-sounding and yet somehow flowing as well. Whatever the language was, it made more of those shivers work their way down my spine. More than anything, I wished I could pull away from Simon and run, but I knew I couldn't. I had to stand there and wait for what was about to happen next.

Into the stillness of the underground room came a wild breeze that caused our robes to flap and the flames atop the black tapers to flicker wildly. With it there was also a strange, creeping cold, one that seemed to seep up out of the ground, freezing my feet in the flats they wore. I could smell a harsh, acrid odor like spent gunpowder, although I supposed that could have come from the candles, which smoked as their flames were bent this way and that.

And out of the center of the diagram drawn on the ground arose an enormous shadowy figure, one with great leathery bat-like wings and long black hair that fluttered in the unnatural wind of his arrival. The being was so tall that he had to bend down, or risk hitting his head against the ceiling eight feet above us.

I knew I wasn't supposed to move or speak, but I couldn't quite hold back the gasp that slipped past my lips.

Red eyes opened, and glared at us. "Why have you summoned me, mortal?"

English. Perfectly good English. I didn't know why I was so surprised, only that I'd thought maybe this being would have spoken to Simon in the same language he'd used for the summoning.

"Lord of Chaos." There was a triumphant note in Simon's voice, one that frightened me almost more than the inhuman figure which stood before us. His ambition was something I knew all too well, and rightly feared, while this demon lord was still an unknown.

"Some have called me that. What is it you want?"

Despite the cold terror pulsing through me, I felt my mouth quirk slightly. The demon sounded almost annoyed, like someone who'd interrupted their dinner to answer a phone call that turned out to be from a telemarketer.

"I have bound you in the circle of air, of fire, of earth, of water. I have—"

"Yes, I can see that. Very pretty artwork. What is it you *want?*"

I couldn't help it. The tiniest of giggles escaped my lips, and at once the demon's red eyes fixed on me. It was hard to make out much of his face in the darkness, because his skin was black as night, but I thought I saw harsh, nightmarish features, a mouth full of jagged teeth.

As I stared at him, I heard his voice in my mind. *You find me amusing, mortal woman?*

No, not you, I replied hastily. *The way you were treating Simon.*

Ah. He is the one who drew the diagram, yes?
Yes.

A pause, and the Lord of Chaos said, *I sense that you are not a willing accomplice in this endeavor.*

No, not at all. He's brought you here to make you his servant, to help give him control of the Castillo clan.

This is not an outcome you wish for?

No, I said firmly. *He has no right to rule this clan, no right to be here in Santa Fe at all. And he has no right to summon you.*

Ah. Another of those pauses. Then the demon

went on, *It was very unwise of him to bring me here. He is a child meddling with things he cannot comprehend. But you—you, young witch, I think I can help you.*

You can? I asked, not daring to hope that the creature's offer might be sincere. Was this demon really offering his assistance?

Yes. You see, this Simon did the summoning, but he performed the ritual using your energy to strengthen it enough that it would actually work. This means you are as bound up in its success as he. You can break the charm that binds me here, set me free.

And you'll go back to—well, to wherever you came from?

That is my hope.

It wasn't a definite yes, but it was better than nothing. But maybe he was lying. He was known as the Lord of Chaos, after all. Maybe he was trying to trick me into setting him free from the binding so he could go out and commit whatever mayhem he chose.

And I have your word that you will go back, that you won't hurt anyone here?

Why on earth would I do that?

Well, you are *a demon,* I pointed out.

A demon lord, he corrected me. *I have no use for the kind of petty vengeance you fear. But yes, I give you my word that I will cause no harm to anyone on this plane.*

That seemed about as good as I was going to get. *What do I need to do?*

It is simple enough. You only need to destroy part of the pattern that binds me here. Then its power will be broken, and I will be free. A pause, and then he went on, amusement clear in the deep voice that had somehow managed to penetrate my very thoughts, *A simple stumble to blur a few of the markings will suffice.*

That did seem easy…almost too easy. What if he reached out to grab my arm as I broke the circle? But I realized then that I couldn't keep dithering over possibilities. Our mental conversation had taken less than a second, since it had traveled at the speed of thought, but very soon Simon would start to realize something was off, and right then I was a lot more frightened of him than I was of the Lord of Chaos.

I understand, I responded.

Then I took a breath, acted as though I was shifting my weight and had gotten my foot caught on the hem of the robe I wore. I stumbled forward, foot scuffing the line that formed the outer perimeter of the chalked circle.

"No!" Simon cried out.

The Lord of Chaos' great wings beat at the air,

and he smiled, showing several rows of sharp teeth. *Thank you, mortal.*

Can you do something to get rid of Simon? I asked desperately. *Even if he fails in this attempt, he's going to try something else.*

I fear I cannot help you in such a way. You yourself just made me swear an oath not to hurt anyone on this plane.

Well, damn, I had. Who would've thought a demon would be so law-abiding? *But you're the Lord of Chaos!* I pleaded.

I am. But that only means I will do what you least expect. He stopped there, terrible head lifted, like a dog catching a strange scent on the wind. *I sense...someone.*

Someone what? I asked.

Someone who can hear me as you do. Perhaps they can help guide me back whence I came, for the way seems blocked. A good night to you, mortal.

Then he was gone, blinking out of existence right in front of our eyes.

Simon rounded on me. "What," he ground out, "the hell did you just do?"

13

WHISPERS IN THE DARK

Rafe

HE STARTED AWAKE, REALIZING A DARK FIGURE stood next to his bed. Visions of demons danced in his head for a moment...until he realized the figure was only his sister. "Jesus Christ, Cat," he snapped. "What the hell are you doing in here?"

She hesitated, looking over her shoulder at the hallway. Faint illumination from a nightlight plugged into one of the outlets in the hall cast a halo over her long dark hair, and it was hard to see her expression clearly. Even so, he could tell she was shaken.

"What is it?" he asked, his irritation melting away. "Has there been another attack?"

That question only elicited a shake of the

head. "No. I mean, everything seems to be quiet. No one's called. Only…."

"Only what?"

Without replying, she went and sat at the foot of the bed, her back to one of the large pillars that made up the bed frame. This had been his room once, but his mother had picked out the furniture, heavy pieces that were intended to work with the Spanish Colonial architecture of the house but had only made Rafe feel as though he slept in a high-end hotel room rather than his own bedroom.

"I heard something," Cat said at last. Once again her gaze shifted to the hallway.

"Here in the house?" Rafe demanded, adrenaline already beginning to pump into his veins. Damn it, if that bastard Simon Escobar was trying to break in somehow—

"No, not in the house." She stopped herself there, then pointed at her temple. "In here."

He stared at her, wondering if all the stress had finally started to get to her. "You're hearing voices in your head?"

"Yes. I mean…one voice."

"Whose was it?"

"I have no idea," Cat responded. She hugged her arms to herself. In her baggy T-shirt and with her hair pulled into two braids for the night, she looked like the little sister who used to sneak into his room after bedtime so they could plot and plan how to deal with Genoveva's next onslaught. "I was asleep—I conked out pretty fast, after everything that happened today."

Rafe couldn't blame her for that, because he'd pretty much passed out the moment his head hit the pillow as well. That had been unexpected, since he was sure that his worry for Miranda would have kept him up half the night. Apparently, weariness had won out over anxiety, though. "And?"

"And then I heard a man's voice in my head. He said, 'Look in the place of the marshes.'"

"That's pretty specific. Are you sure you weren't dreaming?"

"Completely sure, because I'd woken up just a second or two before I heard the voice. I was staring up at the ceiling, watching the shadows of the tree branches move, and then there was this voice in my head, talking to me."

Strange, but definitely not the weirdest thing that had happened this week. Rafe sat up a little straighter and ran a hand through his hair. "What did he sound like?"

"I—I don't know. Like a man. It was a deep voice." Cat played with one of her braids, head cocked to one side as she appeared to contemplate Rafe's question. "He didn't have an accent or anything."

"But the voice wasn't familiar to you."

"No."

"Do you think it might have been a ghost?" Considering speaking to spirits was his sister's talent, Rafe wondered why she hadn't thought of that possibility right away.

"Well, that's what I thought at first, but usually I can see ghosts as well as talk to them. There wasn't anyone there…just this voice in my head."

"Did you talk to it?"

"Yes. I said, 'What do you mean?' and he said, 'That is all I can tell you. I'm sure you're clever enough to figure it out.'"

"So a sarcastic ghost."

Cat shot him an annoyed look. "I just told you it wasn't a ghost. At least, I don't think it was. This voice felt like it belonged to someone real… corporeal, I mean."

Leaning back against the headboard, Rafe said, "Are you suddenly developing psychic powers or something?"

"No. I mean, I don't think I am." She closed her eyes for a moment, then asked, "Can you hear what I'm thinking?"

"No."

"Well, then." She picked at the hem of her T-shirt, frowning so deeply that her expression was clear even in the semidarkness. "I think I only heard him because he wanted me to. After that exchange, I asked him, 'Who are you?' And he said, 'I don't think I will tell you that. It's probably better if you don't know. This is all the help I can give you.' Before I could say anything else, he added, 'I have a quest of my own, you see. Good luck.' And then he was just…gone."

"How could you know he was gone if you couldn't see him?" Rafe asked reasonably.

"I don't know. I just could. Like…there was a presence somewhere near, even if I couldn't see him. It was just sort of a feeling."

That sounded creepy as hell, although Rafe refrained from making a comment on the subject. Clearly, Cat was already shaken enough, and he didn't need to add to her unease by making her think there might have been an actual stalker somewhere nearby.

"'The place of the marshes,'" he repeated. Something was tickling at his brain, but he couldn't quite figure out what he was overlooking. "I wonder what it means."

"I don't know. I was hoping you'd have some insight."

It could mean nothing at all, although Rafe somehow doubted that Cat's invisible visitor would have taken the time to stop by and offer that handy hint if it weren't significant in some way. "I guess we could try looking up the phrase online. I'll try it in Spanish first, just because that makes the most sense for someplace in or around Santa Fe." He leaned over and retrieved his phone from the nightstand, unlocked it, and then entered "the place of the marshes" in the phone's built-in search engine. What popped up made his eyes widen.

"What is it?"

Rafe angled the phone so she could see the screen. "This is what we get for not studying Spanish."

Because in Spanish, "the place of the marshes" was *la cienaga*. The spelling of the location here in Santa Fe was slightly different, but this had to be what Cat's visitor had meant.

"So Miranda is in La Cienega for sure?" Cat asked, eyes wide. "How did he know?"

Good question. Maybe the visitor had been Miranda's guardian angel. Things had been crazy enough lately that Rafe wasn't about to overlook any possibility, no matter how outlandish. "I have no idea. But at least now we know there's no reason to look anywhere except La Cienega for strange real estate transactions…assuming your invisible friend was telling the truth."

"He was," she said immediately, her tone all conviction. "Or at least, I'm about ninety-five-percent sure he was. Why would he come here and lie to me about something like that?"

Good question. Unfortunately, since they didn't know who "he" was, they couldn't really make too many assumptions about his relative trustworthiness. Then again, while Rafe and Cat and Eduardo had all agreed that it was better for Daniel to focus on La Cienega, they hadn't specifically told him not to poke around in other places. As soon as the hour was decent the next morning, they'd have to get in contact with him and let him know where to focus all his efforts.

Assuming, of course, that the person who'd given Cat that little bit of intel wasn't simply trying to mess with them.

Still, it wasn't as if they had any other leads, so they might as well go with it. If nothing else, at least concentrating on La Cienega for the time being would allow them to cross it off the list and move on to other prospects if they didn't turn up anything useful.

"I have no idea," Rafe said. "But we don't know who 'he' is, so it's hard to guess at his motivations. This is something to go on, though. In the morning, I'll get in touch with Daniel, and we'll go from there. But now we'd probably better both go back to sleep."

"All right." Cat pushed herself off the bed and stood, then hesitated for a moment.

"What is it?"

Silhouetted by the faint light coming in from

the hallway, her shoulders lifted. "It was strange, having his voice in my head like that. But also…."

"Also what?"

"I kind of liked talking to him. I hope I can do it again sometime."

Despite his resolve to get up early and fire off a text message to Daniel first thing, Rafe slept late, not cracking an eyelid until it was almost eight-thirty. He was irritated by his sloth, while at the same time he had to wonder whether his late night—or early morning, depending on how you looked at it—convo with Cat might have had something to do with his oversleeping.

Still, there wasn't much he could do about the hour, except shower hastily, put some clothes on, and get downstairs for some coffee as soon as he could. To his annoyance, Cat was already there, dressed and done, sipping at a mug of French roast.

"There's plenty more in the carafe," she said blithely as he shot her an irritated look.

Of course, she couldn't know that concern about there not being any coffee left was not the main reason for his annoyance. Without replying, he went over and filled his mug. As he stirred the tiniest bit of cream and sugar into it, he asked, "Where's Dad?"

"John called and asked if he could come over and sit with Malena for a while. I guess he had to take Elisa somewhere. Of course Dad said he would—he left about twenty minutes ago."

"Any change?"

Cat didn't have to ask what "change" he was talking about. "I don't think so. I guess Yesenia texted Dad early this morning to let him know that both Louisa and Malena were stable, but that they also didn't show any signs of waking up. They were both able to get some water down, though."

Which was something, but if this went on for too much longer, they'd have to do something about getting some nutrients into them. He let out a sigh. "I guess it's better than taking a turn for the worse, but Jesus. I wonder why they both went into comas when you only passed out."

Cat gave a small shrug and glanced away, which meant she was probably feeling guilty over the situation, even though there was absolutely nothing she could have done to make things any different. "I don't know. There isn't much about any of this that makes sense."

No, except that Simon Escobar still had Miranda held captive somewhere. Hopefully somewhere in La Cienega, but they didn't even know that for sure. All they had to go on was the advice of some disembodied voice who'd decided it was a good idea to visit Cat's bedroom in the middle of the night to dispense advice.

Rafe came over and sat down at the kitchen table, then got out his phone and shot off a quick text to Daniel, letting him know they were almost positive Miranda had to be somewhere in La Cienega, even if they couldn't yet pin down the exact location. Daniel responded almost immediately, thanking Rafe for the tip and telling him he'd be in touch as soon as he had something.

"What now?" Cat asked.

"I don't know. All we can really do is sit and wait."

"Which is excruciating."

That was a word for it. Rafe drank some more coffee and contemplated their options…not that they had many. La Cienega wasn't a big place, but they still couldn't exactly go door to door, inquiring whether the residents had seen anyone who matched Miranda's description. If nothing else, they'd let Simon know they were closing in on him, and that would only give him a chance to grab Miranda and find another hiding place. The only way they'd be able to get her away from him was to utilize the element of surprise as best they could.

Which meant sitting tight, even though every

minute that passed felt more like fifteen, or twenty.

Or a hundred.

"What about Lorena?" he asked. "Do we know if she's set out for San Antonio yet?"

"Yes," Cat replied. "Dad said she left a little after seven, so even allowing for a couple of pit stops, she should get to San Antonio by around three or so. Which means we still have about six hours to kill before we hear anything.

"Great," Rafe grumbled. Maybe they should have told Lorena to fly to San Antonio. Was there even an airport in Clovis, though? Flying wouldn't save them any time if Lorena had to backtrack all the way to Albuquerque.

"Maybe we should go visit Louisa," Cat suggested. When Rafe lifted an eyebrow at her, she went on, "You know, to give Oscar a break. I'm sure he'd appreciate it if we stopped by. And it would give us something to do rather than just sitting around here and waiting for Daniel to call. What he's doing could take hours, or it could take days."

God, it had better not. Rafe reassured himself that Daniel tended to work quickly, even though he was also thorough. He'd figure this out today.

In the meantime, it was probably better to take Cat up on her suggestion. Oscar would no doubt like the chance to step away from his wife's bedside, run some errands or go down to Rio Rancho and visit his two kids where they were staying with relatives, and a change of scenery might help to keep Rafe's thoughts from running in the same troubling channels.

"Okay," he said. "Why don't you text Oscar, and I'll make us some breakfast. You okay with toast and eggs?"

"Sounds perfect," she replied, then picked up her phone from where it sat on the kitchen table by her elbow.

While Rafe wouldn't call himself a gourmet cook, he was pretty good at scrambled eggs. He got the carton of eggs and some butter from the fridge, and started prepping the pan while Cat sent out a text to Oscar. Just as Rafe began to crack the eggs into a bowl, she looked up from her phone.

"He says that would be great, and he really appreciates it. I told him we'd probably be over in about forty-five minutes."

"Okay." That would give them enough time to eat their breakfast and then drive out to Las Campanas. Although Rafe wasn't really looking forward to seeing his sister still trapped in a coma, it would be good to get out of this house. Louisa's place was much friendlier, with big picture windows that offered gorgeous views of the Sangre de Cristos, and a feeling of light and space.

Once he was done with breakfast prep, Rafe brought the plates of eggs and toast over to the table. Cat smiled at him as she took hers and set it down.

"This is nice," she said, and he shot her an unbelieving look.

"'Nice'?" he repeated. "With everything that's going on?"

"Well, I wish the circumstances were different, but it's been a long time since you and I sat at this table and had breakfast together. That's all I meant. Plus," she added as she lifted a forkful of eggs to her mouth, "you make some mean scrambled eggs. You'll have to make some for Miranda after we get her back."

"If we get her back," Rafe said darkly.

"We will."

The way Cat made that statement, she clearly thought the outcome was nonnegotiable.

He hoped she was right.

Oscar greeted them enthusiastically, relief at their presence in every plane of his face. "Thanks for coming over—Rosalie and Lewis have been watching the kids, but they really needed to go into Albuquerque today on some business, so it helps that I can go down and spent that time with William and Crystal, if only for a few hours."

"We're glad to help out," Cat said as Oscar closed the door behind them and led her and Rafe farther into the house. "And if we need to leave for some reason, we'll make sure someone else can come over and take our place. You need a chance to get out."

"I don't like to say it, but I think you're right. And I know the kids would like a chance to go to the park. I think I'm going to take them over to the Bosque, see if there are any birds left to watch. We'll probably have lunch, too, if that's okay."

"Take as much time as you need," Rafe told his brother-in-law. He figured that the eggs and toast he and Cat had just eaten for breakfast should keep them satisfied for a while. "We'll hold down the fort."

"Great. Our room is just down the hall at the end."

Rafe nodded, and Oscar hurried off, phone in one hand as he lifted it to his ear. Probably he was making a quick call to either Rosalie or Lewis, letting them know that he was on his way. If traffic cooperated, he should probably be down there in less than forty-five minutes.

And he'll be back in a lot less than that if there's any change with Louisa, Rafe thought. He and Cat went down the hallway to the master suite, where their sister lay in bed, half propped up against some pillows. She looked better than Rafe had expected; someone had brushed out her long, dark hair, and it lay neatly over her shoulders, which were covered by a long-sleeved T-shirt in a cheerful turquoise hue. Her color was natural, and really, it appeared more as though she was just deeply asleep, rather than in a coma.

"She looks good," Cat said in a half-whisper, as though she feared the sound of their voices might wake up their sister.

"I know." Maybe too good? His sister's healthy-looking flush made him think of Snow White, lying asleep after taking a bite from a poisoned apple. No glass coffin here, though. Rafe had a feeling that Oscar had probably kissed his wife as she lay there, and yet she still remained locked in unconsciousness, taken away from them all.

"You might as well sit down," Cat told him. "We're going to be here for a while."

True. There were two chairs grouped together with a small side table in front of the gas fireplace embedded in one wall; Rafe picked them both up and brought them over closer to the bed. He and Cat sat down, then gave one another a pair of uneasy looks.

"So...." she began, clearly not sure what the protocol was in a situation like this.

Not that Rafe knew, either, but he'd always heard it was comforting for people in comas to hear the voices of their loved ones. He certainly wouldn't say anything he didn't want Louisa to overhear, of course, but having her there as a silent audience shouldn't keep him and Cat from talking. "I wish Daniel would get back to us."

"He will…when he has a reason to call." Cat set her backpack-purse on the floor, glanced over at the bed, and added, "It's just going to slow him down if we keep bugging him every five minutes for an update."

"I know that," Rafe replied, not bothering to hide the irritation in his voice. "But between the radio silence from him, and knowing that Lorena's on her way to San Antonio but won't have anything to tell us for hours—"

"And having Miranda held captive by Simon Escobar and us not knowing what's going on," she cut in. "I get it. Just remind yourself that you're doing a good deed here."

"I know." Then again, if he were really doing a good deed, he probably wouldn't feel as grudging about it. Family was supposed to look out for family, especially in a witch clan, and it wasn't as though they had anything else they could be doing. That was probably the part which bothered him the most. He always got antsy when he couldn't be actually doing something. Sitting and waiting wasn't part of his nature. Unfortunately, he couldn't change his current situation, except to hope that Daniel would come up with something very soon.

"I wish I knew who he was," Cat said, her tone musing.

"Your 'friend' from last night?"

"Yes. I mean, obviously he was trying to help…but if he actually knew where Miranda was, why didn't he just come out and tell me?"

"I have no idea. I'm more interested in how he knew in the first place. You're sure it wasn't someone from another witch clan?"

"Of course I'm not sure," Cat replied. She rubbed nervous hands over the knees of her jeans, then shook her head. "I wish I did know, because if it had been someone from the McAllisters or the de la Pazes or whatever, then it would have proved that witches and warlocks from outside can get into New Mexico somehow, even if we can't get out. But I don't think it was a warlock. He felt…different."

"Different how?"

"I don't know," she said irritably. "I'm just going on my gut with this one. But I don't think it was a warlock, and I know it wasn't a ghost, so I don't know who this guy was. About all I can hope is that he wasn't leading us on a wild goose chase."

"Well, we were checking out La Cienega anyway. All he did was confirm that our hunch was right."

"True."

Cat went silent then, her gaze focused on the still figure lying in the bed. Rafe didn't think he'd ever seen his sister Louisa so motionless, because she always seemed to be involved in something—chasing after her kids, or helping Genoveva to organize the numerous get-togethers and gatherings that involved the Castillo clan throughout the year. Now, though…she wasn't dead, but the next thing to do it.

From down the hallway, Rafe heard Oscar call out, "I'm going now—I'll be back in a few hours," followed by the bang of the door that led out to the garage. Now the house felt truly empty, even though it really wasn't.

Cat's phone buzzed, and she hastily pulled it out of her purse and looked at the screen. "It's a text from Daniel," she said. As Rafe waited impatiently, she scanned the contents of the message, then nodded to herself. "He says there aren't any houses in the La Cienega area that have been up for rent as long-term rentals during the past three months, and also that there haven't been any listings on the various vacation rental sites. He's checking property records now to find out what's been bought and sold there over the past year."

"Of course it couldn't be that easy."

"Is it ever?" Cat returned her attention to the screen, then tapped out a message, probably acknowledging receipt of the information and thanking Daniel for sending it over. When she was done, she didn't put the phone away, but left it sitting on her knee—presumably so she could get to it immediately in case Daniel got back to her in the near future. If he was going on to do a title search, Rafe doubted they'd have any new information anytime soon. Even with digital record-keeping, digging through that kind of stuff could be tedious and time-consuming, especially if you were hunting for someone who so far had shown a real talent for flying under the radar.

It would make sense that Simon might buy a house rather than renting one, just because if you were paying cash, you wouldn't have to be quite as much under the microscope as you would if you were applying for a mortgage. And once the house was yours, you might have to deal with nosy neighbors, but there wouldn't be a property management company to come sniffing around.

In La Cienega, neighbors probably weren't too much of a problem. The properties there tended to be spaced widely, and if, as he and Cat had speculated, the place where Simon had hidden Miranda had a lot of trees around it, no one would be able to see much, if anything, of what was taking place there.

Rafe really didn't want to think about that.

He was about to tell Cat that maybe they should have Daniel limit his searches to properties of two or more acres, but he didn't get much further than opening his mouth when something completely unexpected occurred.

Louisa yawned, stretched, opened her eyes, and said, "What happened?"

14

DARING TO FLY

Miranda

I STARED AT SIMON, MIND WORKING furiously. "I—I'm sorry," I stammered, hoping that I sounded frightened and confused and utterly, utterly harmless. "I don't know exactly. I guess my foot got caught on this stupid robe you made me wear. It's too long."

Which it was, although I doubted Simon would gracefully accept that explanation.

My intuition proved correct.

His grip tightened on my arm, and even in the semidarkness I could see the way his eyes glinted with fury—and, I thought with a note of satisfaction, a measure of fear as well, although I doubted he wanted me to know that. "Do you have any idea what you've just done?"

"I broke the spell?" I asked, all innocence.

"Yes, you broke the spell, and the binding. Now the Lord of Chaos is free on this plane, untethered by any sort of magical control."

If I hadn't gotten the strange but distinct impression from the demon in question that havoc wasn't what he had in mind, Simon's statement would have been very worrying. As it was, I could only stammer once again, "I'm—I'm sorry, Simon. I didn't even know something like that could happen. Maybe you should have warned me, told me what the risks were, instead of bringing me down here and using me as your magical battery or whatever without letting me know any of the important stuff."

His eyes narrowed. "I thought you at least would have enough sense to know how to act during such an important ritual."

"How exactly would I know that?" I shot back. "The only 'rituals' I've ever participated in were the ones the McAllisters performed at Samhain and at Beltane, and they weren't exactly summoning demons, you know? I obviously couldn't have learned anything on my own, considering I didn't even have magical powers to work with until a week ago."

Simon went quiet for a moment, probably because he wanted to continue giving me a dressing-down but had realized some of this might actually be his fault. Finally, he said, "Ignorance doesn't excuse what you did. But let's go upstairs. I need to think."

No doubt he wanted to go over his contingencies…assuming he'd planned for any. But then, it seemed that Simon was the sort of person to consider multiple angles of a situation and determine how they all might go wrong, so surely he must have guessed there was the possibility—however small—that this summoning might not go the way he wanted. Even if that were the case, though, he probably had thought that the worst-case scenario would be the spell not working at all, not that a high-level demon lord was now free to roam around Santa Fe to do as he pleased.

Would he, though? After all, even in a city as diverse and colorful as Santa Fe, an eight-foot-tall winged demon with a long mane of black hair would be pretty hard to miss.…

Simon sort of pushed me toward the stairs, and I stumbled for real this time. I hadn't been lying about that damn robe being too long. Holding back a curse, I gathered it up as best I could and climbed the steps, while behind me Simon snuffed the candles and blew out the incense, then followed me up the stairs. By that point I was almost back up to garage level. The thought flashed through my mind that I could blink myself away now, when I was out of reach.

Reluctantly, I pushed the notion aside. Simon was already angry, and if I disappeared on him, I would only invite quick retaliation toward the Castillo clan.

Nice trap I was caught in.

I stood off to one side as Simon lowered the door to the basement. He'd left the light on up here, so now I could clearly see the glower on his face as he turned back toward me. "Come on."

Without waiting for me to reply, he caught me by the bicep and dragged me inside the house. I wished I could yank my arm from his grasp, but I told myself that I still needed to act meek and scared. The last thing I wanted was to seem like a threat to him.

He didn't pause in the kitchen, but continued to the staircase and brought me up to my room. "You'll stay in here," he said. "Until I figure out what to do next." And before I could reply, he slammed the door in my face. As I stood there, I could hear his footsteps loud on the polished tile floor.

Well, fine by me. If I had to be stuck here, I'd rather be alone in this room than have to endure Simon Escobar's company. At the same time, though, I had to wonder what he was going to do now that his prize had flown the coop, so to speak. It was too much to hope that he would give up his plans for domination of the Castillo clan—

and, possibly, the world—but I didn't know how he thought he could manage task that without some serious supernatural help. The lesser demons he'd been summoning to do his dirty work weren't nearly powerful enough.

Knowing Simon, he'd come up with something. But since he obviously had no further ritual use for me tonight, I pulled that stupid robe over my head and tossed it onto the room's single side chair. That felt a bit better.

The clock on the bedside table said it was 3:48. It didn't feel that late, but clearly more time had passed while we were down in the basement than I'd thought. The sensible thing to do would be to try to sleep, although I didn't know if I could manage to do so. It would be hard to relax, knowing Simon was downstairs, still seething over my apparent incompetence.

Then again, since I had no idea what the next day might bring, it was probably smarter to get some rest. I was on edge enough that just about any stray sound would be enough to rouse me from slumber, so I wasn't too afraid of Simon sneaking up on me in my sleep.

That seemed to decide the situation. I was already basically wearing the same things that had been packed in my duffle to sleep in, which meant all I had to do was climb under the covers and close my eyes. Light from the nearly full moon was enough to illuminate the room, and so I didn't bother to leave on the bedside lamp.

I closed my eyes, and was gone.

When I woke up the next morning, the sun was high in the sky. I looked over at the clock next to the bed, saw it was almost ten, and blinked. I rarely slept in that late. Then again, I usually didn't stay up until four in the morning, either.

The good part was that it seemed Simon had decided to let me sleep—or possibly he was occupied enough with other matters that he'd left me alone. That thought wasn't too reassuring, since I could only imagine what Simon might be busy with right now.

I got up from the bed and went to the door, then tried to turn the knob. It wouldn't budge. Cursing under my breath—I really needed to go to the bathroom—I rattled the knob again, this time using the simple magic that had been mine even before far greater powers had awoken in me.

Still nothing. As far as I could tell, Simon had put some kind of locking spell on the door, one I didn't seem able to break.

Fine.

"Simon!" I called out. "Let me out of this goddamn room—I need to pee!"

No reply.

Was this his way of torturing me? It was certainly the kind of petty revenge he would take pleasure in, especially after my performance of the night before.

Asshole.

"Simon!"

At last I heard footsteps on the stairs, and then in the hallway outside my door. When it opened, Simon stood there, smirking at me. He was dressed, and looked like he'd showered and shaved, which meant he must have been up for a while. "Nature calls?"

"Yes," I replied, refusing to be embarrassed. "Can you please let me out?"

"Sure," he said, and stepped out of the way. "I was wondering when you were going to wake up. Trying to sleep away the guilt from the way you fucked up last night?"

"Yes, that's exactly what I was doing. I just couldn't bear to face you and be reminded of my incompetence."

The smirk he'd been wearing disappeared, replaced by the same angry glower I'd seen the night before. "It's not funny, Miranda," he said. "Do you have any idea how badly you screwed up?"

"Not really, but I'm sure you'll keep reminding me about it until I have it figured out." I lifted an eyebrow at him. "But can we hold off on all that until I go to the bathroom? If you keep me talking here, I'm going to end up peeing on your shoe."

His mouth pressed down into a flat line. "Funny. Go ahead and do whatever you need to do. Meet me downstairs afterward—there's still some coffee left."

I nodded and dashed into the bathroom. From the way the floor in the hallway creaked, I guessed that he had turned and headed back downstairs. Good.

Since I'd taken that "ritual" bath late the night before, I didn't bother with a shower. I took care of business, washed my face, put on some mascara and lip gloss, brushed my hair. Then it was back across the hallway to get on some real clothes. Not that I was terribly eager to go down to the kitchen and be subjected to more haranguing, but I knew I needed some coffee—and food, too, for exactly the same reason I'd done my best to get a good night's sleep. I had to be prepared to face whatever Simon planned to dish out.

Thus prepped for the day, I went downstairs. As I'd thought, Simon was loitering in the kitchen, staring moodily out at the bare yard through the large picture window over the sink. As soon as I entered the room, however, he turned toward me and said shortly, "The coffee mugs are in the cabinet above the coffeemaker."

I nodded, then went over and got a mug from the indicated cupboard and poured myself some coffee. Since it had been sitting around for a while, it wasn't exactly at its peak of freshness, but I didn't care. Even though I'd gotten nearly six hours of sleep, I still felt far more tired than I should.

Probably just the influence of Simon's scintillating presence.

Neither of us spoke for a moment, which was fine by me. I kept concentrating on sipping my coffee and doing my best to avoid his gaze, which felt like a pair of lasers trying to bore their way into the side of my head.

At last he said, "I'm going to try again."

This statement made me look up from the coffee mug I held. "Try what again?"

He gave me a pained look. Clearly, he was getting tired of my deliberate obtuseness. "Getting the Lord of Chaos back here. He's already on this plane, which means the summoning shouldn't be as difficult."

"You sure that's such a good idea?" I asked. I was about to add that it sounded as though his lordship had business of his own he wanted to conduct, but then I recalled how our conversation had been entirely telepathic. Simon hadn't heard any of what the two of us had said to each other, and so he didn't know that the demon he'd summoned might not be too keen on getting called back here to be his lackey. I wondered why Simon hadn't been able to hear any of my exchange with the Lord of Chaos. The best explanation seemed to be that the demon lord had wanted it that way, and who was I to argue?

"It will work," he said, deliberately ignoring my question. "And because he's on this plane, the spell will not require as much energy…which means I won't have to rely on your questionable help."

"I said I was sorry."

His eyes narrowed for a second, sooty lashes nearly obscuring his coal-black eyes. Funny how once I'd thought Simon was fairly good-looking, although not as model-handsome as Rafe. Now, though, all I could see was the evil behind those eyes, the ruthless determination overlaid on his sharp features. "Not good enough," he replied. "Maybe I'll forgive you…if I can get the spell to work a second time."

I wanted to tell him that I didn't give a crap about his forgiveness, but again, I managed to hold my tongue before any ill-considered words slipped out. Although I highly doubted that he thought I would fall into his arms anytime soon, I guessed he still had plans for me, still wanted me at his side—if for no other reason than I was the most powerful witch he'd ever met. To his twisted way of thinking, that was enough to indicate that we should be together. Never mind love or affection or caring. For Simon Escobar, those concerns only betrayed weakness.

After taking another sip of coffee, I smiled sweetly at him and said, "Then I hope the spell works. When are you going to try? Tonight again?"

"No," he replied after a slight pause, as though trying to gauge whether my comment required a pithy response. "I'll do it at three this afternoon. It's not as strong a time as three in the morning, but the number has a power of its own, one that should help with the summoning."

"Okay." I hesitated for a moment, then asked, "And what am I going to do during all this? Are you going to lock me up in my room to make sure I don't screw up your summoning again?"

"The thought had crossed my mind, but it's probably better to keep you where I can see you. That said, I'm going to tie you to a chair so you can't possibly interfere with what I'm doing."

"Seriously…a chair?" Not that I would put that sort of act past Simon—he'd done far worse already—but it seemed almost amusingly old school, the sort of thing a villain in an old black and white movie might have done to the heroine.

"Yes, a chair. You won't try to fight me on this, will you, Miranda?"

The threat was clear in his voice—I'd better cooperate, or he'd surely find a way to take out his anger on the Castillo family. "No, I won't fight you."

To tell the truth, I wanted to make sure I was an audience to that summoning. I had a feeling the Lord of Chaos wasn't going to appreciate being called back to this house like he was Simon's errand boy or something.

"Good." But even though Simon sounded satisfied enough with my response, from the way he continued to watch me narrowly, I could tell he had guessed there was something motivating me beyond fear of retaliation against the Castillos.

However, all I did was stand there with my coffee, staring back at him with as bland an expression as I could manage. After a moment, he gave the tiniest lift of his shoulders, then said, "What do you want for breakfast?"

And I knew he wasn't going to question me further.

It was a long and strange day. Simon disappeared into the garage, saying he needed to prepare for the ritual. However, he'd fixed me with a flat stare as he made that announcement, clearly letting me know that just because he wasn't within eyeshot didn't mean he wasn't still keeping tabs on my presence. For all I knew, the house had a video surveillance setup, even if I didn't see much evidence of one. Cameras these days could be smaller than my pinkie fingernail, and hidden inside a light fixture or an air conditioning vent.

I only told him I planned to watch TV while he was working, if that was okay, and he seemed to relax a little. No way was I going to take off now; I wanted to see what happened when the Lord of Chaos returned.

In the meantime, I watched some shows off the satellite feed, went and made myself a sandwich when I got hungry. During all this time, Simon didn't make an appearance. Maybe he was fasting, but since I wouldn't be taking part in the demon-calling ceremony, it didn't really matter whether I stuffed myself full of pastrami. I figured if he was having to redraw all those summoning circles and sigils to accommodate this new ritual, it might take hours and hours, which was fine by me. If he was occupied with that particular task, then he wouldn't be up here, giving me more grief over the way I'd botched the first ritual the night before.

Eventually, though, he reappeared, looking tired but determined. Once again, he was wearing the long black robe, although he hadn't yet pulled up the hood. I paused the television, noting that it was ten minutes until three. "Is it time?" I asked.

"Yes," he replied.

"Do I need mine?" I pointed at the robe he wore. "Because it's still up in my bedroom."

"No, you're not actually taking part in the ceremony, so it's not necessary. Come on."

Dutifully, I shut off the TV and put the remote on the coffee table, then got up from the sofa. Even though I was curious to find out what was going to happen, I still didn't much like the idea of being tied up to a chair. Well, nothing ventured and all that.

Simon led me out of the family room and down to the basement ritual chamber. Once again candles flickered, and it still felt very cold in here, almost colder than it had the night before. Maybe the silk robe had provided more insulation than I'd thought.

Chalk markings again covered most of the floor, although the patterns looked subtly different this time. It was hard for me to say for sure, since I had no experience with this kind of magic and couldn't begin to guess what all those symbols and arcane letters even meant. I didn't like looking at them for very long, even though I now under-stood their purpose, because I knew there was a damn good reason why this magic had been forbidden.

The main difference in the room this time was the hard-backed chair that sat off to one side. "Over there?" I asked, pointing at it.

"Yes. Go ahead and sit down."

Even though I'd been expecting this, I couldn't quite hold back a sigh as I walked carefully around the perimeter of the chamber and then sat demurely down in the chair, which was narrow and uncomfortable, with a hard seat. At least it was a lot easier to avoid smudging the pattern this time, since I had on jeans and boots and not that stupid too-long robe. Once I was seated, Simon came over, several lengths of rope in his hands. At least it was the silky synthetic kind, something that felt soft enough against my wrists as he bound my arms behind me. Once he was done with that, he knelt and tied my ankles to the legs of the chair. During all this, I didn't try to struggle, only stared straight ahead.

Once he was done, he straightened up and surveyed his handiwork. The smirk was back, along with a glint in his black eyes that I didn't much like. Still wearing that unpleasant smile, he said, "You know, I think I like you like this."

"Oh, really?" I returned, which as rejoinders go was pretty weak. But even though I'd agreed to being tied up, I realized I really didn't like being so much at his mercy.

"Yes, really."

In the next second, he bent toward me, pressed his lips against mine. I wanted to pull away, but since I couldn't move, there wasn't much I could do except try to turn my head to escape the unwanted kiss.

At once his fingers were gripping my jaw, holding me in place as he forced my mouth open with his tongue. He didn't taste bad—if anything, he tasted of mint, as though he'd brushed his teeth right before he came to get me—but it was still foul to have him violating me in that way, to know there wasn't anything I could do to stop him with my arms and legs bound as they were. All right, I supposed I could have bitten down on his tongue, but I knew if I pulled a trick like that, he'd only be that much angrier with me, and would retaliate in some sort of unspeakable way. Teleporting wasn't an option, not if I wanted to keep him from going after the Castillos the way he'd threatened.

After a moment, he pulled away from me and stepped back. "Very nice," he said. "I think I've already begun to forgive you, Miranda. You're just too sweet to stay angry at for very long."

The sandwich I'd eaten was roiling in my stomach, but somehow I managed to reply, "I'm glad to hear it. You know, you're a pretty good kisser."

The glint was back in his eyes. "You liked it like that…being forced?"

Think fast, Miranda! "You know, I think I did. It was sort of kinky."

He grinned then, clearly pleased by my reply. "Well, I guess we'll need to explore that later. For now, I've got work to do."

I smiled back at him in what I hoped was a lascivious way. Really, what I wanted to do was tear myself out of that chair and find the nearest bottle of mouthwash. Since that wasn't an immediate possibility, I settled myself into the most comfortable position I could manage, thanks to having my arms tied behind me, and watched Simon as he turned away and took his place at the far side of the circle he'd drawn.

Once more he recited some kind of spell in that strange harsh language, arms held theatrically out to either side. This time, though, I wasn't nearly as frightened as I had been the night before. I'd met the Lord of Chaos, after all, and he wasn't nearly as fearsome as I'd thought he would be. Oh, to look at—absolutely. But otherwise, I'd have to say the demon lord was…kind of cool.

This time it wasn't so much a wind that came out of nowhere as a boom as harsh and loud as a thunderclap going off nearby. I winced and wished I could put my hands up to cover my ears. Almost as soon as it had come, though, the sound was gone, and standing in the basement was the Lord of Chaos.

However, he wasn't standing in the middle of the circle, which was where Simon had meant him to show up. Only if he was trapped in the circle could he be commanded. Standing off to one side, as he was now—I could tell that wasn't supposed to happen.

Even in the candlelight, I saw the way Simon went pale.

"Are you bothering me again, boy?" the demon demanded.

"I—" Simon broke off there, then seemed to recover himself. Standing a bit more upright— although I didn't see how that could do much good against someone a good two feet taller than he was—he said, "You have been summoned to the circle, demon lord. I—"

"No, I haven't," the Lord of Chaos said. With one taloned finger, he pointed at the chalk circle on the ground. "Considering it is over there, and I am over here."

"But you are here, which means you came in response to my summons."

"I came because I was curious what you were up to." The red-eyed gaze moved from Simon to me, and once again I heard the demon lord's deep voice in my mind. *It seems you are in an awkward position, young woman. Would you like to be free?*

Oh, yes, I told the demon, sending my thoughts to him. *Could you take me to Rafe?*

Who is Rafe?

Apparently this Lord of Chaos was powerful, but not all-seeing. I found that vaguely reassuring. *He's—he's my fiancé.* Concentrating as hard as I could, I sent the demon a mental image of Rafe as I'd last seen him, standing in the church with his hands clenched at his sides, face taut with worry and anger. *He has to be someplace in Santa Fe, although I'm not sure exactly where.*

A pause, and then, *Ah, yes. I know where he is.*

I wanted to sag with relief, but I really couldn't because of the way I was tied to the chair. As I watched, the demon deliberately skirted the circle drawn on the ground, then came and paused next to me. It was hard not to flinch, having him that close, but I held myself still as he touched a finger to the ropes binding my legs, and then my arms. Each time his finger rested on its surface, the rope in that spot turned to dust.

"What are you doing?" Simon demanded. "You can't—leave her alone!"

The Lord of Chaos cast a negligent glance over his enormous shoulder. "I fear you are in no posi-tion to tell me what I can or cannot do. You had one attempt at controlling me, and it failed. I am my own master now." He extended an arm toward me, and I went to him and let him pick me up and hold me against him, even though all my instincts were screaming that I needed to run far away from this enormous, frightening creature.

However, I knew he meant me no harm. The long sleeveless robe he wore smelled of smoke, but it was almost a pleasant scent, like the perfume of a campfire that's settled into your clothes after an evening in the wilderness. His impossibly muscled arm held me fast against him, and in the next instant we were gone.

The last thing I heard was Simon screaming at us in denial.

15

AWAKENINGS

Rafe

"Louisa!" Cat exclaimed, getting up with such haste that her cell phone fell to the floor. Luckily, the bedroom was carpeted, so the phone didn't suffer any harm.

Their sister pushed herself up against the pillows and looked around in some confusion. "I'm home. When did I get home? I don't remember Oscar driving me back from the service."

Rafe and Cat looked at each other. Her shoulders went up in an almost imperceptible shrug, and he said carefully, "Do you remember the attack at the church?"

"Attack? I don't—" Then she stopped, one hand going to her forehead as her eyes widened. It looked as though some of her memory was beginning to come back. "Oh, my God. The demons. Is Malena all right?"

"She's…she's still unconscious," Cat replied. "But Yesenia says she's doing okay, all things considered."

"How long was I out?"

"Not too long," Rafe said, still using that careful tone. "It happened yesterday morning."

"Yesterday?" Louisa glanced around, probably trying to determine the level of light outside to give her a clue as to how long she'd been out. "What time is it?"

"Just around three in the afternoon."

"My God." She sagged against the pillows, brows knitted together, as though she was trying to piece some meaning together out of the fragments of darkness that remained after the demon attack. "I—I don't remember anything. That is, I remember these creatures swooping down at us, but it's all a blur after that. A dark blur."

"We're not exactly sure what happened to you and Malena," Rafe said. "You just sort of… collapsed, as though the demons were attacking you both mentally and physically, and we think they had something to do with Malena's coma, too, even if we don't know exactly why yet. Do you remember anything of the attack?"

Louisa shook her head. "Not really. I

remember a horrible kind of pressure, like someone was tightening a band of metal around my head. And then everything went blank."

At those words, Cat glanced over at Rafe, her mouth tight, although she didn't say anything. Louisa's description sounded too much like the same sort of reaction Cat had experienced whenever Simon was mucking around with his demons, but Rafe couldn't begin to guess why she hadn't succumbed the same way his other sisters had when subjected to a physical attack. Maybe it was only that Cat's very talent was communicating with ghosts, spirits, and what-have-you, and so her mind had already grown accustomed to working with strange energies. It wasn't the sort of thing either Malena or Louisa had ever encountered before, although one would have thought that Louisa's *prima* abilities might have made her a bit more resilient.

"Well, you're back now," Rafe said. "That's the important thing. And if you're waking up, then maybe Malena will be soon as well."

"I can try calling Dad," Cat said, and bent down to retrieve her phone. "He's watching her right now," she added for Louisa's benefit.

That comment only made Louisa frown. "Where's Oscar?"

"He's on his way down to Rio Rancho to see the kids—they're staying with Rosalie and Lewis,"

Cat told her, trying to make her tone as soothing as possible. "He's been at your side ever since you collapsed, but he really needed to get down there and spend some time with Crystal and William."

The explanation seemed to reassure her, because she smiled and relaxed a bit against the pillows. "That sounds like Oscar. He's so conscientious."

Cat unlocked her phone, saying, "Then I'll text him now, and get in touch with Dad later. Oscar's going to be so relieved to hear you're okay."

Rather than comforting Louisa, Cat's offer only made her frown. Not looking at either one of them, she said, "I've failed you both."

Cat paused with her finger hovering over her phone's screen, even as Rafe felt himself frown as well. Trying not to sound too upset with her self-defeating tone, he asked, "What are you talking about?"

Louisa was still staring at the fireplace set into the opposite wall. "If I were a *prima* like Mother, or like Grandmother Isabel, I would have fought back against those demons. I would have made them pay for entering a house of God. Instead, I fainted like some idiot heroine in a historical drama."

Oh, shit. Rafe tried to tell himself that Louisa had just come out of a coma, wasn't quite herself yet, but at the same time, he couldn't quite suppress a stir of annoyance. They didn't have time to waste on self-recrimination right now. They needed Louisa to get up out of that bed and be the leader of the clan she was meant to be.

"That wasn't your fault," Cat protested. "I mean, I collapsed, too. For some reason, the effects of the demon attack didn't hit me as hard as they did you. No one knows why—we're all in uncharted territory here. But you can't beat yourself up over it."

Judging by the way Louisa's lips clamped together, Rafe got the impression she wasn't buying it. And the horrible thing was, he didn't know whether he bought it, either. On some level, Louisa was right. She should have been strong enough to stand up to those demons, to face them down, to fight back.

Sort of the way Miranda had.

As best he could, he pushed those thoughts out of his head. He had to focus on what they could do now to get themselves out of this predicament, not what had happened the day before. "Cat's right," he said. Whether he sounded convinced of that fact, he wasn't as sure.

"Exactly," Cat chimed in. "Let me text Oscar. He can't have gotten too far down the road yet."

At least this time, Louisa didn't protest. She

sat there in bed, expression troubled, as Cat sent off a quick message to Oscar.

Just as she was pressing the icon to send the text, something like a sonic boom sounded in the room. The glass in the mirror that hung above the dresser shattered, falling with a tinkle to the wooden surface immediately below it. Cat let out a little gasp of a scream, even as the most nightmarish figure Rafe had ever seen—or could have ever imagined—materialized a few feet away from them.

It stood well over eight feet tall, its hideous black-maned head far closer to the beamed ceiling above them than it was to the floor below. Black leathery wings flapped at the air. From them came a scent of things burning, although there was no fire anywhere.

And in its arms was Miranda. Even while Rafe and Louisa and Cat stared at her in shock, she actually smiled up at the hideous creature as she extricated herself from its grasp. She seemed to pause for a moment, taking a quick measure of her surroundings, and then she ran to Rafe. He retained enough presence of mind to gather her in his arms, although his mind was reeling. "Miranda! What the—?"

"It's all right," she said quickly. She turned back toward the demonic apparition who'd been holding her only a moment before. "This is the

Lord of Chaos. Simon summoned him to do his bidding, but that didn't work out so well."

Somehow Rafe was able to remark, "I guess not."

"He saved me from him, brought me here." She paused, and even smiled at the demon. "Thank you again. This is Rafe, and those are his sisters Cat and Louisa."

To Rafe's shock, the creature bowed slightly, his gaze for some reason lingering on Cat. "I am honored," he said gravely. His voice was deep and resonant but didn't sound much different from a human's, except for the odd way it seemed to echo around the room.

Louisa's face was nearly as pale as the sheets she lay upon, but Cat took a step forward, surprise and curiosity clear in her expression. "It —it was you, wasn't it?"

"Yes," the demon lord replied. "Your street numbers and addresses mean nothing to me, but I had hoped I could provide enough information to help you find Miranda."

Astonished, Rafe looked from Cat back to the demon. Its features were so monstrous that he couldn't begin to read the creature's expression, but it almost seemed that this Lord of Chaos appeared pleased with himself for throwing a monkey wrench into Simon Escobar's plans. As to why he'd reached out to Cat, Rafe could only guess that her ability to speak to ghosts had probably made her more receptive to contact from this otherworldly creature than other witches and warlocks in the clan might be. Why she wasn't suffering from his presence now, when ordinary demons seemed to have such an effect on her, Rafe wasn't sure. Maybe a demon lord's vibrations were different from those of the rank and file.

"We were working on it," Cat said. "But it looks as though we can stop now."

"I am not so sure about that," the demon replied. His blood-colored gaze, which seemed to glow with its own inner fire, moved from Cat to Rafe. "Miranda is safe, but you still have an enemy who seeks your destruction."

"He's right," Miranda said. "I think I saw enough of the property where Simon is hiding that I could probably recognize it from a satellite map or something, though."

"In which case, I will leave you to your hunt," the Lord of Chaos said. "I have my own search to attend to. Good luck."

Then he disappeared, leaving all of them to stare at one another for a moment.

Cat was the first to speak. "What did he mean by 'his own search'?" she asked, expression puzzled.

"Simon summoned him here," Miranda told her. "I guess the demon lord needs him to send him back. However, since Simon is sulking over the way the demon who was supposed to be his servant rebelled against him, he's not going to be much use in that. So the Lord of Chaos is going to go elsewhere to look for help."

"That's kind of sad, actually," Cat said. She hesitated there for a moment, looking at the spot where the demon had materialized just a few moments earlier. "To be trapped here through no fault of his own."

Rafe thought that was just like his sister—feeling pity for some demonic creature who'd probably never pitied anything or anyone in his life. "Well, he looks like he can take care of himself," he remarked. "I think the more immediate concern is dealing with Escobar."

A rustle came from the bed as Louisa began to cautiously slide out from beneath the covers. Rafe looked at her in some alarm.

"Are you sure you should be getting up?"

"I'm fine," she replied, although he noticed the way she put one hand on the edge of the bed to steady herself before she straightened all the way. "Maybe a little shaky, but that's not enough to keep me from doing what I need to do. My laptop's in the study—let me go get it, and then Miranda can look at some satellite maps of La Cienega and see if she can narrow down where Simon's house is."

"Okay," he said reluctantly. It didn't seem right to let Louisa go wandering around the house after she'd been in a coma for more than a day, but he could tell she needed to do this, needed to feel as though she was contributing in some way.

She went out, and Miranda turned back to Rafe and wrapped her arms around his waist, hugging him close. It felt so good to have her this near, to look down at her beautiful face and realize that a miracle had somehow brought her back to him.

All right, technically, it was a demon lord who'd brought her here, but a Lord of Chaos seemed pretty miraculous all on his own.

"You're okay?" he murmured, while Cat got her phone and appeared to be typing out another text message, probably to their father to let him know about Louisa's recovery.

"I'm fine," Miranda said. She paused for a few seconds, obviously thinking something through. "Simon didn't—he didn't do anything to me, if that's what you're worried about. I think the main reason he wanted me there was to tap into my power so the summoning spell would be strong enough."

"I guess it was." Rafe thought again of the demon lord, of the strange way he'd offered his help, had reached out to Cat to pass along what he knew. "If the spell was that strong, though,

I'm surprised our demon lord is still a free agent."

"Well, I *might* have done a little something to sabotage the spell," Miranda admitted, her full mouth quirking a bit at the corners. "Then again, that was mostly because of some advice the Lord of Chaos gave me."

"You two were plotting right in front of Simon?"

"Yes, but here." She touched her index finger to her temple. "I guess that's a talent he has— communicating telepathically. Anyway, he gave me a suggestion, and it worked. I guess he was grateful enough that when Simon tried to summon him back—without my help that time— he decided to steal me away, since that was the thing that would piss Simon off the most."

Rafe couldn't really argue with this explanation, because it was probably right. And Cat said the demon lord had communicated with her the same way, mind to mind. He recalled the way the Lord of Chaos had looked at his sister and thought he didn't like it very much, although he tried to tell himself he was reading way too much into the situation. More likely, the demon had focused on Cat for a moment because this was the first time he'd talked to her in person rather than reaching out via telepathy.

The phone in Rafe's pocket rang, and he

murmured an apology to Miranda as he pulled it out. Looking down at the screen, he saw that the call was coming from Lorena Castillo.

Lorena. Jesus, he'd almost forgotten about her errand to go speak with the Montoya clan in San Antonio and find out whether they'd be able to provide any assistance. "Lorena?"

"Hi, Rafe," she said. Her voice sounded tired, but he didn't know for sure whether that was just her natural intonation, or whether she'd really worn herself out getting to San Antonio from Clovis. Since it was now only a little past three, she'd made very good time. "I just met with Lupita Montoya, the *prima*."

"And?"

A little sigh before Lorena replied, "They send their apologies, but they don't think it's a good idea to interfere right now."

"It's not interfering if we're asking for their help," he said quickly, although, judging by the defeat he heard in Lorena's voice, he had the impression he was already arguing a lost cause.

"I know. I tried to say something along those lines, but Lupita told me that the risk was too great and that it was better for her people to stay in their own territory and defend it—if the situation comes to that."

"Well, shit," he said, as Miranda looked up at

him in concern. "I was really hoping they'd help out."

"I know." A pause, and then Lorena asked, "What do you want me to do now?"

"Come home," he replied. "There isn't much else you can do."

Sure, there was the Calhoun clan, whose territory was far southeast Texas and part of western Louisiana, but their lands didn't even adjoin those of the Castillos. They would have even less reason to help than the Montoyas. For just the briefest moment, Rafe considered having Lorena try to call Miranda's parents in Arizona, but he pushed that thought aside. He'd already asked enough of his cousin's wife. The last thing he wanted was to get her phone blown up while she was five hundred miles from home in an unknown city and state.

"Okay," Lorena said. "I'm going to grab something to eat, and then I'll get back on the road."

"I'm sorry I sent you on a wild goose chase."

"It's okay. We had to try. Take care, Rafe."

She hung up then, and he shoved his phone back in his pocket as Miranda gazed up at him, big green eyes filled with concern.

"What's going on?"

"Not that much," he said. "We sent a civilian wife of one of our clan members over in Clovis to talk to the Montoyas in San Antonio, see if they would be willing to help us. But it sounds as though Lupita, their *prima,* is set on being as isolationist as possible…and I can't even say if that's a bad thing. Maybe they're right to stay out of something that isn't their fight."

"We can do this," Miranda said, giving him another of those brief hugs. "I've got Simon's number now, and he's already partly failed because he can't count on having a big, bad demon lord to do his dirty work for him. We'll be okay."

Rafe wanted to believe her. After all, she'd survived this latest round with Simon, had even managed to thwart one of his terrible plans. Problem was, that meant he would come after them with everything he had, once he'd recovered from this latest setback.

Cat had been standing off to one side, texting on her phone. Now she came closer, phone still in her hand. "Dad says there still isn't any change with Malena, but of course he was relieved to hear about Louisa." She hesitated for a few seconds, then asked, "Are the Montoyas really bailing on us?"

All Rafe could do was lift his shoulders. "I don't know if you can really call it 'bailing,' since they were never exactly with us in the first place, but yeah—it looks like we're on our own."

Her mouth twisted. "Great."

Louisa came in then, laptop tucked under her arm. "What was that about the Montoyas?"

"They're not going to help," Rafe said tersely. "Which means that we need to find Simon Escobar as quickly as we can."

"Well, let's see what Miranda can do." Louisa set the laptop on the bed, opened it up, then placed her thumb against the scanner to unlock the device. Working efficiently for someone who'd just been in a coma for more than a day, she opened the browser and then navigated to a map of the La Cienega area, switching over to satellite view once she'd gotten the object of their search more or less centered in the screen. "What can you tell me about the property?"

"It definitely backed up to the creek," Miranda replied. "And as far as I could tell, the lot the house was built on had to be around four or five acres, maybe a little more. No fences, but there were rows of trees on either side that I think marked the property boundaries. The house itself was two stories, which I guess is a little unusual for Santa Fe, right?" As Louisa nodded, Miranda went on, "It was pueblo style, though, with at least one chimney. I didn't get to see the whole house, though—just the kitchen and family room, and the room upstairs where I slept."

Even though Miranda had assured him nothing had happened between her and Simon,

Rafe still couldn't keep himself from feeling relieved at those words. It sounded as though Simon had put her in a secondary bedroom. Why, he wasn't exactly sure. Maybe the dark warlock had been more focused on using Miranda's powers for his demon summoning, and had figured he could get around to the fun stuff after he had the Lord of Chaos in his back pocket. It was definitely good to know that none of those plans had panned out.

Louisa was using the touchpad on her laptop to maneuver around, looking for a property that matched Miranda's description. She paused for a moment. "What about this one?"

Rafe peered over both their shoulders to look at the place in question, an expansive piece of land with a sprawling house on it and several outbuildings. Although trees crowded around on all sides, it did look as though it backed up to Cienega Creek.

Expression thoughtful, Miranda stared down at the screen for a moment. "No, I don't think so. I know you can't see property lines on something like this, but I got the feeling that the piece of land Simon's house was built on was longer and narrower than this one, which looks almost square, judging by where the trees are and where the road curves past the house. Also, I don't remember seeing any sheds, or whatever those little buildings are, and I did get a chance to walk around the yard a bit."

Disappointed flitted over Louisa's face, but she only nodded and went back to moving around the map, following the line of the creek, since it was the most easily distinguishable landmark in the area. On the other side of Miranda, Cat, too, was looking down at the screen, although probably just because she wanted to be involved in some way and not because she had anything terribly meaningful to contribute to the conversation.

"Oh, wait!" Miranda said suddenly. "Scan back to the right a little bit."

Louisa obliged, and Miranda stood there for a long moment, arms crossed as she studied the satellite image that now filled the screen.

"I'm pretty sure that's it," she said. "It's the right orientation, and the house looks like it's the right size, too."

"Fourteen Los Gatos Lane," Louisa read off the screen. "That's easy to remember." But instead of looking pleased, she straightened up and took a step back from where the laptop sat on the bed. Her gaze moved to Miranda and became even more brooding, as if she wrestled with an idea she didn't want to acknowledge, even though she knew she had to.

"What's the matter?" Rafe asked. He didn't like seeing that expression on his sister's face, mostly because he knew it meant she was about to bring up a topic none of them wanted to hear.

At first she didn't answer, only stood there, this time not seeming to look at anything or anyone in particular. When she spoke, her voice wavered a bit. "You're going to have us go up against Simon Escobar."

"Yes," he replied, wondering why she would be questioning something so obvious. If a rabid dog moved onto your property, you didn't debate what to do with it. You got a gun and you put it out of its misery. Or, he supposed, you called animal control, but there was no "animal control" the Castillos could bring in to handle their particular problem. They had to take care of this one themselves. "We don't have much of a choice, do we?"

"I guess not," she replied.

"We're going to need as many people in your clan with defensive capabilities as we can gather quickly," Miranda put in. Unlike Louisa, she didn't appear listless or conflicted, but rather charged up and ready to go after Simon Escobar so they could put an end to all this and get on with their lives. "He has to know that the Lord of Chaos brought me to you...or at least, he can probably guess, since he must realize that pissing off a demon lord is a good way to get him to do the exact opposite of what you were hoping for by summoning him in the first place. And that means we need to strike fast, before he has a chance to try something else to increase his strength and improve his chances."

"You see?" Louisa said, this time speaking directly to Rafe. The two of them might have been the only people in the room. "Miranda knows what we need to do, and she has the strength to back up her plans. I don't think I'm capable of that. I'm not some warrior witch."

"No one expects you to be—" Rafe began, but Louisa held up a hand, stopping him.

"That's exactly what a *prima* needs to be if she's going to lead her clan effectively. And that's why"—she stopped, as though attempting to gather herself, then drew in a deep breath, obviously steeling herself for what she needed to say next—"that's why Miranda should take over from me as *prima*."

16

CHANGING OF THE GUARD

Miranda

About all I could do was stare at Louisa, aghast. What in the world was she trying to say? I couldn't be the Castillo *prima*—I hadn't been born to it. Hell, less than two weeks ago, I hadn't known I even possessed any real magic.

Judging by their stunned silence, it seemed clear enough that Rafe and Cat were thinking just about the same thing.

"I know it sounds crazy —" Louisa began, and Rafe cut in,

"Yes, because it *is* crazy. Miranda's a powerful witch, but she's not our *prima*. She—"

"She's the most powerful witch I've ever seen," his sister cut in. "Definitely more powerful than anyone else in our clan. And Simon Escobar is probably the worst threat we've ever had to deal with. You really want me leading you in a fight against someone like that? I couldn't even face a few of his demons without falling over in a coma."

"Louisa," I said carefully, "I know you're trying to do what's best for your clan, but this can't work. I mean, everything else aside, I'm not even a Castillo."

"You will be," she said, her gaze moving from me to Rafe, "if you two get married today."

"*Today?*" Rafe and I demanded in a single shocked voice.

Our combined response only made Louisa give a rueful chuckle. "You see? You two were meant to be together. Your getting married was only a matter of when, not if."

I glanced up at Rafe. His jaw was set, his warm brown eyes hot with emotion. Yes, Louisa was right about us knowing that we were going to get married soon, but like this?

"You can't get married like you're ordering a pizza or something," he said.

"Yes, you can," she responded, unruffled. Now that she'd stated her worst and gotten it over with, she sounded more relaxed, more like the Louisa I had first met. "The courthouse doesn't close until four-thirty. You can go over there right now and get it taken care of. They'll waive the blood test if you submit it within thirty days of getting your license."

"You seem to know a lot about it," Rafe commented. Now his arms were crossed, tension radiating from every inch of his body.

Louisa smiled. "You think I didn't help Mom arrange a few quickie courthouse marriages for those Castillos who couldn't keep their hands off each other and weren't responsible about birth control?"

"I never heard about anything like that," Cat put in, sounding offended that she'd been left out of the loop.

"Exactly," Louisa told her. "That was sort of the whole point. Anyway, if you two get married, then Miranda is officially a Castillo, and I can make her *prima*."

"You can't just 'make' someone *prima*," I argued. "The gift is only passed down—" And then I stopped myself, because everyone standing in that room knew how you became *prima*—the former *prima* had to die. That was how it had always been, since we witch clans first began keeping any kind of records.

"I know that," Louisa said. Her tone was firm, her expression calm but resolute. In that moment, she looked very much like her mother. "And no, I don't plan to commit suicide in order for Miranda to take over, so you can all wipe that look off your faces. There is another way, something I read about in one of our former *prima*'s journals. She lived in the early 1800s, and apparently she had some kind of terrible cancer that their healer couldn't cure. This *prima* worried about what would happen to her clan as she became more and more ill and began to waste away—back then, the world was a less civilized place, and the threat from other clans was much greater than it is now. She came up with a way to pass her gifts on to her daughter, who was young, only nineteen and so two years away from finding her consort. And that was what she did—her daughter became *prima* and took over the clan, even though the mother lingered for another few months after that." Louisa stopped there and looked around at all of us, dark eyes glittering. "I know what I need to do. And you know what you have to do."

For a long, terrible space of time, none of us said anything. Worry—yes, and a good measure of guilt—were both churning away inside me. And beneath all that was a sort of horrible understand-ing, one that had just begun to awaken in me.

This was what Isabel Castillo had seen all those years ago. She'd seen that her clan would be in danger, and that their *prima* would be of no use to help protect them. And she saw the child my mother was carrying, and realized it was that very girl who would come to this clan and help save them.

My fingers were cold, but I still slipped my hand into Rafe's. He took hold, his grip strong, reassuring. "We have to do this," I said. "I understand now. It's—it's what your grandmother wanted."

He stared at me for a few seconds, and then comprehension flared in his eyes. "I understand, too." His mouth lifted in a crooked smile. "It's what we were planning anyway. I just thought we'd have something besides a courthouse quickie."

No doubt that was what everyone had expected, but we didn't have time for elaborate ceremonies now. "It's all right," I assured him. "The important thing is for us to be together."

"Then go," Louisa said. "You have less than an hour before the courthouse closes."

"I'll come with you," Cat offered. "You'll need a witness."

Right. I vaguely remembered hearing something about that part of the ceremony, although knowledge of courthouse weddings was not exactly my forte. I'd always known I would marry Rafe Castillo, but I'd imagined a big church wedding, full of the sort of pomp the marriage of the Castillo *prima*'s only son required. Well, I'd almost had one like that, except one of Simon's horrible spells had interfered.

So Rafe and Cat and I hurried out to the driveway, where we got in Rafe's Jeep and set out for the courthouse. As we were turning onto the main road, Oscar's Subaru passed us. I could just barely see him staring at our vehicle in confusion —no doubt he was wondering why the hell we were all leaving now that Louisa was awake—but we didn't try to roll down the window and offer any explanations. Louisa would be able to fill him in on everything that had happened once he got home.

Within fifteen minutes, we were downtown. Fate smiled on us, because someone was pulling away from one of the meters on the street right in front of the courthouse just as we approached. Rafe slid into the open parking space, and then we all got out and hurried into the building.

"Upstairs," Cat said after quickly reading the directory.

The three of us headed up to the second floor, where we obtained the necessary paperwork, got our names added to the list, and hurriedly began filling out the forms, which to my surprise were paper and not an electronic file that could be sent to our phones. At least Rafe and I had gotten there before the cutoff, and so didn't have to worry about not making it in time.

My writing was cramped and messy; I couldn't remember the last time I'd had to fill out anything by hand, rather than having a form autofilled on my computer or phone. But as long as the clerk entering the information could read it, I supposed it didn't matter all that much whether the paperwork was neat and clean.

Most of the other couples waiting their turn had tried to dress up for the occasion. I saw men in suits or at least in ties and dress shirts, women in cocktail dresses or actual wedding gowns. Looking down ruefully at my sweater and jeans, I said to Rafe in a murmur, "Sorry about my clothes. When I got up this morning, I didn't think I would be getting married this afternoon."

He offered me a flash of a grin, the kind that always managed to make my knees weak. "It's all right," he replied. "I'm not exactly dressed up, either."

No, he wasn't, since he had on a long-sleeved T-shirt, faded jeans, and scuffed hiking boots. But he looked so handsome, I really didn't care one way or another. The important thing was that very soon he would be my husband, although under circumstances I could never have imagined.

We'd just finished filling out the paperwork when our names were called. Almost at once, my heartbeat began to speed up, and I could feel a sort of eager, nervous tension fill my body. No, I wasn't worried about being married to Rafe—not so very long ago, that prospect had filled me with trepidation, but now I knew he loved me and I loved him. I knew what it was like to have our bodies joined in ecstatic union. We were meant to be together.

What worried me was the prospect of becoming the Castillo *prima*. Louisa had sounded sure of herself, but was this even going to work? And if it didn't, what then?

Although maybe I should have been more worried about what would happen if her crazy plan did work. I wasn't sure what frightened me more—having to confront Simon and somehow prevail, or facing the Castillo clan and trying to explain that I, someone not even of their blood, was now their new *prima*.

One step at a time, I told myself as Rafe and I went to stand in front of the judge, Cat a little off to one side. *Louisa hasn't transferred her powers to you yet.*

In a way, it was almost reassuring to hear the familiar words of the wedding ceremony spoken by the judge. He was a balding Hispanic man, probably in his early sixties, with friendly brown eyes and a way of speaking that made it seem as though this was all new and exciting, even though he must have performed hundreds of these ceremonies over the years.

When we got to the part about the ring, however, Rafe looked blank for a moment, right before his features became a study in consternation. "We didn't think about that," he murmured to me.

My hands were bare. I wasn't even wearing a ring on my right hand that could have stood in for a wedding band.

Cat stepped forward, pulling a garnet ring off her finger. "Here," she said. "You can borrow this."

"I'll get you a real one," Rafe promised me, "as soon as all this is over."

I nodded. "It's fine."

He took the ring from Cat and slipped it on the ring finger of my left hand. Luckily, it fit pretty well. "With this ring, I thee wed," he said quietly.

A little shiver went through me. We hadn't made it this far in the abortive ceremony in Loretto Chapel, because Simon's terrible spell had kicked in and forced Rafe to say all those awful things to me. This time, though…this time I knew it would be real.

I didn't have a ring for Rafe, either. We sort of fumbled our way around that part of the ceremony, and then at last got to the part I'd been waiting for.

"I now pronounce you husband and wife," the judge said. "You may kiss the bride."

Rafe bent and touched his lips to mine, and a welcome warmth moved all through me. How I wished we could go straight back to his house and make love again, reaffirm our connection to one another! Unfortunately, we didn't have that luxury at the moment. Once this was all over....

If we succeeded. That was what frightened me the most. Louisa was willing to relinquish her *prima* power to me, but what if it turned out that wasn't enough?

I couldn't allow myself to dwell on such defeatist thoughts, however. The only way to make this work would be to trust in myself, in the powers that had been awakened within me, and trust that combining Louisa's *prima* gift with those powers would be enough to beat Simon.

Even as we thanked the judge and left the courtroom so the next lucky couple could slip in before the four-thirty cutoff, I couldn't prevent my brain from churning away at the confrontation that loomed. Would I have to kill Simon? *Could* I, despite everything he'd done?

The whole way back to Louisa's house, Rafe drove one-handed so he could hold my left hand in his right. I could tell he was nervous, too, wanted to stay as connected with me now as he could. Despite his obvious tension, it was reassuring to feel his fingers entwined with mine, to look over at his fine profile and know that he truly was my husband now. Simon hadn't been able to prevent our joining, despite all his machinations.

I could only hope his defeat would be just as inevitable.

When we got to the house, we could hear raised voices inside. Oscar and Louisa, quarreling. I didn't have to guess what they were arguing about, although they stopped as soon as Rafe rang the doorbell. Oscar answered the door, his expression tight with anger.

"You're married?" he asked, although I noticed he only looked at Rafe, seemed to be doing his best to ignore my presence.

"Yes," Rafe said. "Look, Oscar, I know this is rough for everyone, but it's Louisa's decision."

"You're right—it is," she put in as she appeared at Oscar's shoulder. "Let them in, for God's sake," she added, an edge to her voice seeming to indicate that she was just as irritated with her husband as he was with her. "We don't have a lot of time to waste."

Reluctance clear in every line of his body, he stepped aside just enough that Rafe and Cat and I could squeeze past him into the foyer. We followed Louisa, who led us into the living room.

"Miranda, go ahead and sit down," she said, gesturing toward the couch. "I'll sit next to you."

This felt more uncomfortable by the minute, but there wasn't much I could do at this point. I'd already agreed to this crazy plan of action, and so I had to go ahead and follow Louisa's instructions.

I sat on the sofa and she took a seat next to me, shifted sideways so she faced in my direction. Realizing she wanted me to do the same thing, I changed my position slightly so I could look directly at her. It was strange to sit this close, staring into her face. I was able to see some of the resemblance to Rafe now that we were only a few inches apart: the fine arch of her brows, the warm brown of her eyes, although her nose was sharper, more like their mother's.

"Give me your hands," she commanded me, and I couldn't do anything except reach out with both hands. She took hold of them, fingers laced tightly with mine. Her skin was cool, her grip stronger than I had thought it would be, considering she'd been in a coma only an hour earlier. "Ready?"

There was a question. Of course I wasn't. How could I be? I'd never heard of such a thing ever happening before, despite her story about that former Castillo *prima* and her daughter. You shouldn't be able to hand over your magical gifts like some kind of white elephant present at a holiday gift exchange, especially to someone whose own powers were so newly awakened.

But because I'd agreed to this, all I said was, "I'm ready."

She closed her eyes. I didn't know whether I should do the same thing, because she hadn't told me to. However, I figured it might be better to shut my eyes as well, partly because it might help me to focus…and partly because I was scared shitless of what was going to happen next.

A second or two passed, and nothing happened. I began to wonder whether this was going to work at all.

But then I felt it—the warm glow of my magic within me, only growing brighter and brighter by the second, a glowing ball of white-hot power unlike anything I'd ever experienced before. It shimmered within, pulsing, a supernova of magical energy that felt as though it wanted to burst out of my fragile human frame.

It didn't, though. After a moment, it seemed to calm down, to withdraw into itself, although I could still feel it there, waiting for the time when I might call on it.

Louisa's fingers still gripped mine. Once a few more seconds had passed, she finally let go of me. "It is done," she said, her voice only a spent whisper.

Oscar made an incoherent sound of despair, even as Rafe came toward the couch and placed a hand on my shoulder. "Miranda, are you okay?"

I tried to laugh, although the sound came out more as a hiccupy little cough. "I don't know if 'okay' is exactly the right word. I'm…I'm all right, I guess. And the power…it's mine, Rafe. Louisa gave it to me. What the hell am I supposed to do now?"

In response, he took me by the hand and raised me from the sofa, then folded me into his arms. "Give yourself a little time to adjust," he said quietly as he held me. Yes, I was thrumming with so much power, I felt like a human nuclear reactor, but it still felt so good to have Rafe next to me, to know that my gifts didn't frighten him. "No one expects you to run off and face Simon Escobar right this second." He looked over at his sister, who had just stood up as well, looking pale and shaky. "Louisa, are you all right?"

She nodded. "I'm fine. My—my own powers are still there. Giving away the *prima* energy doesn't seem to have changed anything. And really, I was only *prima* for a few days. It wasn't enough for me to really get used to having those powers."

Was she telling the truth, or merely putting a brave face on things? I suddenly got the sense that, if I wanted to, I could look inside her mind and see for myself whether she was lying to herself…and to the rest of us.

No. If I did something like that, I would be

no better than Simon. Louisa should be allowed her privacy. If she was trying to fool herself, well, she should be permitted to do so without any interference. I had taken on these extra powers to help protect the clan, and that was the only reason I would use them. The implications of anything else were far too frightening.

"You're sure?" I asked, and she nodded again.

"I'm sure. They're in better hands with you."

I was relieved to see Oscar come up and wrap his arm around his wife, offer her his own comfort. Whatever harsh words they might have exchanged over her decision, it seemed that now he was willing to put their differences aside and accept what she had done. In the long run, he would probably be relieved. As the daughter of a *prima,* I could safely say that it wasn't always that fun to be the head of a clan. Everyone looked to you for guidance, came to you when disputes arose that couldn't be solved by the elders. And I realized that the Castillos apparently didn't even have elders, so all that responsibility would end up on my shoulders.

It was overwhelming. I wished I could push it all away, say that I was only going to use the magic Louisa had given me to fight Simon, and that I had no interest in being the head of their clan. Unfortunately, it didn't work that way. I had the *prima* powers...and that meant being the *prima* in word and deed, not just in name.

But I could push that aside for later. Right now, I had something far more deadly and dangerous to focus on.

Simon Escobar.

"Okay, I'm locked and loaded," I said, gently pulling away from Rafe. He let me go, although he still held on to one hand—the one with the ring I'd borrowed from Cat. "What next?"

"Well, we know where Escobar is," Rafe replied. "I guess what we have to figure out is the best way to approach him."

"I could teleport in—" I began, but he immediately shook his head.

"That won't work, because none of the rest of us have that ability, and you can only carry one person at a time, right?"

"I think so," I replied. When I'd grabbed Rafe and gotten the hell out of Simon's compound in Tesuque, I hadn't been thinking about much more than fleeing as fast as I could. However, it was probably safe to assume that I could only carry one person with me when I teleported.

"And there's no way you're going in alone," he said. "Simon might not have the Lord of Chaos to do his dirty work, but I'm sure he can still call in his flying monkeys."

"'Flying monkeys'?" I repeated, not sure what he was talking about.

"His demons," Cat said.

"Right." I'd almost forgotten about them, since they paled in comparison to the demon lord Simon had called to this plane. However, since his lordship was occupied elsewhere and no longer under Simon's control, he wouldn't be a factor. Those demons, however…. "Who in your clan has the kind of magic that might work against them? We need offense, not defense."

Louisa and Oscar looked at each other. He cleared his throat and said, "I can call the fire, direct it where it needs to go."

"Good," I said, although I hated to have Louisa's husband dragged into this. Still, I couldn't scruple at bringing him along. We needed all hands on deck for this confrontation. "Who else?"

"Our cousin Arturo can call lightning…but he's all the way down near Las Cruces."

"How far is that?" I asked. I was still hazy on a lot of New Mexico's geography.

"About a four-hour drive from here," Rafe said. "We can't afford to wait that long."

"I could teleport and get him—"

"You need to save your strength to face Escobar. If you teleport all over the place gathering your troops, how much energy are you going to have left?"

Good question. I honestly didn't know, because at the moment I felt absolutely bursting with energy, thanks to the *prima* powers Louisa had given me. However, I couldn't consider them inexhaustible. As Rafe had said, I needed to conserve my energy, know that I had enough in reserve to make sure Simon didn't prevail.

"I'm not sure," I said. "But you're probably right. I need to be careful. So I guess the question is—who's local who has a helpful power?"

"Our cousin Tony," Cat suggested. "He's not a weather-worker, per se, but he can control the wind."

Wind control against airborne creatures could be very helpful. Then again, Tony didn't strike me as the kind of guy who would necessarily be all that good in a fight. His careless attitude could get him in trouble.

But maybe I wasn't being entirely fair. After all, the only time I'd had any real interaction with Tony had been at his Halloween party, when he'd been—well, "drunk" was too strong a word, but definitely elevated. I couldn't judge how he'd act when sober and in a fight, based solely on that one encounter.

"That's good," I said. "I guess we'd better contact him."

Cat nodded and dug out her phone, and

began texting away. Rafe said, "You know my talent is helpful."

Yes, it was. I wished I could keep him out of this—I worried that Simon would try to target him specifically—but there was no way to prevent him from coming along. In a confrontation between a wolf and a demon, I wasn't sure who would prevail. About all I could do was hope for the best.

"I know," I said. "Of course you'll be there with me. Anyone else?"

Cat stopped typing. "I'm coming."

"No," Rafe said, his voice flat.

"You can't tell me what to do," she retorted.

"Maybe not, but Miranda is the new *prima,* and *she* can."

Great. The last thing I wanted was to get in the middle of an argument between brother and sister. As I looked at them, at the rebellious spark in Cat's eyes and the angry set to Rafe's jaw, I realized that Cat should come along. Her talent for speaking with otherworldly creatures could come in handy—now that she knew to be on her guard, she might be able to reach out and help to at least partially block Simon's control of his demons.

"Cat comes along," I said. At once Cat grinned, and Rafe treated me to a fearsome scowl.

"Seriously?"

"Seriously," I told him. I really didn't want to

get into an argument with my new husband, and so I laid a hand on his arm and looked up at him with imploring eyes. "She might be able to talk to the demons...control them. Or at least distract them enough that they're not as much of a threat."

For a long moment, Rafe didn't reply. He just stood there, staring down at me, until at last I saw his expression soften a bit. "Okay," he said. "I don't like it, but...okay."

"Anyone else?" I asked.

A silence, and Louisa gave a helpless shrug. "It's much the same in our clan as it is in most others. Possibly we possessed more warlike talents long ago, but over the years, those gifts have sort of disappeared, their places taken by magical skills that are more useful now."

"It's all right," I said. "That's still five of us against one of him."

Cat still looked thrilled that she was being included. "And you're more like four or five people on your own anyway."

I had to hope she was right. The *prima* energy burned within me, and I prayed it wasn't giving me false confidence when it came to assessing my ability to take on Simon Escobar. I still didn't know exactly what everyone expected me to do. Despite his horrible crimes, deep down I wanted this to end with him fleeing. As long as he knew he couldn't prevail here, he'd never come back. That should be good enough...shouldn't it?

But then I thought of what his father had done to the Santiagos, what Simon had wanted to do to the Castillos. He'd never believe it was enough to live quietly, concealing his warlock powers. Forever an outcast, he wanted to take a clan for his own, and he didn't care who stood in his path.

And I knew then that this could only end one way.

17

SHOWDOWN

TONY APPEARED AT THE HOUSE ABOUT FIFTEEN minutes after Cat had texted him. His expression was much more subdued than it had been when we'd met at the Halloween party at his house, and he looked different, too. Then again, I supposed the change in his appearance shouldn't have been too much of a surprise—he was wearing an untucked flannel shirt and jeans, and his hair wasn't slicked back. Gone was the fake pencil mustache he'd sported as part of his Gomez Addams costume. As I thanked him for coming over, I realized he had been present at the wedding, too, as one of Rafe's groomsmen, but honestly, that afternoon had been such a hideous blur that I'd erased huge chunks of it from my memory.

"Just the five of us, huh?" he asked as he looked at the assembled group.

"Five of you with unique talents," Louisa said. "It should be enough."

I didn't know exactly what Cat had texted to him, but it seemed that she'd explained the situation, since Tony didn't bother to ask why Louisa would be hanging back here at the house rather than coming with us. Her talent for tracking down where and what kind of magic had been used in a particular place was handy, but in this case, it wouldn't help much. We already knew where Simon was hiding…and we also knew exactly what kind of magic he planned to use.

Or at least I could guess. He'd call his demons, of course, and would probably use fire and wind and anything else to strike out at us. The real question was whether I would be strong enough to protect everyone, while at the same time giving them the freedom to utilize their own particular skills to help neutralize our mutual enemy.

"We'll go in one car," I said. "We can all squeeze in your Wrangler, right?" And I looked up at Rafe.

He gave a small lift of his shoulders. "It'll be tight, but sure. Why my car, though?"

"Because it's not automated like a newer one would be," I replied. "I'm not saying that Simon might not try to interfere with it in some way, but it might be harder for him to take control of a vehicle that doesn't have a self-driving mechanism."

"Makes sense." He glanced around the room at everyone. "I don't see much point in waiting. Are we all ready to go?"

I knew I wasn't. Every muscle in my body was tense, bracing for our final confrontation. Unfortunately, there was no way past this battle. We had to go through it, had to face Simon Escobar once and for all.

Tony was the first to respond. "Ready as I'll ever be, I guess. But if we all survive this, you owe me a beer."

"Just one?" Rafe quipped.

"Okay, a six-pack."

"I'd like in on that, too," Oscar said.

Rafe grinned. "Done."

Louisa didn't look entirely thrilled by this exchange, but she didn't say anything. Maybe she knew—as I did—that they were all just doing their version of whistling in the dark.

"Cider for me," Cat put in. "But let's go do this thing. The sooner we kick Simon's ass, the sooner we can all head out for happy hour."

Her remark elicited a round of chuckles, which I assumed was her reason for making it in the first place. But it served another purpose—it got us all moving toward the door, Oscar pausing so he could give Louisa a kiss before he went out. Her expression was almost preternaturally calm, and I guessed that she was exerting every ounce of will she possessed to conceal her fear for him… and her frustration that she couldn't come along.

Right then, I would have given a lot to be in her position.

However, fate had decreed that I needed to be the leader of this little expedition. Oscar and Tony and Cat all piled into the back seat, with Cat squeezed in the middle because she was the shortest. I took shotgun, and Rafe got behind the wheel. A pause while he put the address of our destination in the nav system, and then we were backing out of the driveway and headed toward the main road.

No one said anything as he pulled onto the 599 and pointed the Jeep south toward La Cienega. Even the ebullient Tony seemed subdued; I caught a glimpse of him staring out the window, his mouth pressed into a flat line. That seemed wrong, since he had one of those quirky, mobile mouths that always appeared to be on the verge of laughter.

There was no laughter about him now, that was for sure.

Far sooner than I would have liked, we turned off toward La Cienega, right before the 599 would have connected with the interstate. Almost at once, our surroundings grew rural, with rolling hills on either side, and homesteads tucked far back from the road. As we drove, the landscape grew golden, trees in their autumn finery clustering on either side of the road so thickly that it felt as though we were traveling through a tunnel decorated in copper and gilt.

Following the nav's commands, Rafe turned down an even narrower road, one that was still paved but so full of potholes, it might as well not be. He slowed so the Wrangler moved along at barely ten miles an hour. "The turnoff for Los Gatos Lane is coming up in a few hundred feet," he said. "What's the plan?"

The truth was, I really didn't have a plan. If Simon had any kind of wards set up to guard his property, he would know we were there almost immediately. Coming in slowly wouldn't help at all.

"I'll cast a spell of protection around your car," I replied. "After that, you might as well go in as fast as you can. Everyone else, just be ready."

"Ready for what, exactly?" Oscar asked.

"Whatever Simon might throw at us," I said. "I don't know what that could be, since he has so many different magical skills. Demons for sure, but after that…?" I let the words trail off and gave a helpless shrug. "Just don't let yourself get rattled, and be ready to use your own magic against him. Okay?"

Everyone in the back seat mumbled an "okay," although none of them looked exactly thrilled. I couldn't really blame them, because I was less than thrilled to be here myself. But, as Rafe had pointed out earlier, we couldn't allow a rabid dog to linger in our territory. He had to be put out of his misery, for all our sakes.

I imagined the bubble of protection encasing Rafe's dusty Jeep Wrangler, making it so no magical attacks could get through, no assault by demons would have any effect. This was simple enough, since we were all together in a confined space. I didn't know what would happen once we had to get out and move individually. Should I cast protection spells on everyone? Could I? Theoretically, I supposed I should be able to manage such a thing, since I'd protected so many individual Castillo families here in Santa Fe, but I'd never had to test my talents under such stress.

You'll do it because you have to, I told myself as Rafe turned down Los Gatos Lane and we began to bump our way along the badly rutted road. *Everyone here is precious. You can't allow any of them to get hurt.*

Easier said than done, though.

Trees lined the little lane, crowding on both sides. The effect was extremely claustrophobic.

Then again, they helped to create something of a barrier. Any demons diving at us would have a hard time getting a clear shot.

I hoped.

We emerged into a wide gravel area. To one side was the detached garage; to the other was the house. Everything appeared dead still, with no signs of life at all.

Rafe stopped near the garage and turned off the engine before he glanced over at me. "Is he even here?"

I gave a helpless shrug. "It doesn't look like it, but—"

My sentence was cut off there, because in the next second, the earth seemed to heave under us, shaking the Jeep like a toy instead of the sturdy off-road vehicle it actually was. I'd never been in an earthquake, but this felt like some kind of 8.5 monster, the kind of temblor that shook buildings off their foundations, collapsed bridges, and exploded gas mains. Cat let out a little shriek as the vehicle started to tip to one side.

"Hold on!" Rafe shouted.

I clung to the "Jesus handle" on the roof, my stomach turning over as the Wrangler capsized, falling onto the driver's side. The seat belts held us all more or less in place, but it was going to be hell trying to get out of there.

"Everyone okay?" I asked once the shaking had subsided.

"Think so," Tony replied from the back seat. He sounded mildly freaked out, and I couldn't really blame him. Yes, I'd expected Simon to attack almost as soon as we appeared, but still—

And I realized then how vulnerable we would all be as we tried to climb out of the upended Jeep. I could teleport myself out, but....

You can get all of them out, I realized suddenly. *Just imagine everyone standing out there in that open area, ready to fight.*

Almost as soon as that image passed through my mind, there was a *blink!*, and all five of us were free of the vehicle, taking up defensive postures next to one another. I thought I heard Cat gasp, but I didn't have time to pay much attention, because Simon had emerged from the front door of the house and began walking calmly toward us. He looked very ordinary—it wasn't as though he'd put on his black robes for this confrontation, was only wearing his usual jeans and a long-sleeved dark gray T-shirt.

When he was about six feet or so away, he stopped and regarded our little group, one eyebrow raised at an ironic angle. "This is the best the Castillo clan could gather to fight me?"

"It's all we needed," I retorted. "No need to

drag everyone into this, not when we can easily beat you."

For a moment, he didn't respond. He only stood there, staring at me, and his eyes narrowed slightly. I lifted my chin and met that black gaze, doing my best to forget how I had once laughed into those eyes, had thought I might possibly have a future with this man. He was very good at deception, this Simon Escobar.

I had to remember that.

When he spoke, his tone was almost musing. "There's something different about you, Miranda. You look almost lit up from within."

"That's just happiness at being reunited with Rafe."

That barb got its hooks in him. His nostrils flared, and he glanced away for a second to look over at Rafe, who stood a few paces from me, his stance making it clear that he was ready to attack at only a second's notice.

Then Simon shook his head. "I don't think so."

I felt him reach for me, his magic moving in my direction and then recoiling almost immediately, like someone touching a surface they realized was far too hot. Again his eyes narrowed.

"How did you do it?"

"Do what?" I asked sweetly.

"Take the *prima* powers into yourself. I can

feel them. Your magic was strong before, but now—"

"But now it's enough to defeat you."

For just a second, I sensed his confusion, a flicker of sudden fear. He hadn't been counting on this particular wrinkle, I could tell that much. The realization relieved me a little, because it told me that even Simon Escobar couldn't guess at our every move.

Almost immediately, though, he took a step backward, and the blue skies overhead darkened. I glanced up and saw a horde of demons appear from nowhere, their terrible shapes blocking out the sunlight. How many? Fifty, a hundred?

It didn't matter.

The bubble of protection shimmered into exis-tence, shielding all of us. A few seconds later, the first of the demons plowed into it and rebounded, shrieking in pain. So it hurt them to come in contact with the shield.

Good.

Simon's lips curled in a snarl. His hands moved in that same pushing gesture I'd seen him use before, back at the house in Tesuque. Something hugely heavy plowed into the bubble, and I could almost feel the way it began to cave in, collapsing before the insane force Simon had directed at it.

Shit. I focused, visualizing the invisible shield

repairing itself, regaining its structural integrity. As I did so, I pushed back against Simon, directing more energy toward him in the hope that it might knock him off his feet, or at least off balance.

He did stumble backward a pace or two before regaining his footing. "Nice trick," he said. Perspiration gleamed on his forehead, even though the day itself was cool enough. "It won't be enough, though."

"Oh—really?" I panted. Even with the *prima* energy buoying me up, this was harder than I'd thought it would be. I honestly didn't know how long I'd be able to maintain the protection spell while also mounting any kind of an assault against Simon.

"Really," he responded. At the same time, he raised one foot and stomped it into the ground.

A shockwave exploded outward from him, one as fierce and violent as the blast from an explosion. It shredded my bubble of protection and kept going, knocking all of the Castillos off their feet. I heard Cat cry out but couldn't allow myself to look back and see what was happening to her, because as soon as the shield was gone, the demons dove toward us once again.

Out of the corner of my eye, I saw Tony push himself to his feet. His dark hair was disheveled, and dirt had smudged his face, but he stood straight and tall, hands raised.

The winds came shrieking from nowhere, a gale-force blast that brought tears to my eyes and whipped my loose hair around my face. Dead leaves scattered everywhere, rose up in their own mini-tornadoes. I lifted a hand to protect my face from the debris, and saw that the wind had caught many of the demons, hurling them this way and that as their leathery wings beat at the violent air.

At the same time, a wall of flame came from nowhere, rising up from the gravel ground and burning between Simon and me. I risked a quick glance to my right and caught a glimpse of Oscar standing a few feet away, his hands outstretched. Sweat dripped down his face, which was taut with effort, high cheekbones standing out as he clenched his jaw.

How long would he be able to hold that wall of flame?

A few seconds later, that question was rendered moot, because out of nowhere rain began to fall on all of us, soaking our clothes and hair, smothering the fire and calming the winds Tony had summoned. Oscar swore, even as Simon stepped toward us, dark eyes gleaming in triumph.

"Nice display," he said. "But it's pretty obvious that you just can't beat me, no matter what you try." He paused, his lip curled in contempt. "Miranda, you know what you have to do."

"No," I replied. "I'm not going down that road again."

"I think you need to." He came closer, gaze lingering on my thin, rain-soaked sweater, which now left basically nothing to the imagination. "In order to save them, that is."

Revulsion rose in me. I opened my mouth to speak, but Rafe was there next to me, furious gaze fixed on Simon's face.

"What did you just say to my wife?"

At once, Simon's fists curled in anger. "Your what?"

"His wife," I said. "We got married this afternoon."

A pause, and then Simon replied, "It doesn't matter. Marriages end every day. Especially," he added, "those caused by a spouse's death."

His hand went out, and before I could call another shield to protect my husband, he'd gone flying backward, traveling at least twenty feet before he hit the ground with a terrible thud.

"No!" The same syllable left both my and Cat's lips at the same time, and she hurried over to him, bending down in the gravel to see how badly wounded he was.

"Stop it!" I cried. "I'll never go with you, Simon, because I don't love you. Nothing you do here will change that. Even"—I pulled in a gasp of a breath and forced myself to say the words —"even if you kill Rafe, that won't make me yours. I'm sorry for you—"

"'Sorry'?" he cut in, voice trembling with rage. "You're *sorry* for me? I have everything I ever wanted!"

"Except people who care about you," I said sadly. "That's not all your fault, but at some point you have to stop blaming everyone else for your troubles. For all our powers, none of us can change the past. Not even you." I risked a quick glance back at Cat and Rafe, saw her slowly helping him to his feet. Thank the Goddess. Whatever Simon had done, it didn't look as though it had been enough to cause any permanent harm. Lowering my voice, I went on, "Have you ever stopped to think what might have happened if you'd been brave enough to come to me before I ever left Arizona, had offered to help me with my talents then, told me the truth about yourself?"

His black eyes glittered. "You would have still hated me."

"No," I replied. "I wouldn't. Because you wouldn't have lied. You wouldn't have concocted a plan specifically designed to hurt the Castillos. You would have only come to me offering an enormous gift, the gift of awakening my talents.

But you didn't. It was more important for you to hurt others than to help me."

For one long, terrible second, Simon didn't respond. His gaze was fixed on my face, and I did everything I could to remain where I was, to look back at him with all the truth of what I had just said, to let him know that—just possibly—things might have been different, if only he had come from a place of healing rather than of hatred.

But then an angry flush suffused his cheeks, and he shook his head. "Pretty words, Miranda. Too bad I don't believe any of them. I gave you a chance. You could've kept all these Castillos from harm. But you thought it was a better idea to tell me everything I've done wrong. Now it's your turn to realize what a terrible mistake you've made."

Darkness began to swirl around him, a whirling maelstrom of hatred, fury, the throbbing resentment of an entire life misspent. The cold from it reached toward me, and I barely had a chance to stumble away before those icy tendrils began to drift in my direction, implacable as the tide coming in.

"Get back!" I shouted at Oscar and Tony, who stood a few feet away, eyes wide in horror. "Get back behind the Jeep!"

In all honesty, I had no idea whether that would help at all. But even turned on its side, the

Wrangler offered the best protection I could think of.

They nodded and then ran, and I hurried over to Cat and Rafe, looping an arm around his waist so the three of us could run after Tony and Oscar.

Rafe had an obvious limp, and I looked up at him.

"Think…my ankle's broken," he grunted as we stumbled along. "No big deal."

"'No big deal'?" I echoed, trying to keep the worry out of my voice. With his ankle broken, there was no point in him transforming into a wolf or coyote, because his animal forms would also be injured.

"Yesenia…will fix it," he gritted.

I supposed a broken ankle was no big deal for the Castillo clan's healer—assuming we lasted that long. But did we even have to wait for her? Compared to some of the other feats I'd pulled off lately, fixing Rafe's ankle seemed relatively minor.

"Wait," I said, and Cat looked at me like I'd just gone mad.

"Wait? That thing's almost on us!"

The whirling darkness was moving ever closer, strange sibilant voices seeming to emerge from somewhere within its depths. The hair on the back of my neck stood up, but I couldn't allow myself to be distracted.

"Just one second."

I leaned down and wrapped my hands around Rafe's injured ankle, imagined a warm, healing glow coming from my fingers, penetrating into the broken bone and healing the fracture. Almost at once, his eyes widened.

"What did you do?"

"I healed you," I said. "Now, run!"

We sprinted the last few yards to the Jeep, then huddled behind it with Oscar and Tony.

"What the hell is that thing?" Tony asked. Under his warm-toned skin, he looked pale as death, and I couldn't blame him.

"I don't know for sure," I said. "All of Simon's hatred, all his resentment, all the years he's spent nursing his wounds, real or imagined. All of it wound up together in some sort of monstrous summoning."

"Jesus Christ."

Next to Tony, Oscar made the sign of the cross. I wished that might do us some good, but I had my doubts.

I had a feeling we were on our own.

"Are you all right now?" I asked Rafe.

"I think so."

"Good."

I pushed myself up from my crouch as he stared at me in consternation. "What are you doing?"

"Going to fight him," I said. That sounded

brave. Too bad I was so knotted up in fear, I worried that I might throw up then and there.

"You can't!"

"Neither can you," I said gently. I glanced around at all of them, at Oscar and Tony and Cat. "None of you can. This is my fight. This is why Louisa gave me her powers."

"Not so you would fight by yourself!" Rafe protested. He got up as well, although he retained enough presence of mind to stay partially bent over so his head wouldn't rise above the protection provided by the Jeep and provide an easy target for Simon's malevolent energy. "You fixed my ankle. Let me transform…get the drop on him like I did in Tesuque."

I kissed my husband then, a swift kiss…all we had time for. "I know you want to protect me, Rafe. But I'm the *prima* now. It's my job to protect you. Your wolf self is strong, but I know it's not strong enough."

He let out a frustrated growl, but I could tell he wouldn't keep arguing the point. As much as he hated to admit it to himself, he knew he was no match for the roiling, hideous presence churning away only a few yards from us.

Cat was shaking her head. "There has to be another way—"

"We tried that. It didn't work."

Before any of them could say anything else, I

stepped out from behind the Wrangler. There, just a yard away, was the monstrous spinning form that had engulfed Simon. Or had it been with him all along, and only now showed me his true face?

His voice echoed from somewhere within, oddly distorted. "You can't win."

"Neither can you," I replied. My skin crawled as though a million ants marched their way across my body, and my fingers were shaking. Even so, I held my ground.

That reply elicited a disembodied laugh, one that was echoed overhead by the screeching of the demons. They hung in the air, watching the scene below. Apparently, Simon was confident enough in the eventual outcome of our confrontation that he'd ordered them to stay back and keep out of the fight. "You're very brave now, aren't you?"

"Not brave," I told him. "Determined."

"Determined to die."

I summoned the shield, but as he moved toward me, those strange, ghostly tentacles that obscured his form reached out to the protective bubble and shattered it as easily as if it had been a real soap bubble. Cold enveloped me, drew me in, as though I was being pulled down into some strange vortex in arctic waters, freezing me, preventing me from doing anything except stand there.

Simon's laughter echoed in my ears. "Not as strong as you thought, Miranda."

Those weren't tentacles holding me now, but his arms. I saw him now, saw him as himself again, while we stood inside the eye of the storm he had conjured and those ghastly clouds swirled all around us.

For all my fear, I could still feel the *prima* energy burning within me. It was warm while all else was cold, telling me of the strength I'd been given, the powers that had come down through countless generations of Castillo witches, and which had finally come to me. Those strange gifts told me what I must do now.

"Strong enough, Simon," I replied.

I reached out and cupped his face in my hands. His night-dark eyes widened, and I saw a flare of terrible hope in them, hope that I might finally be succumbing to him.

That wasn't why I touched him, though.

No, I let the *prima* energy flow through me and into him. His body jerked, but I wouldn't allow him to pull away. I held on, showing him every crime he'd committed, every person he'd hurt, every piece of his soul he'd given up to summon his dark powers. And as he began to writhe and twist in my grasp, I showed him every-thing he could have had—love, and acceptance, and a peaceful heart…if only he'd been able to look past his hate.

He let out a terrible cry, even as the ghostly tornado that had surrounded us melted away like morning mist under the sun's heat. Hands clutched to his head, he sank to his knees in the gravel.

In pain, in torment…but still alive.

"Simon—"

He looked up at me, eyes blazing in fury. "You bitch!"

And his hands lifted.

I steeled myself for the attack—and startled when once again a shadow passed over the sun. Looking up, I saw great leathery wings beating against the air.

Not Simon's demons, though. The Lord of Chaos dove toward us in a terrible dark streak. One hand pushed outward, driving Simon a few steps backward, his balance lost. Free of his grasp, I stumbled and nearly fell to the ground, breath catching in my throat. The demon lord bent toward me and murmured, "Now, young witch."

I had this one moment. That was all the Lord of Chaos had given me. I had to hope it would be enough.

Not out of revenge, but out of sorrow for what he should have been, and never would be.

"Goodbye, Simon," I murmured.

I raised my hands, and the *prima* energy flared within me, combining with the gifts that had been there since I was born—even if I hadn't known they existed until a short time ago. A flare of light, golden as sunrise, warm with life…but bearing death with it now.

The surge of light hit Simon full in the chest. He gasped, eyes widening. For one terrible second, I saw that magical illumination flow through his body, overloading his every vein and muscle and cell. Then the light went dark—and he fell to the ground, limp, a trickle of black blood flowing from the corner of his mouth.

Above me, the demon horde shrilled in terror. What they planned to do next, I had no idea, because the Lord of Chaos raised both his hands and extended them toward the sky. All at once, the demons who hovered there shivered away into puffs of dark smoke that were quickly carried away by the wind.

What the—?

I stared at the demon lord as he approached me, then, to my surprise, bowed slightly. "You are uninjured?" he asked once he had straightened up.

"I—" This had all happened far too fast. Was Simon really dead?

One glance seemed to confirm that he was. Surely if he had a single breath remaining, he would have tried to come after me, but he hadn't moved for more than a minute. I was thankful that he'd fallen facing away from where I stood, though. As much as I hated what he'd done to me, to so many others, I wasn't sure I was ready to see his dead eyes staring at me, accusing.

The world seemed to spin around and around. I pulled in a breath and said, "I think I'm okay."

Oscar, Tony, Rafe, and Cat emerged from behind the Jeep. Both Tony and Oscar were staring at the Lord of Chaos as though they were caught in a nightmare from which they desperately wanted to awaken. Rafe came to me, took my hand.

"You're all right?"

"I'm fine…I think."

He looked from me to the Lord of Chaos, who stood a few feet away, watching all of us. "How did you know to come?"

The demon lord's gaze moved to Cat, who suddenly seemed very interested in scrutinizing her chipped fingernail polish. "I came because I was asked," he said.

"'Asked'?" I repeated. Then I realized why the Lord of Chaos had made Cat the object of his attention. "Cat, did you call him?"

She hesitated for a second, then flashed us all a brilliant smile. "Well, you brought me along because you thought I could help with the demons. I tried to control them, or block them, but that didn't work. So I thought of the one demon I *had* been able to talk to, and I asked him to come help. And thank you for that," she added, looking directly at the demon lord.

"It was nothing," he said. "Or rather, it was an opportunity to get my revenge on the one who brought me here against my will. I could not raise my hand against him directly, but at least I could give some small assistance."

"And—and the other demons he summoned?" I glanced upward again. The sky was clear now, with only a few clouds floating serenely past. "You destroyed them. Why?"

A negligent shrug of his massive shoulders. "They betrayed me by answering to a different master, so they deserved their fate. Besides," the Lord of Chaos added, "you would not have much liked having those demons loose in your world, would you?"

No, I most certainly would not. It still surprised me that the demon lord would strike out against his own kind like that, but I would be the first to admit that I didn't know much about demons' codes of conduct.

"But with Simon dead, how will you get back to your world?" Cat asked. She sounded genuinely concerned. "Aren't you stranded here now?"

The Lord of Chaos gave another of those careless lifts of his shoulders. "Perhaps. Perhaps not.

He cannot have been the only warlock in this world with the gift of summoning demons." A pause, and then he went on, his tone quieter, "It is better for your *prima* not to have that death entirely on her conscience."

How he knew I was now the Castillos' *prima*, I had no idea. Possibly his otherworldly nature could detect such things when ordinary mortals— or not-so-ordinary witches and warlocks— couldn't. There were so many things I still didn't know. I knew one thing, however.

I couldn't have defeated Simon if the Lord of Chaos hadn't given me that little bit of an assist.

"Thank you," I said.

A flash of those terrible fangs. Was that the demon equivalent of a smile? "You are most welcome. But now I must go."

His enormous wings flapped, stirring up dust and dead leaves. He hung in the air for a second, and then he was gone.

We all looked at one another. I couldn't help but glance over at Simon's lifeless form. Someone would have to come out here and take care of him, I supposed. I could worry about that later, though. For the moment, I was only aware of a bone-deep weariness.

My hand slid into Rafe's. His fingers locked around mine, strong and warm.

"Take me home," I whispered.

18

HOMECOMING

RAFE AND OSCAR AND TONY MANAGED TO TIP the Jeep over so it sat on all four wheels. The passenger side was horribly dented, but to all our surprise—Rafe's included, I thought—the Wrangler started right up when he pushed the ignition button.

"That's my baby," he said with an affectionate pat on the dashboard.

Other than that, none of us seemed inclined to say much. I could tell that Tony and Oscar were still trying to wrap their heads around the notion of a demon lord loose in the world, and I couldn't really blame them. Even though I'd known such beings truly did exist, since the McAllisters had had a run-in with them before I was even born, it was one thing to understand something on an intellectual level and quite another to be confronted with it in the flesh.

But the Lord of Chaos had given me the opening I'd needed, and in doing so had possibly been just as responsible for saving us as I was. I'd wounded Simon when I'd shown him the truth of his existence, but it hadn't been enough. Somehow I'd known all along that it would have to be my hand which brought him down, even if I hadn't wanted to admit it to myself. Despite my seeming lack of magical powers growing up, I'd been wanted and loved and accepted by my family, while Simon had only been an outcast. Yes, he had done terrible things, had killed and lied and used magic that had been forbidden for centuries…but he was also someone I'd laughed with, had shared meals with. Simon had given me my magic. True, he'd only done so because he wanted to use me just as he used everyone else he encountered, and yet….

I didn't want to feel guilty. No one in the world could blame me for taking Simon's life, not when he'd presented such an obvious danger to the Castillo clan, and very likely all the other witch clans as well.

A witch wasn't supposed to use her powers to harm another, but what if by harming that one person, she could save so many more?

I pulled in a breath, watched the golden landscape pass by outside the car window, and told myself it would be all right.

It had to be.

Just as we were pulling onto the 599, Cat got a text. She dug her phone out of her purse, looked down at the screen, and let out a happy little sigh. "Dad just texted me," she said. "Malena woke up about ten minutes ago. She can't remember much of what happened to her, but she seems to be fine."

"Just like Louisa," I commented. "Do you think she came out of it because Simon—" I stopped there, letting the words hang on the air. It had probably been exactly ten minutes earlier when the Lord of Chaos pushed Simon away from me and I had sent the *prima* power into him, ending his life.

"Maybe," Cat said. "Although that doesn't explain why Louisa woke up so much earlier."

No, it didn't. Then again, magic wasn't an exact science. Whatever dark spell had sent the two sisters into their comas, it didn't necessarily have to have worked on them both in exactly the same way. Louisa was the stronger witch all on her own, and when she'd fallen into the coma, she'd still possessed her *prima* powers. For all I knew, that was why the spell hadn't weighed on her as heavily.

I said as much, then paused as a thought

suddenly came to me. "What if—what if I can give Louisa her powers back, now that Simon isn't a threat any longer?"

Because I knew I really, really didn't want to be the Castillo *prima* if I didn't have to be.

Oscar replied almost at once, "I don't think that's how it works, Miranda." His tone was gentle, as though he knew he was giving me unwelcome news. "Even if it was physically possible, I doubt Louisa would agree to something like that. She gave you her powers because she knew you were stronger, were the one best suited to lead our clan. What if she took her powers back, and then a threat just as bad as Simon Escobar—or worse—appeared? The *prima* talent isn't something that should be passed back and forth like a football."

No, I supposed it wasn't. Rafe glanced over at me, although briefly because he needed to keep his eyes on the road. "It's going to be okay," he said quietly. "I'm here for you. We'll deal with this whole *prima* thing together."

I shot him a grateful smile. Really, this couldn't be all that easy for Rafe, either. He'd spent most of his life struggling against the future fate had planned for him, and now he was going to have to be the consort of the *prima*. Our lives would never be completely our own again after this, but he looked singularly untroubled at the moment.

Maybe he was just relieved that he would never have to worry about Simon Escobar again.

We pulled down the long driveway at Oscar's house. Louisa must have heard the tires on the gravel, because she came running out the front door, her long black hair—loose for once—blowing in the brisk breeze. Rafe had barely stopped before Oscar was out of the Jeep and going to her, taking her in his arms. She held on to him for a long moment, then looked over at Rafe, who rolled down the window.

"It worked, didn't it?" she asked.

"Yes," he replied. "Although we had a little unexpected help."

"'Help'?" Louisa repeated, a puzzled frown pulling at her brows. "From whom? Did the Montoyas come through for us after all?"

"No, no one like that," he said. "Oscar can tell you all about it."

She still looked confused, but she didn't seem inclined to ask any more questions. Tony opened the door on his side of the Jeep and got out, saying, "Well, it's been real, but I think next time I'm going to sit out saving the world. That thing is going to give me nightmares for weeks."

"He's not a *thing*," Cat protested. "He's the

Lord of Chaos—and he helped to save all our butts. Show a little respect."

"Okay, I'll show some respect...from a safe distance."

Cat shook her head at Tony, and he grinned before he closed the door behind him. He went over to say something to Louisa, but I couldn't hear what it was.

"Well, let's get back home," Rafe said. He raised a hand and waved toward Oscar and Louisa, then again to Tony, before he turned the Jeep around and headed up the driveway.

"Which home?" Cat asked. Her tone wasn't exactly plaintive, but when I glanced in the rearview mirror, I could tell that her expression was troubled. "You're the *prima* now, Miranda— you'll have to come live in the big house."

Oh, hell. I'd forgotten all about that. Just the very thought of having to live in that elegant mausoleum made me shudder slightly. "Do I have to? I mean, we're kind of breaking tradition just to have me as your *prima*. Can't we break it just a little more?"

To my surprise, Rafe shook his head. "That's exactly why we should follow this particular tradition. It's going to be difficult enough for everyone to accept what we've done. But at least if they see you living in the *prima's* house, they'll begin to think of you as their clan leader. It will feel like more of a natural transition to them."

I supposed his logic made sense, even though I really didn't want to acknowledge it to myself. "We don't have to move in right away, though, do we?"

He chuckled. "No, of course not. My dad will need someplace to go, although the logical thing to do would be to have him move into my place. That way, he'll still be close by everything he knows, and the transition won't be as difficult."

"And then there's me," Cat said. "I suppose I could go with Dad, but I'd rather have something of my own."

"We're not kicking you out," I protested. "You can stay as long as you want. That house is so big, it's not as though we'd be tripping over each other."

But she only shook her head. "No, I was only staying there because my mother wouldn't hear of me moving out on my own when I wasn't married. Now…." She hesitated for a moment, her big dark eyes sad. "Now I don't have to worry about that. I can get an apartment or rent a little house or something until I figure out what I *really* want."

"Your green place?" Rafe asked. Something about the way he phrased the question made me think he was referring to a conversation he and Cat had had previously, one I hadn't been privy to.

"Yes," she said. "It might take me a while to find it, but I know it's out there, waiting for me." She shifted, her eyes meeting mine in the rearview mirror. "I told Rafe a while back that what I really wanted was a place of my own someplace green, someplace out in the country. Now I guess I can go look for it, since I don't have my mother telling me what to do." A pause, and then she shook her head. "That sounded terrible, didn't it? Like I was glad my mother was gone."

"No," I replied at once. "I don't think so. I understand."

My response elicited a relieved smile. "Thanks, Miranda. I think I'm going to like having you as my *prima*—and my sister-in-law."

Her words warmed me. Of course I had a sister of my own already, but Emily and I had never been super-close, partly because she'd always been very conscious of her role as *prima*-in-waiting and the future leader of the McAllister clan. How she'd react to finding out that I was now the *prima* of the Castillos, I had no idea. First, though, I'd need to call my parents, let them know I was all right, that all of us were all right. I could only imagine how frantic they must have been, not knowing what was happening behind the barrier spell Simon had cast.

Smiling at Cat, I said, "I think I might be able to live through this whole *prima* thing with you and Rafe to help me out."

"You won't just live through it," Rafe said, his voice ringing with confidence. "You'll make it a roaring success. I have faith in you."

He lifted one hand from the steering wheel and reached over to wrap my fingers in his. His touch, the warmth of his skin, gave me so much reassurance, so much confidence that this was all going to be okay. After all, we'd just faced down one of the darkest warlocks the world had ever produced. Everything else would feel like a piece of cake after that.

We dropped Cat off at the house, promising her we'd return for a sit-down with her and Eduardo once we went home and got cleaned up and took a little time to let everything sink in. She waved goodbye before turning to let herself in through the garden gate. I shifted toward Rafe.

"Is she going to be okay?" I asked. "The last thing I want to do is kick her out of her own house."

"She's going to be fine," Rafe replied. "If it weren't for our mother, she would have been out of there a couple of years ago. Her plan sounds like a good one to me—she'll find a place here in town to be on her own for a while until she can get herself her little country retreat."

"Doesn't she ever want to get married?" Because of course, now that I was married to Rafe, I felt as though everyone should be able to experience something so wonderful.

"Eventually," he said. "When the right person comes along. He just hasn't crossed her path yet."

I supposed I had to be satisfied with that. Right then, I resolved to be nothing like Genoveva Castillo. I wouldn't tell people what to do, or try to make them get married to someone just because it was a match that would be good for the clan. Cat was only twenty-four; she had all the time in the world. And after spending her whole life under her mother's thumb, it was probably a good thing for her to have some time on her own before she even thought about settling down.

We pulled into the garage, and Rafe turned off the Jeep. For a second, we both just sat there, neither one of us wanting to move. It was as if we both knew that once we got out of the car, we'd be taking the next step toward our future. At last, though, he put his hand on the door handle and let himself out, and I reluctantly followed suit.

To my surprise, though, he came around the back of the Wrangler and scooped me up in his arms before carrying me into the house. I looked up at him, wondering if he'd just lost his mind, and he grinned down at me.

"Well, I had to carry my new wife over the threshold, didn't it?"

"Dork," I said fondly. "Does anyone even do that anymore?"

"I just did." Relenting, he set me down in the hallway just outside the laundry room. "I wanted to make it official."

"It *is* official. We have a piece of paper to prove it and everything."

"True, but it doesn't feel quite real." He took me by the hand, leading me into the kitchen. Once there, he got out a couple of glasses and poured us some water, then handed one of the tumblers to me. I took it from him and drank gratefully. Until that moment, I hadn't realized how thirsty I was. "And it might not feel real to the rest of the clan." A pause, and he went on, "You know we're probably going to have to have a real wedding, just to prove to everyone that we actually are married."

Somehow I'd known that might be a possibility. "Okay, but hopefully they'll let us have a little breathing space to prepare. After everything that's happened over the past week, I don't think I can jump right into wedding planning."

"Oh, I'm sure they'll give you a few days."

"It had better be more than that."

He bent and kissed me then, the feel of his lips against mine so warm, so true, so real that I forgot everything else, except that he was my husband and we truly were meant to be together. No matter what we had to face in the days ahead, it would be all right, because we wouldn't have to do it alone.

When he pulled away, he was smiling.

"What is it?" I asked.

His warm brown eyes caught mine and held. I looked up at him, thrilling at every line and angle of his face, from the high cheekbones to the ironic lift of his eyebrows to the curves of his mouth. "Just that…I spent most of my life trying to figure out how I could get out of marrying you. Now I am married to you, and all I want is to get married again so I can show everyone how proud I am to say that you're my wife."

Oh, how I loved him. The words didn't exist to show how happy I was to be here with him, even though I knew this house would never really be mine. Fate had other plans for me, and I realized I was okay with that.

I tilted my head. "How soon do you think Cat and your father will be expecting us to come over?"

"I don't know. An hour, maybe. I didn't really set a time."

"Good," I said. "Because we were married

today, and I want my wedding night...or at least my wedding afternoon."

A certain heat entered his eyes. "I think that can be arranged."

Before I could react, he'd bent and scooped me up again, was taking me upstairs to the bedroom. We would make love again, this time as husband and wife. And sometime in the not-too-distant future, we'd have a real wedding to make the clan happy...and I realized I was just fine with that as well.

After all, that meant we would have a second wedding night. We would go live in the big house, and I would throw open the heavy draperies and let the sunlight in, and I would do my best to become *prima* to this clan that was now my own, in this land that had once been strange to me and was now my home.

And maybe...just maybe...Isabel Castillo would look down at us and smile, and know that the vision she'd had once upon a time had now come to pass, and all was settled and as it should be, and her clan safe again.

The End

The Witches of Canyon Road will continue with

A Canyon Road Christmas in late November 2018, followed by Cat's story in *Demon Born,* due out in January 2019.

Don't miss out on any of Christine's new releases —sign up for her newsletter today!

Darknight

Darkmoon

Sympathetic Magic

Protector

Spellbound

A Cleopatra Hill Christmas

Impractical Magic

Strange Magic

The Arrangement

Defender

Bad Blood

Deep Magic

Darktide

THE DJINN WARS*

(Paranormal Romance)

Chosen

Taken

Fallen

Broken

Forsaken

Forbidden

Awoken

Illuminated

THE WATCHERS TRILOGY*

(Paranormal Romance)

Falling Dark

Dead of Night

Rising Dawn

THE SEDONA FILES*

(Paranormal Romance)

Bad Vibrations

Desert Hearts

Angel Fire

Star Crossed

Falling Angels

Enemy Mine

TALES OF THE LATTER KINGDOMS*

(Fantasy Romance)

All Fall Down

Dragon Rose

Binding Spell

Ashes of Roses

One Thousand Nights

Threads of Gold

The Wolf of Harrow Hall

Moon Dance

The Song of the Thrush

THE GAIAN CONSORTIUM SERIES

(Science Fiction Romance)

Blood Will Tell

Breath of Life

The Gaia Gambit

The Mandala Maneuver

The Titan Trap

The Zhore Deception

Refugees (October 2018)

* Indicates a completed series

ABOUT THE AUTHOR

Christine Pope has been writing stories ever since she commandeered her family's Smith-Corona typewriter back in the sixth grade. Her work includes paranormal romance, fantasy romance, and science fiction/space opera romance. She fell under the Land of Enchantment's spell while researching her Djinn Wars series and now makes her home in Santa Fe, New Mexico.

Don't miss out on any of Christine's new releases —sign up for her newsletter today!

Christine Pope on the Web:
www.christinepope.com

www.ingramcontent.com/pod-product-compliance
Lightning Source LLC
Chambersburg PA
CBHW070836260626
47170CB00007B/2399